Stories

Stories

Joaquim Maria
Machado de Assis

Edited, translated, and with an introduction by
Rhett McNeil

DALKEY ARCHIVE PRESS
CHAMPAIGN / LONDON / DUBLIN

Library of Congress Cataloging-in-Publication Data

Machado de Assis, 1839-1908.
[Short stories. Selections. English]
Stories / Joaquim Maria Machado de Assis ; edited, translated, and with an introduction by Rhett McNeil. -- First edition.
pages cm
Collected stories representing the period dating from 1878-1886.
Includes bibliographical references.
ISBN 978-1-56478-899-3 (alk. paper)
1. Machado de Assis, 1839-1908--Translations into English. I. McNeil, Rhett, editor
translator II. Title.
PQ9697.M18A2 2014
869.3'3--dc23
2013049052

Partially funded by a grant from the Illinois Arts Council, a state agency, and by the
University of Illinois at Urbana-Champaign.

Obra publicada com o apoio do Ministério da Cultura do Brasil, Fundação Biblioteca
Nacional, e Coordenadoria Geral do Livro e da Leitura.

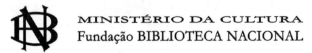

MINISTÉRIO DA CULTURA
Fundação BIBLIOTECA NACIONAL

The publication of this book was partially supported by the Ministério da Cultura do
Brasil, the Fundação Biblioteca Nacional, and the Coordenadoria Geral do Livro e da
Leitura.

www.dalkeyarchive.com

Cover: design and composition by Mikhail Iliatov

Printed on permanent/durable and acid-free paper

Table of Contents

Machado in English

At this point in American letters, Machado de Assis has been deemed an under-recognized master of prose fiction so often that perhaps he can now simply be referred to as one of the great writers of the nineteenth century, without any qualification. To be sure, there have been good reasons to include these qualifiers, especially outside of Brazil. For instance, it took around half a century before his works began to be widely translated throughout the rest of the Americas and Europe. Furthermore, he happened to write in Portuguese, a so-called "minor" language that often isolates Brazil, linguistically and culturally, from even its closest geographical neighbors; many have said that, had he written in English, French, or Russian, he would be ranked alongside Dickens, Flaubert, and Gogol.

However, in the second half of the twentieth century, his work has finally begun to garner the worldwide attention and praise that it received in Brazil during his lifetime, some hundred years earlier. In 1970, Helen Caldwell began her English-language monograph, *Machado de Assis*, by stating that Machado was no longer in need of discovery, that he is "no longer unknown among us." All of his novels, save his first, have been translated into English, and some have even been retranslated. Three collections of his short stories have previously appeared in English translation, and although these only represent a small portion of his total output in this genre, they have helped to further confirm his international reputation and position in the world canon. In fact, he has now been championed by some of the foremost critics and cultural arbiters in the English-speaking world. No less than Susan Sontag called him a "prodigy of accomplishment [. . .] deserving of a permanent place in world literature." Harold Bloom, a critic who is self-consciously engaged in the project of canonization and *weltliteratur*, includes Machado among the one hundred exemplary creative writers he catalogs in *Genius*, stating that "the genius of irony has given us few equals of the African-Brazilian Machado de Assis," and calling Machado "the supreme black literary artist to date." Salman Rushdie has cited him as an important influence and a precursor to the Latin American magical realism that is so closely connected to his own work, and even Woody Allen included Machado's novel *Epitaph of a Small Winner* (alternatively translated as *The Posthumous Memoirs of Bras Cubas*) in a list of his top five books, citing its "great wit" and "great originality." In short, it appears that Machado has finally found his place in English, on bookstore shelves and university syllabi, as well as on the tongues of prominent critics, writers, and cultural commentators.

A Life

It is important to note, however, that Machado de Assis's oft-mentioned obscurity only holds true outside of Brazil. Within his own country and during his lifetime, Machado achieved widespread fame and prominence, which is almost miraculous given his extraordinarily humble origins and the socio-political state of Brazil during his lifetime. Joaquim Maria Machado de Assis was born in Rio de Janeiro on 21 June 1839 to Francisco José de Assis, a *pardo forro* or free mulatto, and Maria Leopoldina Machado da Câmara, a white woman from the Azores who had immigrated to Brazil with her parents when she was a child. Both his parents earned a living working on the estate of Senator Bento Barroso Pereira in the Morro do Livramento area of Rio, his father as a house painter, his mother as a seamstress and embroiderer. He was the grandson of freed mulatto slaves in a society where black slaves outnumbered whites more than two to one, where there were more mulattos in slavery than free mulattos, and where slavery would not be abolished until 1888. Little is known of his formative years in Morro do Livramento, but he certainly faced many hardships. His only sibling, a sister named Maria, two years his junior, died at the age of four, the victim of a smallpox outbreak in Rio de Janeiro. His mother died of tuberculosis roughly five years later, when Machado was only ten, and his father remarried five years after that. Not much is known about his early education, save that he did not even complete grammar school. Machado himself never wrote about his childhood. One of the most extensive remarks we have on the subject—published during Machado's lifetime, in 1893—comes from his close friend and fellow member of the Brazilian Academy of Letters, Artur Azevedo: "His studies were very irregular. Having left grammar school barely able to read and write, he set about teaching himself without teachers or advisors." Machado was an avid reader at a young age, and his first jobs indicate a predilection for a life of letters. In addition to his frequent visits to the Royal Portuguese Cabinet of Reading (a lavish temple to books and reading that is still standing, inconspicuously, on a narrow side-street in downtown Rio), Machado took various jobs in the publishing industry: first, in 1854 at the age of fifteen in the typography shop of Francisco de Paula Brito, then as a typographer's apprentice, and eventually as a proofreader for Brito. Around the same time, Machado had his first publications, the earliest on record being a poem published in the inauspiciously named *Periódico dos Pobres* (*Poor Man's Paper*), simply titled "Sonnet." He followed this with a number of other publications in his teenage years, mainly poetry, often published in one of Brito's literary journals, *Marmota*

Fluminense. His first foray into fiction—the genre that would eventually make his fame in Brazil—came a few years later, in 1858, with a short story called "Three Lost Treasures." In 1861 he published his first book-length volume, a loose translation/adaptation of a French play by Victor Hénaux. Throughout his career he worked in a variety of genres—poetry, drama, criticism, short fiction, novels—but his later output focused increasingly on fiction. Although he rarely left his hometown of Rio de Janeiro, and never left Brazil, he read a variety of languages, including English and French—which was the language of high society of the time (a fact that is mocked in the story "Trio in A Minor")—and in his later years he also taught himself German and Greek (we have facsimiles of his copybooks). We also have a partial catalog of his library, which contained volumes in French (over half of his collection), English, German, Spanish, and Italian, in addition to Portuguese. Machado was a voracious reader, judging from the wide range of his allusions and his extensive library, and read many works of world literature in the original: Dickens, Sterne, and Shakespeare in English; Flaubert, Balzac, and Stendhal in French; Dante, Leopardi, and Ariosto in Italian; Goethe, Heine, and Schopenhauer in German; as well as Cervantes in Spanish. He also translated works from many of these languages, including Victor Hugo's *Toilers of the Sea*, Poe's "The Raven," Canto XXV from Dante's *Inferno*, a large portion of *Oliver Twist*, and poems by Heine and Schiller.

In 1864, after a period of intense publication in newspapers and literary magazines, he published his first volume of poetry, *Crisálidas* (*Chrysalises*). Over the next fifteen years he went on to publish two more volumes of poetry, two volumes of short stories, and four novels. These works comprise what is usually referred to as Machado's first phase, characterized by the high Romantic style that dominated the Brazilian literary scene at the time. The serial publication of *The Posthumous Memoirs of Bras*

Cubas in 1880 in the literary journal *Revista Brasileira* marks
the beginning of a radical stylistic departure from his first phase,
marked by self-reflexivity, formal playfulness, intense irony, and
pitch-black pessimism. All of the stories in the present volume
were published in this period, from 1880 until Machado's death
in 1908, save one, "On the Ark," which was published in 1878
and already contains many of the hallmarks of the second
phase, including a playful, experimental form (biblical chapter
and verse) and his characteristic Schopenhauerian pessimism;
in fact, this story may provide a bleaker view of the human
condition than any other in the volume. His style and narrative
voice during this second period are so drastically different from
what was in vogue at the time—both in Brazil and Europe
(Zola's *Nana* was also published in 1880)—that scholars have
had a hard time putting a label on it. His works from this phase
have been variously described as Realist, Modernist, Proto-
Modernist, and even Proto-Postmodernist (this last formulation
is by John Barth, another of Machado's late-twentieth century
American champions). During this period he published five
novels and four volumes of short fiction, as well as a volume of
previously uncollected writings. It was also during this period
that Machado reached the height of his fame in Brazil. In
1896 he helped found the Brazilian Academy of Letters, and
in 1897 he was unanimously elected as its president, a position
he held until his death. His wife, Carolina Augusta Xavier de
Novais, died in 1904 after thirty-five years of marriage; they
had no children. Machado died on 29 September 1908 after
suffering from a variety of illnesses, including a bad relapse of
the epilepsy that had afflicted him during his childhood. He
was given a state funeral with full civil and military honors, a
first for a man of letters in Brazil and a testament to his national
fame and stature.

The Stories

Although he worked in various genres, fiction eventually became his primary focus, and the novels and short stories from his second phase are his greatest legacy. The stories collected here represent a selection dating from 1878–86 and range in tone from elegiac ("Wedding Song") to philosophical ("The Immortal") to impishly ironic ("On the Ark"). They were chosen for their formal playfulness, ironical pathos, and stylistic subversiveness. A few of the stories are clear allusions to other works: "Voyage around Myself" is a reworking of Xavier de Maistre's "Voyage around My Room," with the self as a stand-in for the bedroom, which was itself a stand-in for a foreign land. "Ex Cathedra" features an old man who is driven mad by books, another Quixote, who attempts to teach his goddaughter, a stand-in for Quixote's niece, about romantic love by starting with a lesson on the cosmos and the universe, then slowly narrowing down the subject matter to love and procreation. "On the Ark" is a parody of biblical form, written in chapter and verse, which claims to present "Three (Undiscovered) Chapters from the Book of Genesis." "The Psychiatrist," a novella-length piece and the longest of this volume, displays Machado's skepticism about scientific progress and human understanding generally. Two of the stories, "To Live!" and "The Immortal" deal with the philosophical implications of immortality, echoing Schopenhauer's essay on the subject in *Parerga and Paralipomena*—"To Live!" is even written in the form of a Socratic dialogue, as is Schopenhauer's essay, with Prometheus playing the role of Socrates. "Wedding Song," "The Dictionary," and "The Priest, or the Metaphysics of Style," are all meditations on the process of artistic creation; Machado is at his most metafictional in "The Priest," in which most of the action centers on a noun and an adjective searching for each other inside the titular character's brain. There's even a detective story of sorts, "A Visit from Alcibiades," written in epistolary form, about Alcibiades, the ancient Greek general and dandy described in Plutarch's *Lives*, coming back to life in nineteenth-century Rio, only to die again soon after. Taken together, these stories provide a good picture of Machado's formal inventiveness, his repurposing of the western canon, his biting sense of humor, and his unshakeable skepticism. Many of the themes, philosophical concerns, and narrative strategies deployed in these stories have counterparts in the great novels of his second phase, and can thus shed new light on their inner workings. Yet these stories are also strong enough to stand on their own, alongside the novels, as art objects in their own right, masterworks of short fiction by Brazil's greatest writer.

THE PSYCHIATRIST

Chapter I: How Itaguaí Came to Have an Insane Asylum

The historical records of the town of Itaguaí indicate that a long time ago a certain physician lived there, one Dr. Simão Bacamarte,[1] whose ancestors were colonial gentry and the greatest doctors of all Brazil, Portugal, and the Spanish territories. He had studied in both Coimbra and Padua, and then, at the age of thirty-four, he returned to Brazil, the king of Portugal having been unable to persuade him to remain in Coimbra to lead the university, or in Lisbon to take charge of the affairs of the monarchy.

"Science," he said to His Majesty, "is my only occupation, and Itaguaí my only university."

Having said this, he returned to Itaguaí and gave himself over, body and soul, to the study of science, dividing his time between treating patients and reading books, proving his theorems through the practical application of poultices. At the age of forty he married a twenty-five-year-old woman named Dona Evarista da Costa e Mascarenhas, the widow of an itinerant circuit judge, who was neither pretty nor charming. One of his uncles, an incorrigible ladies' man known for his frankness, was surprised at his choice and told him so. Simão Bacamarte explained to him that Dona Evarista possessed first-class physiological and anatomical traits, had a healthy digestive system, regular sleeping

1. "Bacamarte" is also the name of an antiquated firearm, called a "harque-bus" or "blunderbuss" in English. Like "blunderbuss," "bacamarte" can also mean "blundering, useless person," although it isn't as thoroughly silly sounding, nor is there an everyday, corresponding verb form like "to blunder" in English. This name, as all others in this text, remains untranslated.

patterns, a strong pulse, and excellent eyesight; as such, she was fit to give him robust, healthy, intelligent children. If aside from these natural endowments—which are the only ones worthy of concern for a wise man—Dona Evarista's physical features were poorly formed, Dr. Bacamarte thanked God for it, rather than lamenting it, since he would never run the risk of neglecting the interests of science in favor of paying ardent and vulgar attention to his spouse.

Dona Evarista dashed Dr. Bacamarte's hopes: she gave him no children, neither robust nor sickly ones. Science is naturally disposed to patience; our doctor waited three years, then four, then five. At the end of this period he made an extensive study of the subject matter, reread all the works of the Arabic writers and others that he'd brought with him to Itaguaí, sent inquiries to universities in Italy and Germany, and ended up putting his wife on a special diet. The illustrious lady, who up to that point had been nourished exclusively on the delicious pork from the pigs of Itaguaí, didn't heed her husband's instructions. It is to her resistance—which is understandable, though not commendable—that we owe the utter extinction of the Bacamarte dynasty.

But science has the ineffable capacity to cure all sorrows, and our doctor immersed himself completely in the study and practice of medicine. It was at this point that one remote corner of this field of study particularly caught his attention: the psychic corner, the study of cerebral pathologies. In all the Brazilian colony— even in the entire empire—there wasn't a single authority on the subject, which up to that point had been only poorly explored or hardly explored at all. Simão Bacamarte understood that, as such, Portuguese science, and particularly Brazilian science, stood to be crowned with "eternal laurels"—a phrase that he himself uttered, but only in a moment of ecstasy in the privacy of his own home. In public he was quite modest, according to those who knew him.

"The health of the soul," he exclaimed, "is the most noble pursuit of a doctor."

"The most noble pursuit of a true doctor," emended Crispim Soares, the town apothecary, and one of Dr. Bacamarte's friends and regular dinner companions.

Among other offenses of which the city council of Itaguaí is accused by historians, it was guilty of neglecting its deranged citizens. Thus it was that all the violent lunatics were locked away in a dark corner of their respective houses and, furthermore, went uncured until death came to cheat them out of the one gift that had been granted to them: life. All the gentle ones walked the streets freely. Simão Bacamarte intended, early on, to reform this abominable practice. He petitioned city hall for permission to house and treat all of the deranged of Itaguaí and the surrounding towns and cities in a building he would have built for that very purpose. All of this would be accomplished by means of a stipend paid to him by the city council, in the event that the family of the patient couldn't afford it. The proposal aroused the curiosity of the entire town and also came up against intense resistance, so pronounced is the difficulty of eradicating absurd customs, even harmful ones. The idea of putting all the deranged in the same house, to have them all living together, seemed, in itself, to be a symptom of dementia, and there was no lack of people willing to suggest as much to the doctor's own wife.

"Look, Dona Evarista," said Padre Lopes, the local parson, "see if you can't get your husband to take a little vacation in Rio de Janeiro. To be always, always studying is no good, it'll fry his brain."

Dona Evarista was aghast and went to speak with her husband, telling him that she was "filled with desires" and one in particular: the desire to go to Rio de Janeiro and eat everything that he deemed well-suited to help obtain that specific result known to them both. But that great man, with the uncommon wisdom that set him apart from others, intuited his wife's true intentions and smilingly replied that she had nothing to fear. From there he went straight to city hall, where the city councillors were debating the proposal. He defended it with such eloquence that a majority of them resolved to authorize what he had requested, and at the same time voted in favor of a tax designed to subsidize the treatment, housing, and meals of those insane citizens who were too poor to pay. Finding something to tax in Itaguaí wasn't easy, since everything already had a tax attached to it. After exhaustive studies, it was agreed that the city would allow for two decorative feathers to be placed on the horses that pulled funeral coaches. Anyone who wanted to put feathers on the funeral coach horses would have to pay city hall two nickels, and this amount would be multiplied by the number of hours that passed between the death and the final graveside benediction. The clerk got mixed up as he calculated the revenue that would result from the new tax, and one of the city councillors—who had little faith in the doctor's endeavor—requested that the clerk be excused from this pointless task.

"The numbers aren't necessary," he said, "since Dr. Bacamarte isn't going to do anything. Who ever heard of putting all the lunatics together in the same house?"

But the esteemed magistrate was mistaken, for the doctor accomplished it all. As soon as he obtained permission, he began construction on the building. It was on Rua Nova, the most beautiful street in Itaguaí at the time, and it had fifty windows on each side, a courtyard in the middle, and plenty of rooms for lodgers. As the doctor was an eminent Arabist, he found a verse in the Koran wherein Mohammed declares that the insane are sacred, given that Allah had taken away their reason in order to render them incapable of sin. The idea seemed beautiful and profound to him, and he had it engraved on the building's facade. However, since he was afraid of the local parson and, by extension, the bishop, he attributed the quote to Pope Benedict VIII. This deception—which was otherwise pious—earned him a lunch with Padre Lopes, who narrated the entire life story of that eminent pope.

The asylum was named the Green House, a reference to the color of the windows, which were the first, and only, in Itaguaí to be painted green. There was much pomp surrounding the inauguration; people came from nearby towns and villages, farther-flung settlements, and even from Rio de Janeiro to attend the ceremonies, which lasted seven days. Many of the deranged had already been committed, and their relatives had the opportunity to see the fatherly care and Christian charity with which they would be treated. Dona Evarista, overjoyed by her husband's glory, dressed luxuriously, covering herself in jewels, flowers, and silks. She was a veritable queen on those memorable days. In spite of the reserved, modest customs of that bygone century, everyone made sure to visit her at home two or three times, and not only did they compliment her, they showered her with praise. They did so because—and this fact is a highly honorable documentation of society at that time—they viewed her as the happy wife of a superior soul, of an illustrious gentleman, and if they envied her, it was but the holy, noble envy of the admirer.

At the end of seven days the public celebrations came to an end. Itaguaí finally had an insane asylum.

Chapter II: A Flood of Madmen

Three days later, during a frank, private conversation with the apothecary Crispim Soares, the psychiatrist revealed his most secret desire.

"Charity, Mr. Soares, certainly enters into the equation of this undertaking, but it enters into it as mere seasoning, just the salt of this operation, which is how I interpret the words of Saint

Paul to the Corinthians: 'Though I have all knowledge, and have not charity, I am nothing.' The most important aim of the Green House project is to study madness and its varying degrees in depth, to classify the various cases, and to discover, finally, the causes of this phenomenon, as well as its universal cure. This is my secret desire. I believe that in doing so I am undertaking a good deed for humanity."

"An excellent deed," the apothecary amended.

"Without this asylum," the psychiatrist continued, "I could do very little. With it, I have a much bigger field for my studies."

"Much, much bigger," added the other.

And they had a point. The deranged from all the towns and hamlets in the region streamed into the Green House. Some were violent, some were gentle, others monomaniacal . . . The whole family of the poor in spirit was present. At the end of four months, the Green House was a small village. There weren't enough rooms in the original building, and a narrow building containing an additional thirty-seven rooms was annexed. Padre Lopes admitted that he could never have imagined that there were so many crazy people in the whole world, much less that some of the more bizarre cases even existed. For example, a young, dim-witted peasant who regularly delivered an academic oration every day after lunch, embellished with tropes, antitheses, and apostrophes, with snatches of Greek and Latin thrown in for adornment, and quotes from Cicero, Apuleius, and Tertullian as decorative tassels. The parson couldn't believe it. How was it possible? This same young man whom he'd seen, not three months earlier, tossing around a shuttlecock in the street!

"I'm not saying you're wrong," the psychiatrist replied, "but the fact is that you're seeing it with your own eyes, Your Reverence. Happens every day."

"To my mind," rejoined the parson, "this can only be explained by the confusion of tongues at the tower of Babel, as the scriptures tell us. Since the languages were confounded long ago, it's probably easy to mix them up nowadays, if one's mind isn't working right . . ."

"This may, in fact, be the divine explanation of the phenomenon," said the psychiatrist in agreement, after thinking it over for a moment, "but it's not out of the question that there may also be a human explanation, a purely scientific one, and that is precisely what I intend to . . ."

"Agreed, and I'm anxious to hear your explanation, truly!"

There were three or four people who had been driven mad by love, but only two of them were startlingly curious cases of delirium. The first, named Falcão, a young man of twenty-five, believed himself to be the morning star and would stand for hours on end with his arms and legs outstretched, mimicking the points of a star, asking if the sun had already risen so he could finally go to bed. The other was constantly walking, walking, walking around the rooms and the courtyard, or along the hallways, looking for the ends of the earth. He was a poor wretch whose wife had run off with a dandy. The moment he found out about it, he grabbed a muzzleloader and went after them; he found them two hours later beside a pond and killed them both with great cruelty.

His jealousy had been sated, but the avenger himself had gone mad. And thus began his anxious desire to get to the ends of the earth, in search of the fugitives.

There were also notable examples of delusions of grandeur. The most noteworthy of these was a poor wretch, the son a of clothes seller, who narrated his entire genealogy to the walls (since he never looked at anybody, ever).

His story went thus:

"God begat an egg, the egg begat the sword, the sword begat David, David begat the color purple, purple begat the duke, the duke begat the marquis, and the marquis begat the count, which is me."

Then he'd slap his forehead, snap his fingers, and repeat, six or seven times in a row:

"God begat an egg, the egg ... etc."

Another of this sort was a scribe who introduced himself as the king's butler; another still, a cattleman from Minas Gerais who compulsively gave out herds of cattle to people: three hundred head of cattle to one, six hundred to another, twelve hundred to another, incessantly. I won't go into the cases of religious monomania. I'll merely mention a subject named João de Deus, who inverted his name and told everyone he was the "God João," promising the kingdom of heaven to all who worshipped him and the sorrows of hell to all the rest. And then there was Garcia, a university graduate, who never uttered a word because he believed that if a single word were to pass through his lips, the stars would fall from the sky and set the world ablaze, such was the power that God had given him.

That's precisely what he wrote down on the piece of paper that the psychiatrist had given him, not so much out of charity as in the interests of science.

For, to tell the truth, the patience of the psychiatrist was even more extraordinary than all the other forms of madness on display in the Green House. It was nothing short of astonishing. Simão Bacamarte's first order of business was to form an administrative staff. It was Crispim Soares, the apothecary, who had given him the idea, and he also gave him two of his nephews, whom the psychiatrist entrusted with a set of instructions—previously approved by city hall—pertaining to the allocation of food and clothing, the bookkeeping, etc. It was just what he needed to be able to focus exclusively on his work.

"The Green House," he told the parson, "has now become its own little world, in which there is both a secular government and a *spiritual* government."

Padre Lopes chuckled at this churchly quip and added, with

the sole intention of joining the repartee, "Enough of that, enough, or I'll have to denounce you to the pope."

As soon as he had relieved himself of the administrative work, the psychiatrist moved on to the colossal task of classifying his patients. First, he divided them up into two main categories: the violent ones and the gentle ones. Then he directed his attention to the subcategories: monomanias, deliriums, and assorted hallucinations. Having accomplished this, he undertook an exhaustive, unremitting study. He analyzed the habits of each of the lunatics: the time of day of their outbursts, their aversions, affinities, words, gestures, and tendencies. He inquired about the lives of the patients, their professions, their habits, the circumstances surrounding their first manifestations of illness, injuries suffered as children or adolescents, other medical conditions, any family history of madness; in other words, an inquest beyond the capabilities of even the most thorough magistrate. Every day he recorded some novel observation, interesting discovery, or extraordinary phenomenon. At the same time, he researched the best diets, medicinal substances, and methods (both curative and palliative); not just the ones he found in the texts of his beloved Arabs, but also those he discovered himself, the results of his own perspicacity and patience. But all this work took up the better part of his time. He hardly slept or ate, and even when he did eat he never really stopped working, now scouring an ancient text, now mulling over a sticky problem; he would often sit through dinner, start to finish, without uttering a word to Dona Evarista.

Chapter III: God Knows What He's Doing!

After two months, that illustrious lady had become the most miserable of women. She fell into a profound state of melancholy, became pale and emaciated, ate little, and sighed at every turn.

She didn't dare complain or offer reproach, for she respected him as her husband and lord; instead, she suffered quietly and visibly wasted away. One night at dinner her husband asked what was wrong, and she sadly replied that it was nothing; later she ventured a little, going so far as to say that she felt as much like a widow these days as she had before they married.

Then she added, "Who would have thought that a half-dozen lunatics . . ."

She didn't finish her sentence; or rather, before she could finish it, she raised her eyes to the ceiling. Those eyes, her most enticing feature: large, dark, and bathed in a dewy light, just as they'd looked when she was still young. As for the gesture itself, it was the same one she'd employed on the day Simão Bacamarte proposed to her. The historical records don't indicate whether Dona Evarista brandished that weapon with the perverse intention of decapitating science in a single blow or, at least, with the intention of cutting off its hands, but that hypothesis has a ring of truth. In any case, the psychiatrist assumed her intention was precisely this. Yet the great man did not become angry, or even dejected. His eyes never varied from their constant state: hard, even, eternal; not a single wrinkle disturbed his face, as placid as the waters of Botafogo beach. Perhaps a smile unsealed his lips, through which these words filtered, as soothing as the ointments in Solomon's song:

"I'll allow you to take a trip to Rio de Janeiro."

Dona Evarista felt the ground beneath her feet fall away. She had never been to Rio de Janeiro, which, although admittedly but a pale shadow of what it is today, was nonetheless something greater indeed than Itaguaí. For her, visiting Rio de Janeiro was tantamount to the dream of the captive Hebrew of old. At that point in her life, especially—after her husband had installed himself for good in that backwoods town—she had lost all hope of breathing the air of our grand city. And at that very moment, he invited her to fulfill the desire she'd felt as a child and a young woman. Dona Evarista couldn't hide the excitement the proposal aroused in her. Simão Bacamarte took her by the hand and smiled a somewhat philosophical smile—and a loving one besides—which seemed to translate this idea: "There are no real remedies for pains of the soul. This lady is wasting away because it seems that I do not love her; I'll give her Rio de Janeiro, and she'll be comforted." Being the studious man that he was, he jotted down this observation.

With this, another arrow pierced Dona Evarista's heart. She contained herself, however, and limited herself to telling her husband that if he didn't go, she wouldn't go either, since she wasn't about to walk the streets of Rio alone.

"Your aunt will go with you," the psychiatrist rebutted.

Keep in mind that Dona Evarista had thought of this very thing, but she didn't want to ask about or even hint at it, because, in the first place, it would cost her husband dearly, and, secondly, it was better, more methodical, and more logical, that the idea should come from him.

"Oh, but it will cost so much!" sighed Dona Evarista, without conviction.

"What does that matter? We've earned a lot," said her husband.

"Just yesterday the bookkeeper showed me the accounts. Would you like to see?"

He took her over to the ledgers. Dona Evarista was entranced. It was a Milky Way of ciphers. Then he led her to the coffers, where he kept the money.

Dear God! There were mountains of gold, coins of *mil cruzados* piled upon *mil cruzados*, gold doubloons upon gold doubloons. These were true riches.

The psychiatrist watched her while she devoured the gold with her dark eyes and whispered into her ear this insidious insinuation: "Who would have thought that a half-dozen lunatics . . ."

Dona Evarista understood his meaning, smiled, and responded resignedly: "God knows what He's doing!"

The trip took place three months later. Dona Evarista, her aunt, the apothecary's wife, her nephew, a priest that the psychiatrist had met in Lisbon who just happened to be in Itaguaí, five or six servants, and four female house-slaves: this was the retinue that the town of Itaguaí saw depart one morning in May. The farewells were sad for everyone except the psychiatrist. Though Dona Evarista's tears were plentiful and sincere, they were unable to shake him. As a man of science and science alone, nothing outside the realm of science could upset him. And if something was bothering him on that occasion, if his eyes seemed to scan the crowd with a restless, policeman's gaze, it was nothing more than the thought that some madman might be found there, intermingling with people who were mentally sound.

"Farewell!" sobbed the ladies and the apothecary, one last time.

And the retinue departed. Crispim Soares returned home with eyes lowered between the ears of the roan horse he rode upon; Simão Bacamarte's eyes scanned the horizon in the distance, leaving the horse in charge of the trip home. What a vivid illustration of the common man and the genius! One with his eyes on the present, with all its tears and longing, the other advancing into the future and its myriad dawns.

Chapter IV: A New Theory

While Dona Evarista made her way to Rio de Janeiro with tears in her eyes, Simão Bacamarte studied all the angles of a bold new idea, which could enlarge the foundations of psychology. Any free time he had outside his responsibilities at the Green House, he would steal away to roam the streets, or go from house to house, talking with people about thirty thousand different subjects and punctuating his speech with a stare that struck fear in the hearts of even the most courageous.

One morning, three weeks later, as Crispim Soares was busy mixing the ingredients of a medication, a messenger arrived to tell him that the psychiatrist wished to see him.

"He told me it's an important matter," added the messenger.

Crispim went pale. What important matter could it be, if not some sad news about the trip, and, specifically, about his wife? I should fully clarify this point, given that the historians insist upon it: Crispim loved his wife, and for thirty years they had never spent so much as a day apart. This fact explains the monologues that he delivered during those days, which his assistant overheard quite often:

"Great, well done! Who told you to agree to this voyage to Caesaria? You lackey, you vile lackey! And all to please Dr. Bacamarte. Well now you have to endure it, endure it, you subservient soul, you weakling, you worm, you wretch! You'll just go along with anything, won't you? Well that's what you get for it, you lowlife!"

All this, as well as many other ugly names that a man should never direct at anyone, much less himself. In light of that, it's easy to imagine the effect that the psychiatrist's message had on him. As soon as he heard it he dropped his chemicals and flew to the Green House.

Simão Bacamarte received him with the happiness particular to the wise, a happiness buttoned up to the neck with circumspection.

"I am very happy," he said.

"News from our people?" asked the apothecary, his voice trembling.

The psychiatrist made a grand gesture and replied:

"This is about something much more elevated: a scientific experiment. I use the term experiment, because I don't yet dare

swear to the truth of my idea, and science, Mr. Soares, is nothing
less than ceaseless inquiry. So, this is about an experiment, but it's
an experiment that will alter the very face of the earth. Madness,
the object of my studies, was, up until now, a forgotten island
on the ocean of reason; I'm now beginning to suspect that it's a
continent."

He said this and fell quiet, in order to bask in the apothecary's
astonishment. He then proceeded to explain his theory at
length. To his mind, an enormous number of brains were beset
with insanity, and he supported this claim with a variety of
arguments, texts, and examples. His examples came from both
history and Itaguaí, but, being the rare spirit that he was, he
understood the danger of describing all the cases in Itaguaí, so
he took refuge in history. Thus he made particular mention of
several famous figures: Socrates, who had an inner demon, Pascal,
who saw an abyss open up beside him at his left, Muhammad,
Caracalla, Domitian, Caligula, etc., a whole series of cases and
people, a mixture of the abominable and the ridiculous. Since
the apothecary was surprised at such an indiscriminate mix, the
psychiatrist told him that it was all one and the same, and even
added sententiously:

"Cruelty, Mr. Soares, is but the grotesque taken seriously."

"An elegant turn of phrase, very elegant!" exclaimed Crispim
Soares, raising his hands in the air in triumph.

As for the idea of expanding the realm of madness, the
apothecary found it excessive, but his modesty—the chief
adornment of his personality—wouldn't allow him to profess
anything other than generous enthusiasm. He declared that the
theory was glorious and true, and added that it was a "case for
the ratchet-man." This phrase has no equivalent in our modern
parlance. In those days, Itaguaí—which, like the other towns,
villages, and settlements of the colony, didn't have a printing
press—had two methods of spreading news: either by means of

handwritten placards, which were nailed to the doors of city hall and the church, or by means of the ratchet-man.

The second method consisted of the following. A man was hired for one or more days to walk the streets of the village with a ratchet—a noisemaker—in his hand. Every now and again he'd swing the ratchet, people would gather around, and he'd repeat the message he'd been entrusted with: news of medicines for malaria, arable land for sale, a sonnet, requests for alms for the church, the best gossip in town, the most beautiful speech given that year, etc. This system disturbed the peace and quiet of the town, but it was kept in place because it was such a powerful way to spread information. For example, one of the city councilmen—precisely the one who was most opposed to the creation of the Green House—enjoyed a reputation as a first-class snake and monkey tamer, yet he had never even trained a single one of these beasts. He did, however, make sure to retain the services of the ratchet-man every month. The town records indicate that some people claimed to have seen rattlesnakes dancing on the city councilman's chest; the claim was completely untrue, but it was a result of the absolute faith in the system. In truth, not all of the institutions of the old regime deserve the disdain of our century.

"Better still than announcing my theory is to put it into practice," said the psychiatrist, in response to the apothecary's suggestion.

And the apothecary, not wanting to disagree with this point of view in any noticeable way, said that yes, it was better to begin with the execution of the plan.

"There will always be time to hire the ratchet-man," he concluded.

Simão Bacamarte reflected on it for a moment more, and said: "Let's suppose that the human spirit is a shell. My intention, Mr. Soares, is to see if I can extract the pearl from it, which is reason itself. In other words, we shall definitively demarcate the limits of reason and madness. Reason is the perfect equilibrium of all the faculties; anything else is insanity, insanity, nothing less than insanity."

Parson Lopes, to whom the psychiatrist confided his new theory, plainly declared that he couldn't quite understand, that it was an absurd endeavor, and, if it wasn't absurd, it was such a colossal undertaking that it wasn't even worth starting on.

"Under the current definition, which is the one we've had since time immemorial," he added, "madness and reason are perfectly delimited. We know where one ends and the other begins. Why move the fence that divides them?"

The faint shadow of a desire to laugh grazed across the thin, discreet lips of the psychiatrist, the sort of laugh wherein contempt is coupled with pity. But nary a word emerged from the depths of his distinguished viscera.

Science was content to merely extend its hand to theology, and with such self-assurance that theology was now unsure if it should believe in itself or the other. Itaguaí, and the universe itself, was on the brink of revolution.

Chapter V: The Terror

Four days later, the townspeople of Itaguaí were aghast at the news that a certain citizen, a man named Costa, had been admitted to the Green House.

"Impossible!"

"Impossible, my foot! He was taken there this morning."

"But really, he doesn't need it ... and after all that he's done ..."

Costa was one of the most admired citizens of Itaguaí. He had inherited four hundred thousand *cruzados*, solid cash in the coin of the realm of King Dom João V, the interest on which would be enough, as his uncle put it in his will, for him to live "until the end of the world." No sooner had he received the inheritance than he began to give out no-interest loans—a thousand *cruzados* to one person, two thousand to another, three hundred to this one, eight hundred to that one—so much so that at the end of five years, he was left with nothing. If destitution had befallen him all at once, the people of Itaguaí would have been greatly astonished. But it came on slowly; opulence turned to abundance, abundance to moderate prosperity, moderate prosperity to poverty, and poverty to destitution, all gradually. At the end of those five years, people who used to beg with hat in hand the moment they spied him at the end of the street would now come up to him and pat him on the back familiarly, flick him on the nose, and call him names. But Costa always remained kind and cheerful. And he didn't even seem to notice that the people who treated him the worst were precisely the ones who still owed him money; on the contrary, he seemed to receive them with ever-greater pleasure and more exalted patience. One day, when one of these incorrigible debtors made a crude joke at his expense and Costa merely laughed it off, a disaffected onlooker remarked underhandedly: "The only reason you let this guy off easy is because you hope that he'll still pay you back."

Costa didn't hesitate for a second. He went up to the debtor and forgave him his debt.

"Don't look so surprised," said the onlooker, "all Costa did was give him a star, already out of reach way up in the sky."

Costa was sharp-witted, and he understood that the man was rejecting the merit of the deed, implying that he was only relinquishing something that was never going to find its way back into his pocket anyway. Furthermore, Costa was honorable and inventive, and two hours later he found a way to prove that this slander wasn't true: he got his hands on a few doubloons and had them sent, as a new loan, to the debtor.

"I hope that now . . ." he thought, without finishing his sentence.

This last display of Costa's generosity persuaded the credulous and incredulous alike. No one else ever doubted the chivalrous intentions of that worthy citizen. Even the most timid of the needy would venture outside and knock at his door, standing there in decrepit shoes and patched-up coats. And yet there was still something that bothered Costa, a worm that gnawed at his soul: the words of that disaffected onlooker. But this, too, soon came to an end. Three months later, that selfsame man came to ask him for one hundred and twenty *cruzados*, promising to pay him back two days later. It was the very last remnant of his considerable inheritance, but it was also a noble way for him to get his revenge. Costa loaned him the money straight away and at no interest. Unfortunately, there wasn't enough time for him to be repaid; he was committed to the Green House five months later.

Just imagine the alarm the people of Itaguaí must have felt when they heard the news. No one talked about anything else. People said that Costa had gone mad during lunch, or in the middle of the night. They talked about his fits, which were violent, dangerous, and terrifying—or else calm and even funny, depending on the version you happened to hear. A bunch of people went over to the Green House and found Costa there, tranquil, a little afraid, speaking very clearly, and asking why he'd been brought there. A few people went to talk to the psychiatrist. Bacamarte applauded them for their feelings of fondness and compassion for Costa, but added that science was science, and that he couldn't leave a madman free to roam the streets. The last person to intercede on Costa's behalf (since no one else dared approach the fearsome doctor after the episode I'm about to narrate) was a poor old woman, a cousin of his. The psychiatrist told her, in confidence, that the mental faculties of this worthy man weren't in perfect equilibrium, as shown by the way he wasted the fortune that . . .

"That's not it! That's not it!" interrupted the kindhearted woman. "Sure, he wasted all he inherited in record time, but it's not his fault."

"It isn't?"

"No, sir. I'll tell you how it happened. My deceased uncle wasn't a bad man, but when he was angry he wouldn't doff his hat to anybody, not even the holy Eucharist itself. So one day, not too long before he died, he found out that a slave had stolen a cow from him. You can imagine how infuriated he was.

"His face was as red as a pepper, and he was shaking, foaming at the mouth. I remember it like it was yesterday. Just then an ugly, long-haired man in shirtsleeves arrived at the door, asking for a glass of water. My uncle, God rest his soul, bellowed that he could get water from the river or from hell itself. The man looked at him, raised his hand in a threatening manner, and pronounced this curse: 'Your fortune shall not last more than seven years and a day, just as surely as this is the Star of David!' And at that he showed him the Star of David tattooed on his arm. You see, that's the problem, sir. It's the curse of that long-haired devil."

Bacamarte impaled the poor old woman with eyes as sharp as daggers. When she finished, he politely extended his hand to her, as if he were holding out his hand to the viceroy's wife herself, and invited her to visit her cousin. And the pitiable woman believed him. He took her to the Green House and locked her up in the wing reserved for the delusional.

News of the illustrious Bacamarte's treachery struck horror in the souls of the townspeople. Nobody could believe that, without motive or enmity, the psychiatrist would lock away a perfectly sane woman in the Green House, a woman who wasn't guilty of any crime other than intervening on behalf of a poor, wretched relative. It was discussed on street corners and barbershops. A whole fiction was developed about how the psychiatrist had once lavished amorous attention on Costa's cousin, and that this was his vengeance. It was all becoming clear. But the psychiatrist's austerity and the life of quiet study that he led seemed to belie such a theory. Lies! All of that was just the villain's facade, naturally. And one of the most credulous even started to spread word that he knew of other things, things he wouldn't repeat, since he wasn't entirely sure. But he knew of them and could almost even swear they were true.

"You're his close friend, can't you tell us what's going on, what happened, what reason he had . . ."

Crispim Soares completely melted. These inquiries from uneasy, curious townspeople and shocked friends were, for him, a public anointing. No doubt about it, the entire town now knew that he, Crispim Soares, the apothecary, was the psychiatrist's intimate friend, that he conferred with the great man on his great endeavors; thus the rush to see the apothecary. All this could be read on the apothecary's big, cheerful face, and in his discreet smile. In his smile and in his silence too, since he didn't proffer a word in response. One or two or three monosyllabic utterances at most, dry and detached, cloaked in that constant, loyal little smile, and full of scientific mysteries which he couldn't, without dishonor or danger, reveal to a single living soul.

"So there really is something," thought the most suspicious.

One of these people limited himself to thinking this, then shrugged his shoulders and left. He had personal business to attend to: he had just built a very luxurious house. The house alone would have been enough to stop passersby in their tracks and grab the attention of the whole town, but there was more. There was the furniture, which, according to him, he'd ordered from Hungary and Holland and could be spotted from the outside, since the windows were always open—and the garden, which was a masterpiece of workmanship and good taste. This man, who'd amassed his wealth in the saddle-making business, had always dreamt of having a magnificent house, a grandiose garden, and exquisite furniture. He didn't give up the saddle business, but whenever he took a break from it he'd gaze upon his new house, the finest in Itaguaí, more magnificent than the Green House, grander than city hall. Amongst the town's upper class there was wailing and gnashing of teeth whenever the house was thought of or brought up or praised—the house of a simple saddler, by God!

"There he is, mouth gaping open," said the passersby in the morning.

As a matter of fact, Mateus had the habit of sitting on the lawn in the middle of the garden for a solid hour in the morning, his eyes fixed on the house, enamored, until he was called in for lunch. The neighbors, who nevertheless greeted him with a certain amount of respect, laughed behind his back out of courtesy. One of them even said that Mateus would save more money and get even richer if he just made those saddles for himself. It was an unintelligible epigram, but people still laughed their heads off.

"There goes Mateus, ready to be looked at," they'd say in the afternoon.

The reason for this other saying was that in the afternoon, when families were out on their walks (they ate dinner early), Mateus customarily stood in front of the window, square in the middle of it, looking stately, standing against a darkened background and dressed in white, with a lordly air about him. And he'd stay there for two or three hours until it was completely dark outside. We can only hypothesize that Mateus's intention was to be admired and envied, since he never admitted as much to anyone, not even the apothecary or Padre Lopes, or his close friends. At any rate, this was precisely what the apothecary claimed when the psychiatrist told him that the saddler perhaps suffered from a love of stones, a mania that Bacamarte himself had discovered and had been studying for some time. That habit of staring at his house . . .

"No, sir," Crispim Soares replied animatedly.

"No?"

"Please forgive me, but maybe you aren't aware that in the morning he's examining the craftsmanship, rather than just admiring the house. And in the afternoon it's other people who do the admiring, staring at him and the house both," continued the apothecary, relating the saddler's habit of standing in front of the window from early afternoon until nightfall.

A scientific ecstasy illuminated Simão Bacamarte's eyes. Either he wasn't familiar with the saddler's habits, or his intention in questioning Crispim, was nothing less than to confirm an uncertain bit of news or a vague suspicion. He was satisfied with the explanation, but since his joys were those concentrated, peculiar joys of a scholar, the apothecary didn't notice anything that might make him suspect a sinister intention. On the contrary, it was in the afternoon, and the psychiatrist asked for his arm so they could take a stroll together. Dear God! It was the first time that Simão Bacamarte had given his good friend such an honor. Crispim felt bewildered and started to tremble, then said yes, that he was ready to go. Two or three people arrived before they left, and Crispim silently damned them all to hell; not only were they delaying the stroll, but it was possible that Bacamarte would invite one of them to accompany him instead, dispensing with the apothecary. Such impatience! Such anguish! At last they left. The psychiatrist led them to the saddler's house, observed him at the window, and passed in front of it five or six times, slowly, pausing to examine his pose, the expressions on his face. Poor Mateus, no sooner did he notice that he was the object of the curiosity or admiration of Itaguaí's most preeminent citizen, than he intensified his expression, made his posture even more distinguished . . . Sad, so sad! All this only served to seal his fate. He was taken to the Green House the very next day.

"The Green House is a private prison," said a doctor in his clinic.

Never had an opinion taken hold and spread so quickly. A private prison: this was repeated from north to south and east to west in Itaguaí. In truth, it was repeated in fear, because during the week following poor Mateus's detention, twenty some-odd people—two of whom were quite prominent citizens—were taken to the Green House. The psychiatrist said that only true pathological cases were committed, but few people took him at his word. Unofficial versions of the stories started to emerge. Revenge, avarice, divine punishment, the monomania of the psychiatrist himself, a secret plot out of the capital city, Rio de Janeiro, with the goal of destroying any seed of prosperity in Itaguaí that threatened to sprout, grow branches, and bloom, that great city wishing to tarnish and starve Itaguaí, and a thousand other explanations which didn't really explain anything. Such was the daily output of the public imagination.

In the midst of this, the psychiatrist's wife returned from Rio de Janeiro along with her aunt, Crispim Soares's wife, and all the rest of the retinue—or almost all of it—that had departed from Itaguaí a few weeks earlier. The psychiatrist went to greet her together with the apothecary, Padre Lopes, the city councilmen, and various other local officials. The moment that Dona Evarista laid eyes on her husband is considered, by the historians of that era, to be one of the most sublime moments in the moral history of humankind, deemed so due to the contrast between their two natures, both extreme, both admirable. Dona Evarista let loose a cry, stammered out a word, and threw herself toward her spouse in a movement that can best be described by comparing it to a mixture of those of a jaguar and a turtle dove. Not so the illustrious Bacamarte. Coldly diagnostic, his scientific rigidity never slacking for an instant, he held out his arms to his wife, who fell into them and fainted. A short-lived episode. Two minutes later, Dona Evarista was receiving the warm welcome of her friends, and the procession set off once more.

Dona Evarista was the hope of Itaguaí. They counted on her to alleviate the scourge of the Green House; hence the public applause, the immense crowds that filled the streets, and the banners, flowers, and silk tapestries in the windows. With her arm resting on that of Padre Lopes—for the eminent Bacamarte had entrusted his wife to the parson and walked alongside them pensively—Dona Evarista looked from one side of the street to the other, curious, restless, bold. The parson inquired about Rio de Janeiro, which he hadn't seen since the reign of the previous viceroy, and Dona Evarista enthusiastically replied that it was the most beautiful thing in the world to behold. The gardens of the Passeio Público were now open and she'd visited them many times, a real paradise, and the Rua da Belas Noites, and the Marrecas Fountain, the fountain of the wild ducks . . . Ah, what a fountain! And, indeed, there were ducks! Made of forged metal, with water flowing out of their mouths. Such an elegant sight. The parson agreed that Rio de Janeiro must be much more beautiful nowadays. It was already lovely way back when! And no wonder, since it's bigger than Itaguaí, and the seat of government besides. But that's not to say that Itaguaí is ugly. It has beautiful houses, such as Mateus's house, the Green House . . .

"Speaking of the Green House," said Padre Lopes, artfully moving along to the topic on everyone's lips, "you've returned to find it quite full."

"Really?"

"Why, yes. Even Mateus is there . . ."

"The saddler?"

"The saddler himself. Costa is there, as well as his cousin, and Mr. So-and-so, and Mrs. What's-her-name, and . . ."

"They're all crazy?"

"Or almost crazy," the priest said, in partial agreement.

"Well, what of it?"

The parson turned the edges of his mouth downward, like someone who knows nothing about a subject, or someone who doesn't want to reveal all he knows; a vague response, which can't be repeated to another person, since there are no words to accompany it. Dona Evarista found it truly extraordinary that all those people could have gone mad. One or another, fine, but all of them? However, it was hard for her to doubt it. Her husband was a scientist and he wouldn't put anyone in the Green House without clear evidence of madness.

"Without a doubt . . . without a doubt . . ." said the parson, stressing this point.

Three hours later, around fifty guests sat down at Simão Bacamarte's table: it was the welcome banquet. Done Evarista was the obligatory subject of toasts, speeches, all manner of verses, metaphors, rhetorical amplifications, and apologias. She was the wife of the latter-day Hippocrates, the muse of science, angelic, divine, the embodiment of youth, charity, life, and consolation; her eyes were two stars, according to Crispim Soares's modest rendition, and two suns, in the opinion of a city councilman. The psychiatrist was somewhat bored as he listened to all this, but showed no outward sign of impatience. The most he did was whisper in his wife's ear that the rhetorical art allowed for much ostentation without literal signification. Dona Evarista tried her best to adhere to her husband's opinion, but even disregarding three quarters of the adulation, there was still much to make her soul swell with pride. For example, one of the orators, Martim Brito, a young man of twenty-five and a dandy through and through, his life brimming with love affairs and adventures, delivered a speech in which Dona Evarista's birth was illustrated by a most singular provocation.

"God," he said, "having given the universe both man and woman, the diamond and pearl of the divine crown"—the orator triumphantly stretched this part out, from one end of the table to the other—"wanted to outdo himself, God surpassing God himself, so he created Dona Evarista."

Dona Evarista lowered her eyes with exemplary modesty. Two women, who found this affected obsequiousness excessive and audacious, examined the eyes of the man of the house, and, in fact, the psychiatrist's expression seemed to them to be clouded over with suspicion, foreboding, and probably even bloodlust. The dandy had been too cheeky, thought the two ladies. And both of them prayed that God would prevent any tragic occurrence—or at least postpone it until the following day. Yes, just postpone it. One of them, the more pious of the two, even admitted—to herself— that Dona Evarista didn't merit suspicion, since she was far from being attractive or pretty. She was simply harmless. Although, on the other hand, it's true that there's no accounting for taste. This second thought made her shudder once more, although less than the first time; less, because the psychiatrist was now smiling at Martim Brito and, everyone having stood up from their seats, had gone over to talk to him about his speech. He couldn't deny that it was a dazzling improvisation, full of magnificent flashes of brilliance. Was the notion about Dona Evarista's birth of his own invention, or had he found it in the works of some author who . . . ? No sir, it was his own creation. He'd happened upon it at that very moment and found it fitting for his oratorical outburst. Besides, his ideas were always bold, never tender or ironic. In the epic style. Once, for example, he wrote an ode about the fall of the Marquis of Pombal, in which he called this diplomat the "cruel dragon of Nothingness" who was crushed by the "vengeful talons of All," among other conceits in the same vein, more or less out of the ordinary. He preferred his ideas unique and sublime, his images grand and noble . . .

"Poor young man," thought the psychiatrist. And, thinking further: "What we have here is a case of cerebral lesion, not a serious phenomenon, but worthy of further study . . ."

Dona Evarista was astonished to find out, three days later, that Martim Brito had been taken to the Green House. A young man with such beautiful thoughts! The two ladies attributed this act to the psychiatrist's jealousy. It couldn't be anything else, really, the young man's speech had been much too bold.

Jealousy? Then how do you explain that, soon after, José Borges do Couto Leme, a person held in high regard, Chico das Cambraias, an illustrious reveler, Fabrício the clerk, and others too, were all rounded up? The terror mounted. No one knew who was sane and who was crazy anymore. When their husbands went out, women would light an oil lamp for the Virgin Mary. And the husbands weren't fearless either; some of them wouldn't leave the house without a bodyguard or two. Terror, pure and simple. Those who could, left. One of the people who fled was captured a mere two hundred paces outside of town. He was a young man, thirty years old, affable, chatty, and polite. So polite, in fact, that every time he greeted someone he would doff his hat and lower it almost to the ground; out on the street, he'd run twenty or thirty meters to shake the hand of a dignified gentleman, a lady, or at times even the hand of a little boy, as happened with the son of the itinerant circuit judge. He had a knack for courtesy. Besides, he owed his good rapport with the town not only to his natural gifts—which were unique—but to the noble tenacity that never let him get discouraged when confronted with one, two, four, six rebuffed attempts, scowling faces, etc. It was usually the case that once he was invited into a home he was always invited back, since the occupants of the home wouldn't let him stay away for long. Such was the charm of Gil Bernardes. And although Gil Bernardes knew he was well liked, he was frightened to learn one day that the psychiatrist had his eye on him. The next day, in the wee hours of the morning, he skipped town, but was quickly captured and conveyed to the Green House.

"We've got to put an end to this!"

"This can't go on!"

"Down with tyranny!"

"Despot! Brute! Goliath!"

This wasn't shouted in the streets. It was sighed indoors, but the time for shouting was drawing nigh. The terror grew, inching closer toward rebellion. The thought of drafting a petition to the government to seize and deport Simão Bacamarte passed through a few heads, until Porfírio, the barber, spelled it out in detail in his shop, gesticulating indignantly. Take note—for this is one of the purest pages of the whole gloomy tale—take note of the fact that ever since the Green House started to get so extraordinarily full, Porfírio had seen his profits increase, due to the constant demand for leech treatments at the asylum. But personal gain, as he put it, should surrender to the public good. And he added: "The tyrant must be overthrown!" Now, take further note of the fact that he unleashed this cry on the very day that Simão Bacamarte locked up Coelho, who had filed a lawsuit against Porfírio.

"Can anyone here give me one reason why Coelho should be deemed crazy?" roared Porfírio.

No one responded. The all merely confirmed that he was a perfectly sensible man. Even the lawsuit that he'd filed against the barber, involving a few plots of land in town, was the result of the ambiguity of a permit, not greed or hatred. A fine sort, that Coelho. His only detractors were a few guys who, claiming to be reserved, or alleging that they were in a hurry, would turn a corner or pop into the nearest store the moment they caught sight of him. The truth is, Coelho loved a good chat, those nice, long discussions that are savored between big gulps from a glass. Thus he was never alone, preferring the company of people who knew how to put a sentence or two together, although never rejecting the company of others. Padre Lopes, who knew his Dante and was one of Coelho's adversaries, would declaim and amend this passage any time he saw someone leave Coelho's side:

La bocca sollevò dal fiero pasto
Quel "seccatore" . . .

But only a few people knew of the Padre's distaste for Coelho. The rest assumed this was a Latin prayer.

Chapter VI: The Rebellion

Around thirty people joined forces with the barber, drafted a petition, and sent a group of representatives to city hall.

The city council refused to accept it, declaring that the Green House was a public institution, and that science couldn't be overturned by an administrative vote, much less by street-level movements.

"Go back to work," concluded the council president. "That's our advice to you."

The agitators were enraged. The barber proclaimed that they would raise the banner of rebellion and march to destroy the Green House, that Itaguaí could no longer serve as a cadaver for the tests and experiments of a despot, that too many well-regarded people—some eminent, others of humble origin, yet all worthy of respect—were languishing in the cells of the Green House, and that the psychiatrist's scientific despotism was mixed with a spirit of greed, since the insane, or those presumed to be so, weren't exactly treated free of charge. Their families, or, in their absence, city hall itself, paid the psychiatrist . . .

"You're wrong about that," interrupted the president.

"Wrong?"

"About two weeks ago we received an official letter from the illustrious doctor, in which he stated that, intending to perform experiments of the highest value to psychology, he would no longer accept the stipend voted into law by the city council, just as he would no longer accept any payment from the families of the patients."

The news of such a noble, pure action somewhat hampered the spirit of the rebels. The psychiatrist could very well be wrong, but he wasn't motivated by any interest outside science itself. And demonstrating that he was wrong would take more than just street riots and general uproar. Thus spoke the president, to the applause of the entire city council. The barber, after a few moments of concentration, declared that he had been given a public mandate, and that peace would not be restored in Itaguaí until the Green House was razed to the ground—"that Bastille of human reason," an expression he'd picked up from a local poet, which he repeated with great pomp. Having said this, he gave a signal and the rebels departed.

Imagine, for a moment, the situation the city councillors found themselves in: they felt compelled to stand in opposition to the horde, the rebellion, the fighting, the bloodshed. To add to the difficulty, one of the city councilmen, who had previously supported the president, heard the epithet the barber used to refer to the Green House—"the Bastille of human reason"—and found it so elegant that he changed his mind. He said that he thought it prudent to pass some measure that would scale back the Green House. The president, fuming mad, expressed his astonishment in forceful terms. Then the city councillor shared this insight:

"I don't know a thing about science, but if so many men whom we suppose to be sane are locked away as lunatics, who is to say that the psychiatrist isn't the real madman?"

Sebastião Freitas, the dissenting city councilman, had a gift for words and spoke a while more, circumspectly but firmly. His colleagues were speechless, and the president requested that Freitas, at very least, set an example of order and respect for the rule of law, and keep his opinions to himself in public, so as not to give shape and soul to the rebellion, which was at that point still just a whirlwind of scattered particles. This figure of speech somewhat balanced out the effect of the previous one, and Sebastião Freitas promised to refrain from any direct action, reserving the right to request, through proper legal channels, that the Green House be scaled back. And he repeated to himself, enamored: "Bastille of human reason!"

Meanwhile, the general uproar grew. There were no longer just thirty, but three hundred people who accompanied the barber, whose nickname should be mentioned at this point, since it lent its name to the rebellion. He was called *Canjica*, or Corn Cake— and the movement became known by the name "The Corn Cakes Revolt." Direct action may have been limited, since most people, either out of fear or habitual good manners, didn't take to the streets, but the sentiment was unanimous, or nearly unanimous, and the three hundred people who marched to the Green House—accounting for the population difference between Paris and Itaguaí—could be roughly compared to those who stormed the Bastille.

Dona Evarista caught wind of the rebellion before it reached the Green House; one of the household servants brought her news of it. At the time, she was trying on a silk gown—one of the thirty-seven she'd brought back from Rio de Janeiro—and she couldn't bring herself to believe what she was told.

"Probably just a group of revelers," she said, changing the angle of one of the pins. "Benedita, make sure the hem looks right."

"It does, ma'am," replied the slave woman, squatting down to check, "it's fine. Will you turn a little, ma'am? That's good. Yes, it's just fine."

"It's not just some revelers, no ma'am, they're screaming 'Death to Dr. Bacamarte! The tyrant!'" said a frightened little black boy.

"Shut your mouth, you half-wit! Benedita, look here on the left side, doesn't it look like the seam runs at a diagonal? The blue stripe doesn't go all the way to the bottom, it's so ugly that way. It needs to be re-stitched so that it looks exactly like . . ."

"Death to Dr. Bacamarte! Death to the tyrant!" came the sound of three hundred voices howling outside. It was the rebellion, pouring onto Rua Nova.

All the blood rushed from Dona Evarista's face. At first she didn't take a step, didn't move a muscle; she was petrified by fear. The slave woman instinctively ran to the back door. As for the little black boy, whom Dona Evarista hadn't believed, he had a moment of triumph, a sort of sudden sensation—imperceptible and deeply internalized—of moral satisfaction, upon seeing that reality had vouched for his story.

"Death to the psychiatrist!" shouted the voices, now closer.

If Dona Evarista had trouble resisting the persuasive call of pleasure, she certainly knew how to deal with moments of danger. She didn't faint. Instead, she ran to an inner room, where her husband was studying. When she entered the room in haste, the illustrious doctor was scouring a text by Averroes; his eyes, cloaked in meditation, rose from the book to the ceiling, then lowered from the ceiling back to the book, blind to any external reality, but clairvoyant for the purposes of profound mental exertion. Dona Evarista called to her husband twice, failing to get his attention. He heard her third attempt and asked what the problem was. Was she were feeling sick?

"Can't you hear the shouting?" asked his worthy wife, with tears in her eyes.

The psychiatrist listened: the shouts were approaching, terrible and threatening. He understood at once. He got up from his armchair, closed the book, and, with a calm, resolute stride, walked over to put it back on the bookshelf. Since the re-shelving of this volume slightly disturbed the neat line of the two books adjacent to it, Simão Bacamarte took care to fix this minor yet interesting flaw. He then told his wife to retire to bed, and that she shouldn't do anything.

"No, no," implored the worthy lady, "I want to die by your side . . ."

Simão Bacamarte insisted that she not do this, that it wasn't a matter of life and death, and that even if it was, she must—in the name of life itself—stay put. The poor thing lowered her head, obedient and tearful.

"Down with the Green House!" yelled the Corn Cakes.

The psychiatrist walked out to the front porch, and arrived there at precisely the same time as the rebels, who stopped in front of the house—three hundred faces, bright with civic pride, yet dark with rage. "Death! Death!" they screamed from every side as the psychiatrist appeared on the porch. Simão Bacamarte made a gesture indicating he wanted to speak; the rebels drowned out his voice with indignant cries. At that point, the barber waved his hat in the air in an attempt to silence the crowd, managed to quiet down his companions, and told the psychiatrist he could speak, but added that he mustn't abuse the patience of the people, as he had already done thus far.

"I'll say little, or even nothing at all, if necessary. First, I'd like to know what it is you request."

"We're not going to request anything," roared the barber in response. "We demand that the Green House be demolished, or at least that the poor things who are locked away in it be set free."

"I don't understand."

"You understand all too well, you tyrant. We want to free the victims of your hatred, your whims, your greed . . ."

The psychiatrist smiled, but the great man's smile wasn't visible to the eyes of the multitude. It was a slight contraction of two or three muscles, nothing more. He smiled and responded:

"Gentlemen, science is a serious thing, and it deserves to be treated with seriousness. I don't explain my actions as a psychiatrist to anyone, save other eminent scientists and God himself. If you wish to change the administration of the Green House, I'm willing to hear you out. But if you demand that I reject my own ideas, you won't get anywhere. I could invite some of you, as representatives of the others, to come see the deranged inmates; but I won't do it, because doing so would reveal my system, which I will not reveal to laymen, nor to rebels."

The crowd was astonished by the psychiatrist's words. It was clear that they didn't expect him to be so forceful, much less that he'd be so calm. But their amazement grew greater still when the psychiatrist, waving to the throng with great solemnity, turned his back on them and slowly walked inside. The barber soon came back to his senses and, waving his hat, invited his friends to go destroy the Green House; only a few weak voices responded. It was at this decisive moment that the barber felt an ambition for government office blossom inside him. It seemed to him that by destroying the Green House and overthrowing the psychiatrist, he would be able to seize power at city hall, control the remaining authorities, and become the ruler of Itaguaí. For a few years he'd fought to get his name on the ballot for the selection of city councillors, but he was rejected because his position in society wasn't deemed fit for such a heavy responsibility. It was now or never. Besides, the riot had gone so far already that defeat would mean prison, or exile, or the gallows. Unfortunately, the psychiatrist's response had tempered the fury of his followers. As soon as he noticed this, the barber felt a twinge of indignation and wanted to scream at them, call them scoundrels, cowards. But he restrained himself, breaking the silence by saying:

"My friends, we'll fight to the end! The salvation of Itaguaí is in your worthy, heroic hands. Let's destroy the prison that holds captive your sons and fathers, your mothers and sisters, your friends and relatives, and you yourselves! If not, you'll die of poverty, or beneath the whip, in the dank dungeon of that scoundrel."

The crowd began to stir, and people started talking, screaming, threatening, and eventually rallying around the barber. The revolt was coming back to consciousness after a brief fainting spell, threatening to raze the Green House.

"Let's go!" yelled Porfírio, waving his hat.

"Let's go!" repeated the others.

Yet something halted their progress: the dragoons, moving double-time, were entering Rua Nova.

Chapter VII: The Unexpected

When the dragoons caught up with the Corn Cakes, there was a moment of stupefaction. The Corn Cakes could hardly believe that the city's police force had been sent after them, but the barber understood it all immediately and waited. The mounted infantry stopped, and the captain ordered the crowd to disperse. And although some of them were inclined to do so, others vigorously supported the barber, whose response consisted of these elevated words:

"We shall not disperse. If it's our corpses you want, you can have them. But only the corpses. You shall not take our honor, our reputation, our rights, and, along with them, the very salvation of Itaguaí."

There was nothing in the world more foolish than the barber's response, and nothing more natural. Chalk it up to the vertiginous feeling of great crises. Perhaps it was also due to an excess of confidence that the dragoons would abstain from using force, a confidence that the captain soon quashed when he ordered the dragoons to attack the Corn Cakes. The moment defies description. The throng let out a frenzied roar. Some of them, climbing into the windows of nearby houses or running off down the street, managed to escape, but the majority of them remained, huffing with rage, indignant, spurred on by the barber's words. Just when the Corn Cakes' defeat seemed imminent, a third of the dragoons, for reasons unknown—the historical records don't state why—suddenly joined forces with the rebellion. This unexpected reinforcement gave the Corn Cakes courage, while at the same time demoralized the ranks of the authorities. The faithful soldiers couldn't bring themselves to attack their own comrades and, one by one, they joined them on the other side, so that within minutes the outlook of the skirmish was completely different. The captain was on one side with just a few people, facing a densely packed crowd that was calling for his head. There was no other option: he admitted defeat and handed his sword to the barber.

The triumphant revolution didn't waste any time. They took the wounded into nearby homes for help and headed straight to city hall. The troops and the people joined forces, chanting "long live the king, the viceroy, Itaguaí, and the 'Illustrious Porfírio.'" He was up front, adroitly wielding the sword as if it were nothing more than an abnormally long straight razor. The victory had lent his visage a mysterious aura. The dignity of government had begun to cause his hindquarters to stiffen.

The city councillors were at the windows watching the approaching multitude, and assumed that the troops had subdued them. Without further examination, they entered the hall and voted on a petition to the viceroy, requesting a bonus equal to a month's salary for the dragoons, "whose courage saved Itaguaí from the abyss, into which it had been tossed by a band of rebels." This phrase was proposed by Sebastião Freitas, the dissenting city councillor, whose defense of the Corn Cakes had scandalized his colleagues. But their illusion soon disappeared. The refrains of "Long live the barber" and "Death to the city councillors" made the distressing reality clear. The president wasn't discouraged. "Whatever may happen to us," he said, "let's remember that we are at the service of His Majesty and the people." Sebastião Freitas suggested that they could better serve the crown and the town by escaping by the back door and conferring with the itinerant circuit judge, but the rest of the city council rejected this proposal.

Moments later, the barber, accompanied by some of his subordinates, entered the chambers of the city council and informed them that they were defeated. The city council didn't offer resistance; they turned themselves over to the barber and were summarily taken to jail. The barber's companions then proposed that he take charge of the city government in the name of His Majesty, the king. Porfírio accepted the position, although he didn't fail to recognize (he added) the difficulties that came along with such a responsibility. He further added that he couldn't do it without the aid of those of his companions there present, to which they quickly consented. The barber went to the window and communicated these decisions to the people, and the people ratified them, applauding the barber. He took on the name of "Protector of the Town in the Name of His Majesty and the People." They soon issued various important edicts, official missives from the new government, including a detailed statement to the viceroy, brimming with asseverations of loyalty to His Majesty's orders. And, finally, there was a proclamation to the people, short, but forceful:

Itaguaians!
A corrupt and violent city council conspired against the interests of His Majesty and those of the people. Public opinion condemned it; a handful of citizens, valiantly supported by His Majesty's gallant dragoons, have just dealt it a disgraceful defeat, and, by the unanimous consensus of the town, I have been entrusted with its supreme command, until the day when His Majesty decides to ordain whatever he deems best for his royal service. Itaguaians! I merely ask

that you surround me with your trust, and that you help me restore public peace and the normal flow of commerce, which were utterly destroyed by the city council that has just now met its end at your hands. Count on me to make sacrifices for you, and rest assured that the crown will be on our side.

The Protector of the Town in the
Name of His Majesty and the People,
Porfírio Caetano das Neves

Everyone noticed the proclamation's absolute silence regarding the Green House, and, according to some, there was no clearer indication of the barber's sinister plans than this. The danger seemed even greater, since, in the midst of all these weighty events, the psychiatrist had committed seven or eight people to the Green House, including two women and a man who was related to "The Protector." It wasn't a provocation, an intentional act of defiance, but everyone interpreted it as such, and the whole town sighed with relief, hopeful that the psychiatrist would be in shackles within twenty-four hours, and that the Green House, that terrible prison, would be destroyed.

The day ended merrily. While the town-crier—the ratchet-man—went from corner to corner reciting the proclamation, the people congregated in the streets and swore that they'd die in defense of the illustrious Porfírio. There were very few shouts in opposition to the Green House, proof of their belief that the government would take action. The barber issued a decree declaring that day a holiday and started discussing the possibility of holding a *Te Deum* with the parson—the union of secular and temporal power seeming particularly advantageous in the eyes of the barber. But Padre Lopes flatly rejected his offer.

"In any event, Your Reverence, you're not going to side with the enemies of the government, are you?" asked the barber, a dark look coming over his countenance.

To which Padre Lopes responded, without exactly responding: "How can I side with them, if the new government has no enemies?"

The barber smiled; it was absolutely true. Save for the captain, the city councillors, and the town's most prominent citizens, everyone had publicly endorsed him. Even the prominent citizens, though they hadn't endorsed him, at least hadn't come out against him. None of the inspectors of weights and measures failed to come take orders from him. Generally speaking, every family in town blessed the name of the man who would finally liberate Itaguaí from the Green House and the terrible Simão Bacamarte.

Capítulo VIII: The Apothecary's Anguish

Twenty-four hours after the events that were narrated in the previous chapter, the barber left the government palace—the name given to the city hall building—with two aides-de-camp and headed to Simão Bacamarte's house. He wasn't oblivious to the fact that propriety dictated that the government should send for Bacamarte; however, fear that the psychiatrist wouldn't heed his order obliged him to appear tolerant and restrained.

I will not describe the apothecary's horror upon hearing that the barber was headed for the psychiatrist's house. "He's going to arrest him," he thought. And his anguish increased. Indeed, the moral torture the apothecary suffered during the days of the revolution exceeds all possible description. Never has a man found himself in such an intense quandary; his close friendship with the psychiatrist pulled him toward his friend's side, while the victory of the barber attracted him to the barber's cause. News of the uprising had been enough to cause his soul to tremble, since he was aware of the unanimous nature of the hatred directed toward the psychiatrist, but their ultimate victory was a final blow to the apothecary. His wife, a strong-willed woman and a friend of Dona Evarista, said that his rightful place was at Simão Bacamarte's side, while his heart screamed the opposite, insisting that it wasn't, that the psychiatrist's plight was a lost cause, and that nobody, of their own volition, ties their fate to a corpse.

"Cato the Younger, did, it's true, *sed victa Catoni*," he thought, remembering some of Padre Lopes's customary sermons. "But Cato didn't attach himself to a lost cause, he *was* the lost cause, the cause of the republic. His action, therefore, was that of a selfish man, a miserable egotist. My situation is different."

Nevertheless, his wife insisted and, at that juncture, Crispim Soares had only one way out: falling ill. He pronounced himself sick, and got into bed.

"There goes Porfírio on his way to Dr. Bacamarte's house," said his wife the following day, at his bedside, "and there are a lot of people with him."

"They're going to arrest him," thought the apothecary.

One idea yields another. The apothecary imagined that, once the psychiatrist was jailed, they would also come after him for his role as accomplice. This thought was better than any recuperative treatment. Crispim Soares got up, declared himself better, and said that he was going out; despite his spouse's protests and efforts to the contrary, he got dressed and left. The town historians of the era unanimously assert that the wife was certain that her husband was going to take his proper place by the psychiatrist's side, and that this thought gave her great solace. Perspicaciously, they make further note of the immense moral power of an illusion, for the apothecary resolutely strode to the government palace, not the home of the psychiatrist.

Upon arriving there, he affected surprise at not finding the barber there, to whom he had come to pledge his loyalty, not having been able to do so yesterday on account of being sick. And he coughed, with some effort. The high-level functionaries who listened to his announcement, knowing full well the apothecary's close ties to the psychiatrist, understood the deep importance of this new supporter and treated Crispim Soares with extreme kindness. They told him that the barber wouldn't be long, that His Lordship had gone to the Green House about an important matter, but that he wouldn't be long. They offered him a chair, something to drink, and their compliments. They told him that the cause of the Illustrious Porfírio was the cause of all true patriots, to which the apothecary responded that, yes, he had never thought about it any other way, and he would even state as much in front of His Majesty.

Chapter IX—Two Beautiful Cases

The psychiatrist didn't take long to invite the barber in. He announced that he had no way to resist, and was thus prepared to obey. He made only one request: that he not be forced to assist personally in the destruction of the Green House.

"You are mistaken, Your Lordship," said the barber, after a brief pause, "you are mistaken to think that the government has destructive intentions. Rightly or wrongly, it's public opinion that the majority of the crazies who are locked away there are perfectly sane. But the government recognizes that the question at hand is a purely scientific one and would never consider resolving scientific matters with governmental posturing. Furthermore, the Green House is a public institution, which is how we received it from the previous, now-dissolved city council. However, there should be, or rather, there must be, some intermediate proposal that can set the public spirit at ease."

The psychiatrist could barely contain his astonishment. He admitted that he expected something quite different, for the asylum to be razed, for him to be jailed, exiled, anything but . . .

"Your Lordship's amazement," said the barber, gravely cutting the psychiatrist short, "stems from you not understanding the serious responsibility of the government. The people, caught up in their blind piety—which in a case like this is manifested in legitimate indignation—may demand a certain succession of actions of its government. But the government, in turn, with the responsibilities incumbent upon it, must not go through with them, at least not all of them; such is our situation. The daring revolution, which just yesterday toppled a corrupt and despised city council, demanded the destruction of the Green House in loud cries of protest. But can a government presume to abolish madness? No. And if the government is unable to abolish it, isn't it at least capable of discerning it, of recognizing it? Again, no; it's a scientific matter. Thus, with such a delicate matter, the government cannot, must not, and does not wish to dispense with Your Lordship's cooperation. What we do ask is that, to some extent, we satisfy the will of the people. If we are united, the people will obey instinctively. One possible solution—if Your Lordship doesn't have another to offer—would be to remove all the patients who are almost cured from the Green House, as well as those lunatics who are basically harmless, etc. In this way, without incurring any grave danger, we'll display some amount of tolerance and benevolence."

"How many dead and wounded were there in the skirmish yesterday?" asked Simão Bacamarte, after about three minutes.

The barber was surprised at the question, but quickly responded that there had been eleven dead and twenty-five wounded.

"Eleven dead and twenty-five wounded!" repeated the psychiatrist two or three times.

He then immediately stated that the proposal didn't seem

right to him, but that he would think up another one and would give them a response within a few days. He went on to ask the barber various questions about the successes of the day before, the attacks, the defensive strategies, the dragoons' change of heart, the resistance of the city councillors, etc., to which the barber responded at great length, emphatically underscoring the disgraceful manner in which the city council fell. The barber confessed that the new government still hadn't received the endorsement of the town's most prominent citizens, but that the psychiatrist could do a lot to change that. The government, concluded the barber, could rest easy if it could count on the goodwill—if not yet the affection—of the most elevated spirit in all of Itaguaí and, to be sure, the entire kingdom. But none of what the barber had to say altered the noble and austere countenance of that great man, who listened silently, with neither pride nor modesty, as impassive as a stone deity.

"Eleven dead and twenty-five wounded," repeated the psychiatrist, after accompanying the barber to the door. "What we have here are two beautiful cases of mental illness. The symptoms of duplicity and insolence are clear as day in the barber. As for the idiocy of those who revolted alongside him, no further proof is needed than the eleven dead and twenty-five wounded."

"Two beautiful cases!"

"Long live the illustrious Porfírio!" shouted the thirty or so people who awaited the barber at the door.

The psychiatrist looked out the window and managed to hear a snippet of the short speech the barber delivered to the thirty people who were shouting his praises:

". . . for I keep vigil, you can be certain of it, I keep vigil to ensure that the will of the people is carried out. Put your trust in me, and all will be carried out in the best possible manner. I only suggest that you maintain order. Order, my friends, is the foundation of government . . ."

"Long live the illustrious Porfírio!" shouted the thirty voices, waving their hats.

"Two beautiful cases!" whispered the psychiatrist.

Chapter X—The Restoration

Within five days, the psychiatrist had locked up around fifty supporters of the new government in the Green House. The townspeople were incensed. The government, bewildered, didn't know how to react. João Pina, another barber, stated openly in the streets that Porfírio had been "bought off by Simão Bacamarte's gold," a phrase that rallied the most resolute citizens around Pina. Upon seeing his old razor-wielding rival at the head of the insurrection, Porfírio understood that his defeat was inevitable if he didn't deliver a decisive blow; he issued two decrees, one abolishing the Green House, the other exiling the psychiatrist. João Pina lucidly demonstrated, with grand turns of phrase, that the action Porfírio had taken was pure ostentation, a facade in which the townspeople shouldn't place their confidence. Two hours later Porfírio fell ignominiously, and João Pina took over the difficult task of governing. He found drafts of the proclamation, the detailed statement to the viceroy, and other inaugural documents of the previous administration in the files of city hall and made haste to have them copied and sent out. The town historians add—and besides, it's to be assumed—that they changed the names on these documents, and whereas the previous barber wrote of a "corrupt city council," the new one wrote of "an intruder contaminated by evil French doctrines, contrary to the sacrosanct interests of His Majesty," etc.

In the midst of this, troops sent by order of the viceroy entered the town and reestablished order. The psychiatrist immediately demanded that Porfírio, the barber, be handed over to him, as well as fifty some-odd other individuals, whom he declared insane.

But the troops didn't stop at this; they guaranteed to deliver him an additional nineteen of the barber's followers, who were recovering from wounds received in the initial rebellion.

This point in the crisis of Itaguaí also marks Simão Bacamarte's highest level of influence. All that he wanted was given him. And the most telling evidence of the illustrious doctor's power is the swiftness with which the city councillors, restored to their seats, agreed to his request that Sebastião Freitas be committed to the asylum. The psychiatrist, knowing the extraordinary inconsistency of the city councilman's opinions, understood that it was a pathological case, and called for his committal. The same happened with the apothecary. As soon as he was informed of Crispim Soares's impulsive decision to support the Corn Cakes rebellion, the psychiatrist weighed that fact against the approbation he'd always received from Soares—right up until the night before the revolt—and took him into custody. Crispim Soares didn't deny what had happened, but rationalized it, saying that he had surrendered to a fear-inspired impulse once he saw that the rebellion had triumphed, and gave as further proof the absence of any other action on his part, adding that he had even gone straight back to bed, ill. Simão Bacamarte didn't contradict him. He did, however, inform onlookers that fear is the father of insanity, and that Crispim Soares appeared to be among the most distinguished of these cases.

But the most obvious proof of Simão Bacamarte's influence was the compliant manner in which the city councillors handed over their own president. This honorable magistrate had declared, in open session, that, to cleanse himself of the Corn Cakes' affront, no less than five hundred liters of blood would suffice; word of this reached the psychiatrist's ears from the lips of the city council secretary, enthusiastic and full of energy. Simão Bacamarte began by tossing the secretary in the Green House, and from there went to city hall, where he declared that the president was suffering from "bull's dementia," a variety of madness that he intended to study in depth, to the great benefit of the townspeople. The city council hesitated at first, but ended up going along with it.

From that day forth there was an unrestrained reaping of people. A man couldn't contrive or spread the simplest of lies, even those that benefited their inventor or propagator, without immediately getting thrown into the Green House. Everything was a symptom of madness. Those who thought up riddles, created puzzles, or invented anagrams; slanderers; people who were curious about the great beyond; dandies who cared only for their appearance; a prideful price-fixer or two; no one escaped the psychiatrist's emissaries. He respected lovers but didn't spare flirts, saying that the former were merely submitting to a natural impulse, the latter to a vice. Miser and spendthrift were both sent to the Green House just the same. All this resulted in the allegation that there was no guideline for complete sanity. Some historians believe that Simão Bacamarte didn't always proceed in good faith and frequently cite in evidence of this claim (which I don't know should be accepted), the fact that he convinced the city council to pass a municipal ordinance authorizing the use of a silver ring on the thumb of the left hand for anyone who, lacking any longstanding belief or documented proof, declared to have a drop or two of Gothic blood running through their veins. These historians claim that the secret purpose of the city council's decree was to enrich a jeweler, a friend or crony of the council. But while it's certain that the jeweler saw his business prosper in the wake of the municipal ordinance, it is no less certain that this measure provided the Green House with a horde of new tenants, from which one cannot determine, without going out on a limb, what the true intentions of the illustrious doctor really were. As for the definitive reason for the capture and detention of all those who wore the ring, it is one of the most enigmatic questions in the history of Itaguaí. The most probable answer is that they were rounded up for thoughtlessly gesticulating everywhere they went: in the street, at home, at church. As everyone knows, the deranged gesticulate wildly. At any rate, it's just a speculation. There's no way to say for sure.

"How far will this man go?" asked the nobility of the town. "Ah, if we'd only supported the Corn Cakes!"

One morning, on the day that the city council was going to hold a grand ball, the town was rocked with the news that the psychiatrist's wife had been committed to the Green House. No one could believe it; it must have been some rascal playing a joke on them. But it wasn't, it was the honest truth. Dona Evarista was taken there at two in the morning. Padre Lopes immediately tracked down the psychiatrist and interrogated him about this turn of events.

"I've had my doubts about her for some time," the husband said gravely. "The modest manner in which she lived throughout both her marriages couldn't be reconciled with the frenzy of silks, velvets, lace, and precious stones that appeared soon after she returned from Rio de Janeiro. I've been observing her ever since. All her conversation has centered around these things. If I spoke to her of ancient courts, she'd instantly ask about the style of the women's dresses. If a lady paid her a visit while I was away, she'd describe the lady's attire before she even told me the purpose of the visit, approving of certain aspects of the attire, criticizing others. One day, which I think Your Reverence surely recalls, she proposed to make a new dress each year for the statue of the Holy Virgin at the church. These were all very serious symptoms. Last night, however, she manifested symptoms of total dementia. She had chosen, prepared, and adorned the outfit she was going to wear to the ball thrown by the city council. But she wavered between a garnet necklace and a sapphire one. The day before yesterday, she asked me which she should wear; I responded that either one would look nice on her. Yesterday she repeated the question over lunch. A little while after dinner, I found her quiet and pensive.

"'What's wrong?' I asked.

"'I want to wear the garnet necklace, but the sapphire one is so beautiful!'

"'So wear the sapphire one.'

"'Ah, but what about the garnet one?'

"Ultimately, the evening wore on without further incident. We supped and went to bed. In the middle of the night, around one-thirty, I awoke and couldn't find her. I got up, went into the dressing room, and found her with the two necklaces, trying them on in front of the mirror, first one, then the other. Her dementia was obvious, and I immediately turned her in."

Padre Lopes wasn't satisfied with this response, but he didn't raise any objections. The psychiatrist, however, noticed this and explained to him that Dona Evarista was a case of "sumptuary mania," not incurable, and worthy of study, at any rate.

"I expect to have her well within six weeks," he concluded.

The illustrious doctor's act of self-sacrifice had great repercussions. Speculations, inventions, and doubts all came crumbling down, since he clearly wouldn't hesitate to lock up his own wife, whom he loved with all the energy of his soul. No one else had the right to oppose him now, much less accuse him of any intentions outside the realm of science.

He was a great, austere man, a mix of Hippocrates and Cato.

Chapter XI—The Astonishment of Itaguaí

And now prepare yourself, reader, for the same astonishment that washed over the townspeople when they learned one day that all the crazies in the Green House were going to be released.

"All of them?"

"All of them."

"Impossible. Some, perhaps, but not all . . ."

"All of them. That's what he said in the official letter he sent to the city council this morning."

Indeed, the psychiatrist had sent a dispatch to the city council, stating:

"1ˢᵗ—that he had examined the statistics relating to the town and the Green House, and that four fifths of the population were residing in said institution;

"2ⁿᵈ—that this population displacement had led him to scrutinize the foundations of his theory of mental illness, a theory which excluded from the realm of reason all cases in which the person's faculties were not perfectly and completely balanced;

"3ʳᵈ—that resultant from this re-examination and the statistical reality, he was convinced that his theory was not the true principle, but that its opposite was true; and that, consequently, those with unbalanced mental faculties should be deemed normal and exemplary, and all cases in which mental equilibrium was undisturbed should be presumed to be pathological;

"4ᵗʰ—that in light of this, he thereby announced to the city council that he was going to grant freedom to all those currently residing in the Green House, and gather into it all those people who found themselves in the conditions now put forth;

"5ᵗʰ—that in order to discover the scientific truth, he would spare no effort of any kind, and hoped for equivalent dedication from the city council.

"6ᵗʰ—that he would return the sum total of the stipend received for the room and board of the supposed lunatics to the city council and private individuals, deducting the amount that had already been spent on food, clothing, etc., the amount of which, the city council could verify in the ledgers and coffers of the Green House."

The astonishment of Itaguaí was great. No less great was the joy of the relatives and friends of the prisoners. Dinners, dances, festive lanterns, music—nothing was spared in the celebration of such a fortunate occurrence. I will not describe the festivities, since they aren't important for our purposes here, but they were magnificent, touching, and prolonged.

Thus proceed the affairs of humanity! In the midst of the mirth produced by Simão Bacamarte's official letter, nobody took notice of the final phrase of section four, which was full of future import.

Chapter XII—The End of Section 4

Lanterns were snuffed out, families were reunited, and everything appeared to be restored to its previous arrangement. Order reigned, and the city council once again carried out the duties of government, without any outside pressure. Even the president and city councilman Freitas returned to their positions. Porfírio the barber, having learned from the events that had taken place, having "experienced all in life," as the poet says of Napoleon— and even one thing more, since Napoleon never experienced the Green House—found the obscure glory of the razor and the scissors preferable to the dazzling misadventures of power. He was arrested, of course, but the townspeople begged His Majesty for lenience, and Porfírio was granted clemency. João Pina was absolved, too, since it was understood that he was toppling a rebel. Historians believe that this is what gave rise to the old adage: "When a thief robs a thief, for a hundred years there'll be no beef." True, it's an immoral adage, but an extremely useful one.

Not only did all the complaints against the psychiatrist come to an end, but there wasn't even any lingering resentment about what he had done. Additionally, ever since he had declared them completely sane, the prisoners of the Green House had felt overcome with a profound sense of gratitude and fervent enthusiasm. Many people felt that the psychiatrist deserved a special display of gratitude and threw a ball for him, followed by several other balls and dinners. The historical records say that Dona Evarista initially thought about separating from her husband, but the pain of losing the companionship of such a great man vanquished any grievances she may have had, and the couple ended up even happier than they were before.

No less intimate was the friendship between the psychiatrist and the apothecary. The latter concluded from Simão Bacamarte's official letter that prudence is the chief virtue in times of revolution and appreciated the magnanimity displayed by the psychiatrist when, upon granting the apothecary his freedom, he held out his hand to his old friend.

"He is a great man," he told his wife, referring to that specific incident.

It's unnecessary to discuss the saddler, Costa, Coelho, Martim Brito, and others who have been named in this work; suffice it to say that they were freely able to get back to their old habits. Martim Brito, who had been locked away for a speech that emphatically praised Dona Evarista, now delivered another one in honor of the distinguished doctor, "whose elevated genius, raising its wings well above the sun, left all other souls on earth, far below it."

"I thank you for those words," the psychiatrist retorted, "and I don't yet regret having granted you your freedom."

Meanwhile, the city council, which had responded to Simão Bacamarte's official letter with the proviso that they would enact a statute relating to the end of section four in a timely manner, finally got down to legislating on the matter. A municipal order was adopted, without protest, which authorized the psychiatrist to gather into the Green House all those who were found to be in possession of perfectly balanced mental faculties. And since the city council had gone through such a painful experience the first time around, it established a clause stating that the authorization was provisional, limited to one year, for the purpose of testing the new psychological theory, and granting city council the authority to shut down the Green House before the provisional year was up, if such a measure was deemed necessary for the maintenance of public peace. City councilman Freitas also proposed a measure stating that under no circumstances could any of the city councillors be committed to the insane asylum; this clause was accepted, voted on, and included in the municipal order, despite city councilman Galvão's objections. This magistrate's chief argument against it was that the city council, in passing legislation about a scientific experiment, couldn't exclude its own members from the consequences of the law; such an exception was odious and ridiculous. He had barely uttered these harsh words when the other city councillors broke out in shouts against the audacity and foolishness of their colleague. Galvão, however, heard them out and limited himself to saying that he would vote against the exception.

"Our position as city councillors," he concluded, "doesn't give us any special power or separate us from the rest of humanity."

Simão Bacamarte accepted the municipal order with all of its restrictions. As for the exclusion of the city councillors, he stated that he would be profoundly sorry if he were compelled to commit any of them to the Green House; the clause itself, however, was the greatest proof that they didn't suffer from a perfect equilibrium of their mental faculties. The same couldn't be said for councilman Galvão, whose insightful objection, as well as the restraint he showed in response to his colleague's invectives, revealed that he possessed a well-organized brain. As such, the psychiatrist pleaded with the city council to hand him over. The city council, still feeling that Galvão had wronged them, accepted the psychiatrist's request, and voted unanimously in favor of turning him in.

It should be understood that, according to the new theory, a single fact or statement wasn't sufficient to send someone to the Green House; a lengthy examination was necessary, an extensive inquest into the person's past and present. Padre Lopes, for example, was only rounded up thirty days after the municipal order passed; forty days for the apothecary's wife. This lady's imprisonment filled her spouse with indignation. Crispim Soares left his house boiling with rage, telling everyone who crossed his path that he was going to rip the tyrant's ears off. Upon hearing this on the street, an enemy of the psychiatrist set aside the reasons for his own animosity and ran to Simão Bacamarte's house to inform him of the danger he was in. Simão Bacamarte thanked his adversary for this kind behavior. It only took Bacamarte a few minutes to recognize the integrity of this man's feelings, his good faith, his respect for his fellow man, his generosity. He shook his hand warmly, then locked him up in the Green House.

"A case like this is quite rare," he said to his astonished wife. "Now we wait for Crispim." Crispim Soares arrived. Grief overcame anger, and the apothecary didn't rip the psychiatrist's ears off. The latter comforted his close friend, assuring him that it wasn't a lost cause. Perhaps his wife just had a cerebral lesion; he promised to give her a thorough examination, but until then he couldn't let her out on the street. The psychiatrist thought it might be advantageous to reunite them, since the husband's guile and deceit could, in a way, cure the moral goodness that he'd found in the wife. Simão Bacamarte added:

"You, sir, can work during the day at your apothecary shop, but you'll take lunch and dinner with your wife in the Green House, and spend the nights there too, as well as Sundays and holidays."

This proposal placed the poor apothecary in the situation of Buridan's ass. He wanted to live with his wife, but he was afraid to return to the Green House. He struggled with it for some time, until Dona Evarista freed him from this quandary, promising that she'd take it upon herself to visit her friend and relay messages back and forth between them. Crispim Soares kissed her hands in gratitude. The psychiatrist found this final display of cowardly selfishness sublime.

By the end of five months there were around eighteen people at the Green House, but Simão Bacamarte wasn't discouraged. He went from street to street and house to house, observing, questioning, and studying. And when he took in a patient, he felt the same glee he used to feel back when he gathered them up by the dozen. This very disproportion confirmed his new theory; at last, he had discovered the true cerebral pathology. One day, he managed to lock up the itinerant circuit judge, but he had proceeded so scrupulously that he only did so after minutely studying all of his actions and interviewing all the prominent citizens in town. More than once he had been on the verge of locking up people who were perfectly unbalanced. Such was the case of a lawyer, in whom he recognized such an ensemble of moral and mental qualities that he thought it dangerous to leave him out on the streets. He ordered him to be detained, but the psychiatrist's deputy, doubting him, asked his permission to perform an experiment. He went to speak with a friend of his, who was being prosecuted over a falsified will; he told the friend that he should use a lawyer named Salustiano, which was the name of the lawyer in question.

"Well, do you think he'll really . . ."

"Without a doubt. Go to him, confess everything, the whole truth, whatever it may be, and ask him to take your case."

The friend went to meet with the lawyer, confessed that he had falsified the will, and asked him to take the case. The lawyer didn't refuse him; he studied the papers, pled his case at length, and proved beyond a shadow of a doubt that the will was absolutely authentic. The judge solemnly proclaimed the defendant's innocence, and the inheritance was turned over to him. The distinguished barrister owed his liberty to this little experiment. But nothing escapes the eyes of such an original, discerning soul. Simão Bacamarte—who had, for some time now, noticed the zeal, wisdom, patience, and restraint of his deputy—acknowledged the cleverness and good judgment with which he had carried out such a delicate and complicated experiment, and decided to send him immediately to the Green House. He did, however, give him one of the best cells.

The arrangement of the lunatics was organized by classification. There was a hallway for the modest—that is, for the crazies in whom this specific moral perfection predominated—one for the tolerant, one for the truthful, one for the ingenuous, one for the loyal, one for the magnanimous, one for the wise, one for the sincere, etc. Naturally, the families and friends of the inmates were against this new theory, and a few of them tried to coerce the city council into revoking the psychiatrist's authorization. The city council, however, hadn't forgotten councilman Galvão's speech, and if they revoked the authorization, he'd be back out on the street and would resume his place on the city council—so they rejected the idea. Simão Bacamarte sent letters to the city councillors, not thanking them, but congratulating them for this act of personal vengeance.

Disillusioned with their legal recourses, some of the town's prominent citizens secretly appealed to Porfírio the barber and guaranteed him their complete support, money, and even influence at the viceroy's court if he would spearhead another movement against the city council and the psychiatrist. The barber replied that he wouldn't, that ambition had lead him to transgress the law the first time, but that he had changed, and recognized the error of his ways, as well as the fickleness of his own followers; and that, furthermore, the city council had decided to authorize the psychiatrist's new experiment for a year: it thus behooved them to either wait until the year was up or to petition the viceroy, in the event that the city council rejected the request. He would never advise them to employ a tactic that he'd seen fail before his very eyes, especially not one that was paid for in lives and wounds, which would cause him eternal remorse.

"What is it that you're telling me?" asked the psychiatrist, when one of his plainclothes deputies told him about the conversation between the barber and the citizens.

Two days later the barber was taken to the Green House.

"Damned if you do, damned if you don't!" cried the unfortunate wretch.

The one-year period came to an end, and the city council authorized a supplementary period of six months for the testing of therapeutic methods. The conclusion of this episode in the history of Itaguaí is of such magnitude—and so unexpected— that it deserves no less than ten chapters of exposition. But I'll be content with just one, which shall be the highest point of the narrative, and among the most beautiful examples of scientific conviction and self-sacrifice.

Chapter XIII—*Plus Ultra!*

It was time for therapy. Simão Bacamarte, who was agile and shrewd in discovering patients, outdid himself in the diligence and sagacity with which he started their treatment. The town historians are in full agreement on this point; the illustrious psychiatrist performed amazing treatments, which aroused the lively admiration of all Itaguaí.

In fact, it was hard to imagine a more sensible therapeutic system. Since the lunatics were divided into categories according to the moral perfection that predominated in each of them, Simão Bacamarte decided to attack the dominant quality head-on. Take a modest person, for instance. Bacamarte would apply a remedy that could instill the opposite sentiment in the person. And he didn't start off with large doses right away; he increased them by degrees, depending on the mental state, age, temperament, and social position of the patient. Sometimes all it took was a dress-coat, a ribbon, a wig, or a fine cane to restore a lunatic to his senses. In other patients, the malady was more stubborn. In such cases he turned to jewel-encrusted rings, honorary titles, etc. There was one patient, a poet, who withstood all treatment. Simão Bacamarte began to give up hope of finding a cure, when he happened on the idea of sending the ratchet-man around to proclaim that the poet rivaled the great ones, even Garção and Pindar.

"It was a miracle cure," said the poor man's mother to a friend, "a miracle cure."

Another patient, also a case of modesty, displayed the same resistance to his medication, but since he wasn't a writer—he could barely even sign his name—he couldn't be given the same ratchet-man treatment. It occurred to Simão Bacamarte to request for his patient the position of secretary in the Royal Academy that had been established in Itaguaí. The positions of president and secretaries had been made by royal appointment, by special dispensation of the deceased king Dom João V, and they included the title "Your Excellency" and the use of a gold plaque on one's hat. The government in Lisbon refused the request, but since the psychiatrist informed them that he wasn't requesting it as an honorary award or legitimate distinction, but rather only as a method of treatment for a difficult case, the government made an exception and complied with his request. Even so, they wouldn't have given in without the extraordinary efforts of the Minister of the Navy and Overseas Territories, who happened to be a cousin of the patient. It was another miracle cure.

"Truly, it's quite admirable!" they said in the streets, upon seeing the healthy, prideful expression on the faces of the two former lunatics.

Such was his system. Imagine the rest of the cases. Each moral or mental grace was attacked at the point where its perfection seemed most solid, and the desired effect was achieved. But it didn't always work. There were cases where the predominant quality resisted all efforts, so the psychiatrist would attack another area, applying a military strategy to his therapeutic method, whereby one attacks a stronghold from a different side, if the first side proves impenetrable.

At the end of five and a half months the Green House was empty; they were all cured! Councilman Galvão, who had been so cruelly afflicted with restraint and fairness, had the good fortune to lose an uncle. I call it good fortune because the uncle left behind an ambiguous will, and Galvão obtained a favorable interpretation of it by bribing judges and deceiving the other heirs. The psychiatrist's sincerity was made manifest on this occasion. He candidly admitted that he didn't have anything to do with the cure: it was a simple *vix medicatrix naturæ*. That wasn't the case with Padre Lopes, however. Knowing that the priest didn't know a word of Hebrew or Greek, the psychiatrist told him to write a critical analysis of the Septuagint. The priest accepted the task and made quick work of it; at the end of two months he stood in possession of both a book and his liberty. As for the apothecary's wife, she wasn't in her cell for very long, and never wanted for kind visitors.

"Why hasn't Crispim come to visit me?" she asked daily.

Her visitors would give her one excuse or another, but they finally told her the whole truth. That worthy matron could not contain her indignation and shame. Vague snatches of speech escaped her lips during her outbursts of rage, such as these:

"Scoundrel! . . . Villain! . . . Ingrate! . . . That coward has built his career on counterfeit ointments and rancid balms . . . Ah, the scoundrel!"

Simão Bacamarte realized that, even though the accusation contained in these statements wasn't true, the words were enough to demonstrate that the eminent lady was finally restored to a perfect imbalance of her mental faculties, and he promptly discharged her.

Now, if you think that the psychiatrist must have been beaming as he watched the last patient leave the Green House, you'll only be showing how little you understand our man. *Plus ultra!*: that was his motto. It wasn't sufficient for him to have discovered the true theory of insanity; he wasn't content with having ushered in a reign of reason in Itaguaí. *Plus ultra!* He didn't become happy, he became preoccupied, contemplative. Something told him that the new theory contained within it another, even newer theory.

"Let's see," he thought, "let's see if I can arrive at the ultimate truth."

He said this to himself as he paced the length of the immense room, wherein sparkled the most splendid library of any of His Majesty's overseas territories. A large damask housecoat, tied at the waist by a silk sash with gold tassels (it was a present from a university) enveloped the majestic, stern body of the illustrious psychiatrist. A wig covered his bald head—broad and noble, but bald as a result of his daily scientific cogitations. His feet—neither slender nor feminine, neither massive nor rough, but proportionate to his size—were covered by shoes that had buckles made of nothing fancier than simple, modest brass. Note the difference: the only noticeable luxury was that which sprang from scientific origins. All that was actually his was marked by restraint and simplicity, fitting virtues for a wise man.

It was in this attire that he, the great psychiatrist, ambled from one end of the library to the other, absorbed in his own thoughts, distanced from all things outside the disturbing problem of cerebral pathology. Suddenly, he stopped. Standing in front of a window, with his left elbow supported on his open right hand and his chin supported on his closed left hand, he asked himself:

"But were they truly insane, and cured by me, or was what appeared to be a cure nothing more than the discovery of their perfect mental disequilibrium?"

And upon digging even further, he arrived at this conclusion: the well-organized brains that he had just finished curing were just as unbalanced as the others. Yes, he said to himself, it's presumptuous to think that I have instilled a new sentiment or mental faculty in them; one thing or another already existed in them, in a latent state, to be sure, but it existed nevertheless.

Upon arriving at this conclusion, the illustrious psychiatrist felt two opposing sensations, one of pleasure, the other of dejection. The pleasurable feeling resulted from realizing that, at the end of his extensive, patient research, constant toil, and intense struggle with the townspeople, he could affirm this truth: there were no lunatics in Itaguaí. Itaguaí did not count a single madman among its number. But no sooner had this idea reinvigorated his soul, than another idea appeared, which neutralized the effect of the first. It was a doubt. But why doubt? Hadn't Itaguaí been purged of all its well-balanced brains? But isn't such an absolute conclusion erroneous for its very absoluteness? And didn't it, therefore, threaten to destroy the grand and majestic edifice that was the new psychological doctrine?

Itaguaian historians describe the affliction suffered by the eminent Simão Bacamarte as one of the most frightful moral maelstroms that ever felled a man. But such tempests only terrify the weak; the strong steady themselves against them and stare into the storm. Twenty minutes later the psychiatrist's countenance was illuminated with a gentle glow.

"Yes, that's got to be it," he thought.

"It" was this: Simão Bacamarte had discovered in himself all the characteristics of perfect mental and moral equilibrium. It seemed to him that he possessed wisdom, patience, perseverance, tolerance, truthfulness, moral strength, loyalty; in short, all the qualities that, together, form a well-wrought lunatic. He soon doubted it, it's true, and even started to think it was an illusion, but since he was a prudent man, he resolved to summon a counsel of friends, whom he questioned candidly. Their opinion confirmed it.

"No defects?"

"None," said the assembly in unison.

"No vices?"

"None."

"Completely perfect?"

"Completely."

"No, it's impossible," shouted the psychiatrist, "I'm telling you, I don't feel within me this superiority that I just witnessed you all describe so generously. You're merely telling me this out of kindness. I've examined myself and don't find anything that would justify your excessive benevolence."

The assembly insisted it was true; the psychiatrist resisted. Finally, Padre Lopes clarified everything with this explanation, worthy of an attentive observer:

"Do you know why it is that you cannot perceive your lofty virtues, while, on the other hand, we all recognize and admire them? It's because you have yet another quality that is raised higher than the rest: modesty."

This proved decisive. Simão Bacamarte lowered his head, both cheerful and dejected, yet still more happy than sad. In one continuous action, he committed himself to the Green House. In vain his wife and friends told him to stay, that he was perfectly sane and mentally balanced; neither pleas nor suggestions nor tears detained him for a single second.

"It's a matter of science," he told them, "it's the new doctrine, of which I am the very first case. Both theory and practice are united in me."

"Simão, Simão, my love!" cried his wife, her face bathed in tears.

But the illustrious doctor, his eyes aglow with scientific conviction, paid no heed to his wife's pleading, and gently dismissed her. With the door to the Green House locked behind him, he applied himself to the study and cure of his own malady. Historians say that he died seventeen months later in the same state in which he entered the Green House, having accomplished nothing. Some go so far as to conjecture that there had never been a single lunatic, save him, in all of Itaguaí—but this opinion, based on a rumor that began to spread after the psychiatrist passed away, had no other basis than the rumor itself. And it's a questionable rumor at that, for it is attributed to Padre Lopes, who had praised the great man's virtues with such fervor. Whatever the truth is, the burial was carried out with much pomp and uncommon solemnity.

THE IMMORTAL

Chapter I

"My father was born in 1600 . . ."

"Excuse me, but you mean 1800, naturally . . ."

"No, sir," replied Dr. Leão, in a sad and solemn manner, "it was 1600."

Astonishment on the part of his listeners, of which there were two: Colonel Bertioga and the town notary, João Linhares. The town was in the interior of the state of Rio de Janeiro, let's say it was Itaboraí or Sapucaia. As for the date, I can say with certainty that it was in 1855, on a November night, pitch-dark and as hot as an oven, just after nine o'clock. Silence surrounded them. The three of them were seated on a patio that gave out onto the backyard. A large lamp with a feeble light, hanging from a nail, underscored the darkness. From time to time the harsh, arid wind would whine, merging with the monotonous sound of a nearby waterfall. Such was the scene and the moment when Dr. Leão insisted on the accuracy of the first words of his narrative.

"No, sir. He was born in 1600."

A homeopathic doctor by trade—homeopathy had just started to make its way into the realms of our civilization—Dr. Leão had arrived in town ten or twelve days earlier, replete with good letters of recommendation, both personal and political. He was an intelligent man, with refined behavior and a kind heart. The townspeople noticed a certain sadness in his appearance, a trace of reservation in his habits, and even a hint of coolness in his speech, although he was perfectly polite. But all this was chalked up to the shyness of his first days in town and his homesickness

63

for the capital city. He was thirty years old, had a slightly receding hairline, copper-colored eyes, and the hands of a bishop. He was traveling around, preaching the new system.

His two listeners remained shocked. Their doubts had been raised by the owner of the house, Colonel Bertioga, and the public notary insisted on this front, explaining to the doctor the impossibility of his father having been born in 1600. Two hundred and fifty-five years ago! Two and a half centuries! It was impossible. Well then, how old was the doctor? And how old was his father when he died?

"I'm not interested in telling you my father's life story," responded Dr. Leão. "You all told me about an elderly man who lives out behind the church. I told you that, speaking of macrobiotic beings, I knew of the most astonishing case in the world, an immortal man ..."

"So your father never died?" asked the colonel.

"No, he died."

"Well then, he wasn't immortal," the notary concluded triumphantly. "Immortal means that the person never dies, but your father died."

"Do you want to hear the story or not?"

"Ok, it's possible," observed the colonel, somewhat taken aback. "It's best to just listen to the story. All I'm saying is that I've never known anyone older than the groundskeeper at the church. He's so overripe that he's nearly falling off the tree. Your father probably looked quite old as well ..."

"He looked as young as I do. But why go on asking questions in this haphazard manner? Just to get more and more astonished? Because, to tell the truth, my father's story isn't an easy one to believe. It would only take a few minutes to tell."

Once their curiosity was whetted, it didn't take much more to get them to be silent. The rest of the colonel's family had retired to their rooms, and the three men were alone on the patio. Dr.

Leão finally began to narrate his father's life story in the manner that you, reader, will soon see, if you go to the effort of reading the second chapter, and the others after that.

Chapter II

"My father was born in the year 1600, in the city of Recife.

"At the age of twenty-five he put on the Franciscan cowl, which was the will of my grandmother, who was deeply religious. Both she and her husband were of noble birth—'of good stock,' as my father used to say, affecting the old way of putting it.

"My grandfather was a descendant of the Spanish nobility, and my grandmother was of the grand house of Alentejo. They married while they still lived in Europe, and years later, for reasons that are irrelevant to the present story, they relocated to Brazil, where they remained until their death. My father used to say that he had seen very few women as beautiful as my grandmother. And take note, he had loved the most radiant women in the world. But let's not get ahead of ourselves.

"My father donned the monk's habit at the Iguaraçu monastery, where he remained until 1639, the year in which the Dutch once again invaded that town. The friars abandoned the monastery in haste. My father, lazier than the others (or already determined to toss his cowl in the bushes), remained in his cell, and the Dutch found him there as he was gathering up a few religious books and some of his personal things. The Dutch didn't treat him poorly. He gave them the best he could find in the pantry of the Franciscans, who live in poverty as a rule. Since the friars took turns in the kitchen, my father was skilled in the culinary arts, and this talent was just one more charm in the eyes of the enemy.

"At the end of two weeks, a Dutch official gave him a writ of safe passage, so he could travel wherever he wished. But my father didn't accept it right away, preferring to think over whether he should remain with the Dutch and, under cover of their shadow, abandon the Franciscan order, or if he was better off seeking out a new life on his own. He chose the second option, not only because he had an adventurous, curious, daring spirit, but also because he was a patriot and a good Catholic—despite his distaste for monastic life—and didn't want to get mixed up with these invading heretics. He accepted the writ of safe passage and left Iguaraçu.

"By the time he told me his story, he could no longer remember how long he spent wandering the wilderness alone, purposefully steering clear of towns and villages, and not wanting to go to the big cities, Olinda and Recife, which were occupied by the Dutch. Having eaten all the provisions he'd taken with him, he lived off wild game and fruits. He had, in effect, tossed his monk's habit into the bushes. He wore Flemish trousers, which the Dutch official had given him, and a leather overcoat or cloak. To make a long story short, he eventually took up residence in a village of idolater Indians, who received him warmly, showing him great kindness and favor. My father was, perhaps, the most enchanting of men. The Indians were smitten with him, principally the chief, an old warrior, a courageous and generous man, who ended up giving my father his daughter's hand in marriage. At this point my grandmother was already dead, and my grandfather had been exiled to Holland; my father learned of all this from a chance encounter with a former servant of my grandparents. So the Indian chief let him stay in their village until 1642, when the old warrior passed away. The events surrounding his death are astonishing, so I ask you to pay close attention."

The colonel and the notary pricked up their ears, while Dr. Leão leisurely took out a pinch of snuff and inserted it into his nostril with the cool detachment of someone luring others in with a dazzling bait.

Chapter III

"One night, the indigenous chief—whose name was Pirajuá—
went over to my father's hammock and declared that he was
going to die shortly after dawn, and that my father should be
ready to accompany him when he left the village in the morning,
before his final moments. My father became alarmed, not because
he actually believed him, but because he thought he must be
delirious. In the wee hours of the morning, his father-in-law
came to get him.

"'Let's go,' he told him.

"'No, not now. You're weak, much too weak . . .'

"'Let's go!' repeated the warrior.

"By the light of a dying fire, my father saw the authoritative
expression on his face, as well as a certain diabolical demeanor,
or, at any rate, an uncommon demeanor, which terrified him. He
got up and followed him toward a small stream. Arriving at the
stream, they walked along the left bank, upstream, for a period that
my father estimated to be around a quarter of an hour. It grew
later, and the moon disappeared with the first signs of sunlight.
Despite the rough years my father had spent in the backlands, he
was frightened by this adventure; he followed his father-in-law
with a watchful eye, wary of some sudden betrayal. Pirajuá walked
on silently, with his eyes on the ground and his visage heavy with
thoughts, which could either have been sanguinary or merely
melancholic. And they walked and walked, until Pirajuá declared:

"'Here.'

They were standing before three large stones, arranged in
the shape of a triangle. Pirajuá sat on one of them, my father on
another. After resting for a few minutes, Pirajuá said:

"'Remove that stone,' pointing at the remaining stone, which
was the biggest of the three.

"My father got up and walked over to the stone. It was heavy and withstood his first attempt, but he kept at it and put all his strength into it. The stone gave way a little, then a little more, until it was finally removed from its original spot.

"'Dig into the earth,' said the warrior.

"My father went and found a broken branch or a bamboo stick or whatever it was and began to dig. At this point he was quite curious to know what he'd find. He was struck by the idea that it might be some treasure that the old warrior, fearing his death was nigh, wanted to entrust to him. He dug and dug and dug until he struck something hard; it was a primitive pot, or maybe a clay urn. He didn't pull it out, or even begin to dig out the dirt around it. The old warrior went over to him and unfastened the piece of tapir hide that covered the top of it, stuck his hand in, and pulled out a two-handled pot. This pot, in turn, had another piece of hide covering its opening.

"'Come here,' said the warrior.

"Once more they sat down on their respective stones. The warrior had the pot on his knees, the leather top still fastened to it, an air of mystery about it—arousing the curiosity of my father, who was burning with desire to know what it contained.

"'Pirajuá is going to die,' he said, 'to die, and never return. Pirajuá loves white warrior, husband of Maracujá, his daughter, and will show him secret like no other.'

"My father was trembling. The old warrior slowly unfastened the animal hide that covered the top of the pot. Once open, he looked inside it, stood up, and went over to my father to show him. It contained a yellowish liquid that had an odd, acrid smell.

"'He who drinks this, even just a drop, will never die.'

"'Oh! Drink it, then, drink it!' my father exclaimed spiritedly.

"He said this out of kindness, a spontaneous act of true filial friendship. But a second later he realized that he had no reason, other than his father-in-law's word, to believe what he'd been told;

what's more, he supposed that his father-in-law's judgment had been clouded by illness. But Pirajuá understood the spontaneous nature of my father's words and thanked him; nevertheless, he shook his head.

"'No,' he said, 'Pirajuá will not drink. Pirajuá wants to die. He is tired and has seen many, many moons. Pirajuá wants to rest in the earth, he is weary. But Pirajuá wants to leave this secret with white warrior. Here it is. It was made by an old shaman a long, long time ago . . . White warrior drinks and never dies.'

"Having said this, he put the cover back on the pot and placed it back in the half-buried urn. My father covered the top of the urn, and replaced the stone. The first strong rays of sunlight were beginning to show, and they hurried back to the village. Before even reaching his hammock, Pirajuá passed away.

"My father didn't believe in the elixir's merits. It was absurd to think that a mere liquid could open up a loophole in the law of death. It was obviously some sort of medicine, if it wasn't also some sort of poison. And in this case, the Indian's fabrication could be attributed to the mental disturbance my father presumed he was suffering. But, despite all these doubts, my father didn't say anything to the other Indians in the village, not even his own wife. He stayed silent about it. He never told me his reason for keeping mum; I don't think it was anything other than the power of the mystery itself.

"Some time later he fell ill, and it became so serious that everyone assumed he was a lost cause. The local medicine man told Maracujá that she would soon be a widow. My father didn't hear this, but he read it on the page of tears that was his wife's face, and felt deep inside that he was done for. He was strong and courageous, able to face any danger, so he wasn't scared of dying. He bid farewell to the living, gave some counsel, and prepared himself for the great voyage.

69

"In the middle of the night, he remembered the elixir and asked himself if it might be wise to give it a try. Since his death was already certain, what did he have to lose by trying it? The science of one century doesn't contain all knowledge; another century comes along after it and surpasses it. Who knows, he said to himself, whether mankind will one day discover immortality, and if the scientific formula might be made from this selfsame wild drug. The first person to cure malignant fever performed a miracle; everything is incredible before it becomes common knowledge. With these thoughts in mind, he decided to make his way back to the place where the stones were, on the bank of the stream. But he didn't want to go during the day, afraid that he'd be seen. So he got up in the middle of the night and left, shaky, unsteady, teeth chattering. He found the stone, pushed it aside, took out the pot, and drank half of its contents. Then he sat down to rest. Either the rest or the medicine seemed to raise his spirits right away. He replaced the pot and was back in his hammock half an hour later. By the following morning, he was well ..."

"Completely better?" asked the notary, João Linhares, interrupting the narrator.

"Completely."

"So it was some kind of remedy for fevers ..."

"That's precisely what he thought when he realized he was better, that it must have been some remedy for fevers and other illnesses. And that's what he kept thinking, although, despite the effect of the drug, he still didn't reveal it to anyone. Meanwhile, years passed, and my father never aged; he remained exactly the same as he was around the time he fell ill. No wrinkles, no gray hairs. A young man, perpetually young. Life in the jungle eventually began to bore him. He had remained there out of gratitude to his father-in-law, but a yearning for civilization eventually took hold of him. One day, the village was invaded by a horde of Indians from a neighboring settlement for reasons unknown, and which, furthermore, have no bearing on our tale. Many people perished in the battle; my father was wounded, and fled into the jungle. He came back to the village the following day, and found his wife dead. His wounds were deep, but he dressed them using standard remedies and was restored to health within a few days. But the recent turn of events had confirmed his resolve to leave the semi-savage life behind and return to civilized, Christian life. Many years had passed since he'd abandoned the monastery in Iguaraçu, and no one around there would recognize him anymore. One morning, he left the village under the pretext of going out to hunt. First he went to the stream, pulled the rock away, opened the earthen urn, and took out the pot where he had left the rest of the elixir. His idea was to have the drug analyzed in Europe, or even in Olinda or Recife, or in Bahia, by someone who was versed in chemistry and pharmacology. At the same time, he couldn't help but feel a sense of gratitude; he owed his health to that medicine. With the pot in hand, youthfulness in his legs, and a firm resolve in his heart, he left that spot, walking toward Olinda and into eternity."

Chapter IV

"I can't dwell on the minute details," said Dr. Leão, as he accepted the coffee that the colonel had a servant bring him. "It's almost ten o'clock . . ."

"What does that matter?" asked the colonel. "The night is ours and, for what we have planned for tomorrow, we can go to sleep whenever we like. For my part, I'm not sleepy at all. You, Mr. João Linhares?"

"Not a bit," replied the notary.

And he further insisted that Dr. Leão tell them everything, adding that he had never heard anything so extraordinary. Keep in mind that the notary fancied himself well read in ancient histories and was perceived, in town, as one of the most learned men in the entire Empire. Nevertheless, he was stunned. He recounted, then and there, between two swigs of coffee, the story of Methuselah, who lived for nine hundred and seventy-nine years, and the story of Lamech, who died at the age of seven hundred and seventy-seven. But he quickly added, since he was a valiant soul, that these and other examples out of the Hebraic chronology had no scientific basis . . .

"Come on, come on, let's hear what happened to your father," said the colonel, cutting in.

The wind, exhausted, had died down and the rain had begun to beat down on the leaves in the trees, intermittently at first, then steadily and forcefully. The night cooled down a little. Dr. Leão continued his narration and, despite having said that he couldn't dwell on the details, recounted them with such rigor that I do not dare set them down on this page exactly as he relayed them. It would get tedious. The best option is to summarize them.

Rui de Leão—or rather Rui Garcia de Meireles e Castro Azevedo de Leão, which was the full name of the doctor's father—remained only a short time in the state of Pernambuco. A year later, in 1654, the Dutch reign there came to an end. Rui de Leão witnessed the joys of victory and then embarked for Portugal, where he married a noblewoman from Lisbon. He had a son, and lost both his son and his wife in the same month, March of 1661. The sorrow he suffered was profound; to distract himself from it, he traveled to France and Holland. But Rui de Leão—either because of some secret love affair, or because he'd incurred the wrath of some Jews who were either natives of Portugal or of Portuguese descent, with whom he had entertained business relations in The Hague, or perhaps even for reasons unknown—didn't lead a peaceful life in Holland for very long. He was imprisoned and taken to Germany, then transported to Hungary and a few cities in Italy, then to France, and, finally, to

England. In England he made a profound study of English, and, since he knew Latin—which he'd learned in the monastery—and Hebrew—which he'd been taught in The Hague, by the famous Spinoza, who had been his friend, which perhaps had given rise to the hatred the other Jews felt for him—in addition to French and Italian, and a smattering of German and Hungarian, he became an object of genuine curiosity and veneration in London. He was sought after, consulted, and listened to, not only by common folk or simpletons, but by scholars, politicians, and members of the royal court.

I should add here that in all the countries he passed through, he had practiced a wild assortment of professions: soldier, lawyer, sacristan, dance instructor, merchant, and bookseller. He even became a secret agent in Austria, a Pontifical Swiss Guard, and a ship rigger. He was energetic and resourceful, but not very persistent, judging from the variety of endeavors he undertook. He refuted this claim, however, saying that this variety was due to the fact that the fates were always stacked against him. In London, where we now find him, he limited himself to the occupations of scholar and dandy. But he didn't take long to get back to The Hague, where some old lovers awaited him, as well as a fair amount of recent ones.

I feel compelled to add that love was one of the causes of our hero's troubled and turbulent life. Personally, he was elegant and charming, endowed with eyes full of power and magic. According to what he himself told his son, he left the Don Juanian figure of *mille e tre* in the dust. He couldn't say exactly how many women he had loved in all those latitudes and languages, from the savage Maracujá in Pernambuco, to the beautiful Cypriots, to the noblewomen of the salons of Paris and London, but he put the number at no less than five thousand. It's easy to see that such a multitude of women would contain all possible variations of feminine beauty: blondes and brunettes, the pale-skinned and those with rosy cheeks, tall ones, medium ones, short ones, skinny ones and full-figured ones, fiery ones and listless ones, the ambitious, the devout, the lascivious, the poetic and the prosaic, the intelligent and the stupid—yes, even the stupid ones, since he was of the opinion that the stupidity of women at least had a feminine touch to it, and was thus endearing, whereas the stupidity of men was channeled into masculine brutality.

"There is a time and place for stupid women," he used to say.

Among his new lovers in The Hague, he fell in with one who captured his attention for a quite a long time: Lady Emma Sterling, an Englishwoman, or rather, a Scottish woman, since was descended from a family from Dublin. She was beautiful, courageous, and daring—so daring that she even suggested to her lover that they mount a military expedition to Pernambuco, to seize control of the region and proclaim themselves king and queen of the new nation. She already had money, could raise even more, and even went so far as to contact outfitters and merchants, as well as some old Dutch soldiers who were dying to get revenge. Rui de Leão was aghast at her proposal, and didn't think she'd really go through with it, but Lady Emma persisted and demonstrated such rock-solid determination that he eventually realized he was in the presence of a truly ambitious woman. He was still, however, a man of sound judgment, and he saw that this endeavor, as well organized as it may have been, was going to end in disaster. He told her as much, pointing out that if Holland had been eventually beaten back, it wouldn't be easy for a private player to achieve stable dominion there, much less instantaneous power. Lady Emma finally gave up her plan, but she never let go of the idea of exalting him to some lofty position.

"You will be a king, or a duke . . ."

"Or a cardinal," he added, laughing.

"Why not a cardinal?"

Lady Emma soon found a way for Rui de Leão to get involved

in the conspiracy that would lead to the invasion of England, the Monmouth Rebellion, and the eventual death of the principal leaders of the rebellion. Although the rebellion was defeated, Lady Emma was not. Around that time, a startling idea occurred to her. Rui de Leão had hinted at the fact that he was the true father of the Duke of Monmouth, the supposed son of Charles II and the leader of the rebellion. The truth is that they looked as similar to each other as two drops of water. It's equally true that Lady Emma, on the occasion of the rebellion, had secretly plotted to kill the duke, if he was victorious, and install her lover in his place, thus placing him on the English throne. Needless to say, our man from Pernambuco had no knowledge of this treachery, nor would he have consented to it had he known. He joined the rebellion, saw it end in blood and execution, and then went into hiding. Emma went with him and, since the desire for the royal scepter had never left her heart, after some time had passed she began to spread the rumor that the duke hadn't really died, that it had been a friend who looked so much like him and was so dedicated to him that he took his place before the execution.

"The duke is alive, and will soon make himself known to the noble people of Great Britain," she whispered in the ears of the people.

When Rui de Leão finally appeared, the people were amazed, their enthusiasm was renewed, and their love for him gave new life to a cause that the executioner thought he had brought to an end in the Tower of London. Donations, gifts, weapons, supporters; all of this was heaped at the feet of the daring Pernambucan, who was proclaimed king and soon surrounded by hordes of men willing to die for his cause.

"My son," he said to the homeopathic doctor, a century and a half later, "if things had gone just a little differently, you would have been born Prince of Wales . . . I ended up ruling several cities and towns, decreeing laws, nominating cabinet members, and, for all that, I still had to withstand two or three armed revolts of people who demanded the dissolution of my last two cabinets. I personally think that these internal dissentions aided the lawful forces that opposed us and led to my eventual defeat. In the end, I wasn't angry with the people who turned on me; I was weary from all the fighting. I'm not lying when I say that my capture came as a great relief. I had witnessed not one, but two civil wars, one inside the other, one cruel, the other ridiculous, both of them senseless. On the other hand, I had done a lot of living, and so long as they didn't execute me, and just tossed me into prison or exiled me to the ends of the earth, I wouldn't ask anything else of mankind, at least not for a few centuries . . . I was imprisoned, tried, and sentenced to death. A fair number of my allies renounced me outright; I think that one chief among them even served in the House of Lords until his death. This great betrayal was like torture to me. But Emma was different. That noble lady never abandoned me. She was imprisoned, sentenced, and later pardoned, but she never abandoned me. On the eve of my execution, she came to be with me, and we spent those final hours together. I told her never to forget me, gave her a lock of my hair, and asked her to forgive the executioner . . . Emma burst into tears, and the guards came to escort her out. Left alone in my cell, I looked back on my life, from Iguaraçu to the Tower of London. It was the year 1686, and I was eighty-six years old, although I didn't look a day over forty. My appearance was one of eternal youth, but the executioner was going to destroy it all in an instant. It was pointless to have imbibed half of the elixir and carried that mysterious pot around with me everywhere I went, only to meet a tragic end on the executioner's block . . . Such were my thoughts that night. In the morning, I prepared myself for death. First came the priest, then the soldiers, and finally, the executioner. I obeyed their orders mechanically. We all walked out together, then I went up on the platform, offering no final speech. I laid my neck on the block, the executioner swung his weapon, and I felt a sharp pain, immense anguish, as if my heart had suddenly stopped. But this sensation was as fleeting as it was intense, and a moment later I was back to normal. There was some blood on my neck, but it wasn't much and was almost dry already. The executioner retreated a few steps, and the people screamed for him to kill me. They pushed my head against the block, and the executioner, calling on the strength of all his muscles and principles, unleashed another blow, even greater than the first, if that was possible, capable of killing me and digging my grave all at once, as they say of a bona fide tough guy. The sensation I felt was the same as the first in intensity and brevity, and once more I raised my head off the block. Neither the magistrate nor the priest would allow a third attempt. The people were stunned. Some called me a saint, others a devil, and both of these opinions were defended in taverns with all the force of fists and rotgut. Devil or saint, I was handed over to the court doctors. They listened to the testimonies of the magistrate, the priest, the executioner, and a few soldiers, and concluded that, once the blow had been dealt, the tissues of the neck quickly reconnected, as well as the bones, although they couldn't offer an explanation for the phenomenon. For my part, I kept quiet, saying nothing about the elixir; I preferred to use the mystery to my advantage. Yes, my son, you can't imagine the impression this made all over England, the love letters I received from the finest duchesses, the poems, the flowers, the gifts, the metaphors. A poet called me Antaeus. A young Protestant demonstrated that I was Christ himself."

Chapter V

Our narrator continued:

"As you can see from what I've already told you, if I were to

77

describe my father's entire life in detail, I wouldn't finish the story today, nor even this week. Someday I'll do this, put it all in writing. I imagine that the whole story would take up five volumes, not counting the additional documents . . ."

"What documents?" asked the notary.

"The corroborating documents I possess: titles, letters, transcripts of judicial decisions, copies of legal documents, statistical documents . . . For example, I have a census certificate from 1742 of a certain neighborhood in Genoa, where my father eventually died. It bears his name, along with his place of birth . . ."

"Does it have his real age?" asked the colonel.

"No. My father always stayed between forty and fifty. Once he reached the age of fifty, or thereabouts, he'd start over at forty again. And this was easily accomplished, since he never stayed in the same place for long. He would spend five, eight, ten, twelve years in a city, and then move along to another . . . Well, I've got a number of documents that I'll compile, including, among others, the last will and testament of Lady Emma, who died soon after the failed execution of my father. My father told me that of all the losses he suffered over the course of his life, the loss of Lady Emma was among the hardest and most profound. He never again encountered a woman so sublime, a love so constant, or a devotion so complete. And her death reaffirmed her life, for Lady Emma named my father as her sole heir. Unfortunately, other people laid claim to the inheritance, and the case went to court. But my father couldn't remain in England, and eventually accepted the proposal of a providential friend who traveled to Lisbon to tell him that the case was all but lost, but that he could, perhaps, salvage a little something, offering to buy my father's problematic stake in the will for a mere ten thousand *cruzados*. My father took the *cruzados*, but such was his luck that the will was eventually upheld, and the inheritance went to my father's friend . . ."

"And your father ended up poor . . ."

"With just ten thousand *cruzados*, plus a little more that he was able to scrounge up. He then had the idea of becoming a slave trader. He obtained the rights, outfitted a ship, and started transporting Africans to Brazil. This part of his life was harder on him than any other, but he eventually grew accustomed to the distressing realities of a slave ship. He grew accustomed to them, then got bored of them, which was a recurring phenomenon throughout his life. He always grew bored of his professions. The long periods of solitude out on the ocean amplified the emptiness he felt inside. One day he reflected on this, and wondered if he might eventually get so used to life at sea that he would end up sailing the seas for centuries and centuries. This prospect frightened him, and he realized that the best way to traverse eternity was by changing things up every so often . . ."

"What year was this?"

"1694, toward the end of 1694."

"Imagine that! He was ninety-four years old, right? But he still looked young, naturally . . ."

"So young that two years later, in that state of Bahia, he married a beautiful lady who . . ."

"Go on, tell us."

"Yes, I'll tell you, since he himself was the one who told me. He married a beautiful lady who was in love with another man. And you won't believe who the other man was! Now just imagine, in 1965, my father participated in the conquest of the famous Quilombo of Palmares. He fought valiantly and lost a friend, a close friend, riddled with bullets, stripped of his skin . . ."

"Stripped of his skin?"

"It's true. The blacks used boiling water to defend their settlement, and my father's friend took a whole kettle full. His entire body was a festering wound. My father recalled this episode with sorrow, and even remorse, since in the middle of the skirmish he ended up stepping on his unfortunate companion. It even seems that he only expired once my father's boots crushed his face ..."

The notary grimaced, and the colonel, to disguise his repulsion, asked what the conquest of Palmares had to do with the woman who ...

"It has everything to do with her," said the doctor, continuing his story. "Even as my father saw his friend die, he was able to save the life of an officer, taking an arrow in the chest in the process. It happened like this. One of the blacks, after shooting down two soldiers, turned his bow toward the officer, who was a kind and courageous young man who had lost his father young and left his mother behind in Olinda ... My father knew that the arrow wouldn't do him any harm, so he jumped in front of it. The arrow wounded him in the chest and he fell to the ground. The officer was named Damião ... Damião something or other. I won't give his full name, because he still has a few descendants in Minas Gerais. Damião will suffice. Damião spent the night by my father's bedside, grateful, dedicated to him, praising him for such a sublime deed. And he wept, too. He couldn't bear the thought of watching the man who had saved his life in such exceptional fashion die. My father healed quickly, to the astonishment of all. The officer's poor mother wanted to kiss his hands.

"'All I ask in return is a simple reward,' he told her. 'Your friendship, and that of your son.'

"The entire city of Olinda marveled at this turn of events. No one spoke of anything else, and after a few weeks the public admiration had started to create a legend. The sacrifice, as you know, was nothing at all, since my father couldn't die, but the people, who were unaware of this, searched for a motive for such a sacrifice, a motive as big as the sacrifice itself seemed to be, and realized that Damião must be my father's son. His illegitimate son, naturally. They looked into the widow's past and found a few recesses that were shrouded in darkness. My father's face started to look familiar to some people, and there was even someone who claimed to have taken afternoon tea at the widow's house once, back when she was still married, and seen my father there. My father got so sick of all these lies that he decided to move to Bahia, where he married . . ."

"The lady you mentioned?"

"Precisely . . . Where he married Dona Helena, as radiant as the sun, as he used to say. A year later the widow died in Olinda, and Damião came to Bahia to bring my father a lock of his mother's hair, as well as a necklace that the dying woman requested be given to his wife. Dona Helena then heard the story of the arrow and thanked him for this memento of his mother. Damião wanted to go back to Olinda, but my father told him that he should stay until the following year. So Damião stayed. Three months later, there was a tumultuous love affair . . . My father found out about their duplicity from a frequent dinner guest. He wanted to kill them, but the same person who denounced them also warned them of the danger they were in, and they escaped with their lives. My father then turned the dagger on himself and buried it in his heart.

"'Son,' he said to me, as he told me this part, 'I stabbed myself six times, each of which was enough to kill a man, but I didn't die.' Despondent, he left his house and threw himself into the ocean. The ocean returned him to solid ground. Death would not accept him; he belonged to life, forever, century after century. He had no other choice but to flee. He traveled south, where a few years later, at the beginning of the last century, we find him involved in the discovery of the gold mines. It was a way to drown his sorrows, which were great, for he had loved his wife intensely, like a madman . . ."

"What ever happened to her?"

"It's a long story, and I don't really have time for it. She moved to Rio de Janeiro after the two French invasions, in 1713, I think.

By that time my father had already become wealthy with the mines and was living in Rio, where he was well respected, and where he even entertained thoughts of being appointed governor. One day Dona Helena showed up at his door, accompanied by her mother and an uncle. The mother and uncle told him that it was time to put an end to the situation in which he had placed his wife. The slanderous rumors had weighed down the lady's life for a long time. Her hair was going gray, but it wasn't so much because of her advancing age, but because of her sorrow, her tears. They showed him a letter written by the dinner guest who had denounced her, in which he begged Dona Helena's forgiveness for the slanderous remark, which he claimed was prompted by his immoral passion for her. My father was a good soul, and he accepted his wife, his mother-in-law, and the uncle into his home. The years performed their task; the three of them grew old, but not my father. Helena's hair turned completely white, her mother and uncle were quickly becoming enfeebled, and none of them took their eyes off my father, looking for the white locks that never appeared, the wrinkles that never showed up. One day my father overheard them say that he must have made a pact with the devil. Strong words! And the uncle added: 'What use is the will, if we're all going to go first?' The uncle died two weeks later; the mother-in-law lost her mind completely about a year later. His wife was the only one left, and she didn't last much longer."

"It seems to me," ventured the colonel, "that those three were after his riches ..."

"Certainly."

"... and that Dona Helena, God forgive her, wasn't as innocent as she claimed. Is it true that the letter from the man who denounced them ..."

"He was paid to write the letter," explained Dr. Leão. "My father found out about this after his wife died, while he was

passing through Bahia . . . Midnight! Let's go to bed. It's late . . .
I'll tell you the rest tomorrow."

"No, no, tell us now."

"But, sirs . . . only if I can just give a quick synopsis."

"A synopsis will do."

The doctor stood up and looked out at the night, sticking his
arm out from under the roof of the back porch, feeling a few drops
of rain on his hand. Then he went back over to the other two, who
were shooting inquisitive glances at each other. He slowly rolled
a cigarette, lit it, and, after taking three short puffs, concluded his
remarkable story.

Chapter VI

"My father left Brazil shortly after this and went to Lisbon,
and from there traveled to India, where he remained for over
five years before returning to Lisbon, with a few treatises he
had written about that part of the world. He put the finishing touches on them and had them published at just the right
time; such good timing, in fact, that he was called before the
government and appointed governor of Goa. Another candidate for this position, upon hearing what had happened, tried
to discredit my father by any possible means, and even some
impossible ones. Plots, schemes, defamatory remarks: he used
every weapon at hand. He was even able, for the right price,
to get one of the best Latinists in the Iberian Peninsula, an
unscrupulous sort, to forge a Latin version of my father's text
and attribute it to an Augustinian friar who had died in Aden.
The stain of plagiarism managed to do my father in. He lost the
governorship of Goa, which ended up going to the other candidate. What's more, he lost all the respect he'd earned. He wrote
a lengthy justification and sent letters to India, but didn't even
wait for the responses, because in the middle of all this work he

got so bored of it all that he thought it best to just abandon it and leave Lisbon. This generation will pass on, he said, but not me. I'll come back here in a century or two."

"Will you look at that," interrupted the notary, "it sounds like some kind of joke! Go back there in a century . . . or two, as if it were a month or two. What do you think, Colonel, sir?"

"Ah! I'd like to be this man! So, did he return a century later . . . or didn't he?"

"Just listen to my story. He left Lisbon for Madrid, where he had love affairs with two noblewomen, one of them a widow and as radiant as the sun, the other married, less pretty, but as amorous and affectionate as a turtle dove. The latter's husband found out about the affair, but didn't want to challenge my father to a duel, since he wasn't a nobleman. But the pangs of jealousy and honor propelled the offended man to commit an act of treachery that was every bit as grievous as the affair: he hired people to kill my father. The hit men stabbed him three times and landed him in bed for fifteen days. Once recovered, they put a bullet in him, which might as well have been nothing. Then the husband found a real way to get rid of my father. He had noticed that my father possessed some objects, notes, and drawings pertaining to the religious practices of India, and denounced him to the Holy Office of the Inquisition as a practitioner of superstitious arts. The Holy Office, which was neither negligent nor lazy in its task, took him into custody and condemned him to life in prison. My father was terrified. In truth, life in prison would have been the most horrifying thing in the world for him. Prometheus, even Prometheus was freed from chains eventually . . . Don't interrupt me, Mr. Linhares, I'll explain who Prometheus was later. But let me repeat: Prometheus was eventually unchained, whereas my father was in the hands of the Holy Office, without any hope. On the other hand, he reflected internally, if he was eternal, the Holy Office was not. The Holy Office will someday meet its end, along with its prisons, and then I'll be free. Then he imagined that as soon as a certain number of years had passed, without him having aged or died, he would become such a sensation that the Holy Office itself would let him walk free of their own accord. Finally, this gave way to another consideration.

"'My son,' he told me, 'I had suffered so much over the course of those many years, had seen such wrath, such misery, such calamity, that I thanked God for the prison and my lengthy sentence. And I told myself that the Holy Office wasn't all that bad, for it had saved me—for a few dozen years, perhaps even a century—from the spectacle of the outside world . . .'"

"Well now!"

"Poor man! He wasn't counting on the other noblewoman, the widow, who made use of all the resources she could get her hands on to arrange for his escape only a few months later. They left Spain together, spent some time in France, then moved on to Italy, where my father remained for many years. The widow died in his arms, and save for one romance he had in Florence, with a young noblewoman with whom he ran off for six months, he was always faithful to the memory of his lover. Let me repeat: she died in his arms, and he suffered greatly, wept often, and even wanted to die as well. He told me of all the desperate measures he took, all because he had truly loved the beautiful Madrilenian woman. Disconsolate, he took to the road, traveling to Hungary, Dalmatia, and Wallachia. He spent five years in Constantinople, where he studied Turkish in depth, then Arabic. I've already mentioned that he knew a lot of languages; I recall once seeing him translate the Pater Noster into fifty different tongues. He knew a lot. And the sciences! My father was versed in an infinite number of subjects: philosophy, jurisprudence, theology, archeology, chemistry, physics, mathematics, astronomy, botany. He was trained in architecture, he could paint, play music. He knew a hell of a lot."

"Truly . . ."

"Yes, he knew a lot. And he did more than merely study Turkish; he adopted Mohammedanism. But he abandoned it soon afterwards. Eventually, he grew bored of the Turks; it was his fate to grow bored easily with any given thing or profession. He left Constantinople, visited other parts of Europe, and then traveled to England, which he hadn't seen for many years. The same thing happened to him there that always happened to him: all of the faces were new to him. And this changing of faces within a single city, the same city he'd left years before, gave him the impression of a play, in which the set never changes, but the actors do. This impression, which was surprising at first, eventually became tedious, but now, in London, it was something worse, because it awoke within him an idea that he had never had before, an extraordinary, terrifying idea . . ."

"What was it?"

"The idea that he would one day go insane. Just think: an eternal madman. The disturbance this thought caused within him was so great that he almost went crazy right then and there. And then something else occurred to him. Since he had the pot of elixir with him, he thought that he should give the rest of it to some woman or man, so they could be immortal together. They would always have company. But since he had plenty of time ahead of him, he didn't rush into anything; he thought it best to wait for the perfect person. The truth is that this idea put him at ease . . . If I were to tell you about all the adventures he had back in England, and later in France, and in Brazil, to which he returned while the Count of Resende was viceroy, I would never finish this story. The hour is late and urging us on, and besides, the colonel is getting sleepy . . ."

"I'm not sleepy!"

"Well, you're at least tired."

"Not tired either. I've never heard anything that interested me more. Go ahead, tell us about these adventures."

"No, I will only say that he happened to be in France during the revolution of 1789 and witnessed it all: the fall from power and death of the king, the Girondists, Danton, Robespierre. He even lived for a while with Filinto Elysio, the poet, you know him? He lived with him in Paris, where he was one of those sharp citizens elected to the French Directory, and met the First Consul ... He even wanted to naturalize and lead a life of arms and politics. He could have become one of the Marshals of the Empire, and perhaps Waterloo never would have happened. But he suffered a few political betrayals and became so disgusted, so exasperated, that he resigned his position before all this took place. In 1808, we find him accompanying the Portuguese royal court to Rio de Janeiro. In 1822 he saluted the newly independent Brazil and was part of the Constituent Assembly, participated in the April 7th events that led to Dom Pedro I's abdication, and celebrated when the young Dom Pedro II reached the age of majority and took office. He was even a member of the Chamber of Deputies for two years."

At this point, the two men redoubled their attention. They understood that they were getting close to the conclusion of the story and they didn't want to miss a single syllable of that part of the narration, in which they would learn of the death of the immortal. For his part, Dr. Leão paused for a moment. It might have been some painful memory, or it could have just been a strategy for whetting their appetite even more. The notary even asked him if his father ever had anyone else drink the rest of the elixir, as he had planned, but the narrator didn't respond. He was looking inside himself. At last, he finished his story, thusly:

"My father's soul had reached a state of profound melancholy. Nothing gave him pleasure, neither the taste of glory, nor the taste of danger, nor that of love. He had at this point lost my mother, and the two of us lived together like two confirmed bachelors. Politics had lost all its charms in the eyes of a man who once had been a pretender to the throne, one of the foremost thrones in the universe. He languished: alone, sad, impatient, and bored. In his happiest hours he worked on projects for the twentieth and twenty-fourth centuries, for he had already revealed the great secret of his life to me. I must confess that I didn't believe him, and I assumed that it must be the result of some mental illness. But the evidence he had was exhaustive, and from my own observations I knew that he was in perfect health. His spirit alone seemed defeated and disillusioned. One day, I told him that I couldn't understand why he was so sad, since I would well have sold my soul to the devil to gain eternal life. My father smiled at me with such an expression of superiority that it seemed to bury me a hundred feet deep in the ground. Then he told me that I didn't know what I was saying, that eternal life only seemed wonderful to me because my own life was limited and short, and that, in truth, it was the most atrocious punishment. He had seen all of his loved ones die and would one day lose me, as well as all the other children that he would have throughout the centuries to come. He would have other loves—not a few of whom had cheated on him in the past—one after another, both good and bad, faithful and unfaithful; he was forced to repeatedly cycle through them all, without respite, unable even to draw breath, because experience could never teach him to overcome the innate desire to hold fast to something in that swift passage of men and generations. It was a necessity of eternal life. Without it, he would descend into madness. He had experienced everything, exhausted everything. Now, all was repetition, all was monotony. There was no hope, nothing. He would have to explain the same things he was telling me now to other children, twenty or thirty centuries later, then to others, and others, and others, without end, ever. He would study new languages, as Hannibal would have done, were he alive today. But to what end? To hear people speak of the same feelings, the same emotions? . . . He told me all this, truly defeated. Isn't that curious? Then one day, as I was giving a presentation on the system of homeopathic medicine to a few friends, I saw an extraordinary, seldom-seen fire flash in my father's eyes. But he didn't say anything to me. That night, I was summoned to his bedroom. He was dying, and told me, with his tongue faltering, that the homeopathic principle had been his salvation. *Similia similibus curantur.* He had drunk the rest of the elixir, and just as the first half had given him life, the second half gave him death. Having said this, he passed away."

The colonel and the notary remained quiet for some time, not sure what they thought of that extraordinary story, but the doctor's solemnity was so profound that they couldn't doubt it. They believed his tale, and they also believed, definitively, in homeopathic medicine. When they told this story to others, there was no shortage of people who assumed the doctor was insane. Others thought his intention was to change the minds of the colonel and the notary, after they both expressed displeasure at not being able to live forever, demonstrating to them that death is ultimately a blessing. But the suspicion that the doctor only wanted to spread the message of homeopathy crept into a few minds in town, and it wasn't an unlikely explanation. But I'll leave that problem to the scholars. Such is the extraordinary story that years ago, under a different name and in other words, I narrated to the good people of this country, who have probably already forgotten both name and tale.

There was once a barrel-maker and demagogue named Bernadino, who, in the realm of cosmography, professed a belief that the world was an enormous tunnel of marmalade, and in the realm of politics insisted that the throne should belong to the people. To that end, he grabbed a cudgel, stirred up the souls of the masses, and brought down the king. But upon entering the palace, victorious and lauded, he noticed that there was only room for one person on the throne, so he resolved this dilemma by sitting atop it himself.

"Through me," he announced, "the masses are crowned. I am you, you are me."

The first act of the new king was to abolish barrel-making, compensating the barrel-makers—who threatened to overthrow him—by granting them the title of "The Magnificent." His second act was to declare that, for the greater glory of his person and position, he would from then on be called by the augmentative Bernardão, rather than the diminutive Bernardino. He personally requested a genealogical document from a great scholar of the subject, who, in a little over an hour, discovered a certain sixth-century Roman general in his line, Bernardus Barrelius. This name gave rise to a controversy, which still remains, with some people claiming that King Bernardão was once a barrel-maker, while others insist that this is nothing more than a lamentable corruption of the name of the family's founder. And we've already seen that the latter opinion is the only true one.

As he had been bald since he was a young man, Bernardão decreed that all of his subjects should be bald as well, either naturally or by the razor, and justified this act by reason of public order. Namely, that the ethical unity of the State required the external conformity of heads. He revealed a similar sort of wisdom in another act, in which he proclaimed that all left-footed shoes must have a small slit near the pinky toe, thus giving all his subjects the opportunity to look like him, since he suffered from a painful corn. The use of glasses throughout the kingdom has no other explanation than the ophthalmitis that afflicted Bernardão early in the second year of his reign. The illness cost him one of his eyes, and this occurrence revealed Bernardão's true vocation: poetry. One of his two ministers, named Alpha, told him that the loss of an eye made him Hannibal's equal, and he was very flattered by the comparison; then his other minister, Omega, took a step forward and declared him superior to Homer, who had lost both his eyes. This act of courtesy was a revelation, and since it is connected to his marriage, let's move straight to the marriage.

He wished, in fact, to secure the dynasty of the Barrelius line. There was no shortage of potential brides for the new king, but none of them enchanted him as much as the young Estrelada, who was beautiful, rich, and of noble birth. This fair lady, who was trained in music and poetry, was courted by a few gentlemen and remained faithful to the deposed sovereign. Bernardão showered her with the most luxurious and exquisite gifts. On a separate front, her family bellowed at her that a crown on the head was worth more than empty longing in the heart, that she mustn't disgrace her family (after Bernardão enticed her with a princedom), that thrones don't just grow on trees, and so on and so forth. Estrelada, however, still resisted his seductive advances.

She didn't resist for long, but she also didn't give in right away. Since among her many suitors she secretly preferred one who was a poet, she declared that she was ready to marry, but that first a contest would be held, and she would marry the man who wrote the best madrigal. Bernadão accepted this stipulation, mad with love and confident in his abilities; after all, he had one more eye than Homer, and had already composed the harmonious arrangement of feet and heads.

Twenty people entered the literary contest, which was anonymous and secret. One of the madrigals was judged superior to all the others; as expected, it was the poem of her beloved poet. Bernardão issued a decree annulling the contest and commanded that another contest be inaugurated. But then, in a flash of remarkable Machiavellian inspiration, he mandated that no word less than three hundred years old could be employed. None of the contestants had studied the classics; it was the most likely way of beating them.

Yet even so, he didn't win, for the beloved poet quickly read whatever he could, and his madrigal was once again deemed the best. Bernardão annulled the second contest as well, and, seeing that the ancient phrases lent a particular charm to the verses of the winning madrigal, he decreed that only modern words could be used, especially those currently in vogue. A third contest, a third victory for the beloved poet.

Furious, Bernardão opened up to his two ministers, asking them for a quick and forceful solution, because, if he didn't win Estrelada's hand, he would cut off the heads of three hundred thousand subjects. The two of them, after discussing the issue for a while, came back to him with this proposal:

"The two of us, Alpha and Omega, are, by our very names, designated for work that deals with language. Our plan is this: that Your Highness should order that all dictionaries be confiscated and command us to compose a new vocabulary that will ensure your victory."

Bernardão did just that, and the two ministers locked themselves indoors for three months, at the end of which they delivered to his kingly hands the completed work, a book they called *The Dictionary of Babel*, because it truly was a confusion of letters. There wasn't a single phrase that bore resemblance to the spoken language.

Consonants scrambled atop consonants, vowels were diluted by other vowels, words with two syllables now had seven or eight and vice versa, everything was jumbled, mixed up; a complete absence of vigor, of elegance: a language of shards and tatters.

"Impose the use of this language by royal decree, and all will be yours."

Bernardão awarded them both with embraces and pensions, instituted the new vocabulary, and declared that he would hold a final contest to determine who would win the beautiful Estrelada's hand in marriage. The confusion of the dictionary spread to the souls of the citizens; everyone was perpetually perplexed. These clowns greeted each other in the street with the new words. For example, instead of "Good morning, how have you been?" they'd say "Pflerrgpxx, rouph, aa?" The lovely maiden herself, fearing her beloved poet would finally fail in his crusade, proposed that they elope. The poet, however, replied that he'd like to see if he could finagle something first. They'd been given ninety days for the new contest, and twenty madrigals were turned in. The best one, in spite of the barbaric language, belonged to the beloved poet. Raving mad, Bernardão ordered that the ministers' hands be chopped off, and that was his sole act of vengeance. Estrelada was so wonderfully beautiful that he didn't dare upset her, and he conceded defeat.

Feeling sorrowful, he locked himself away in his library for eight days, reading, pacing, and meditating. It appears that the last thing he read was a satire by the poet Garção, specifically these verses, which seem written just for the occasion:

". . . the singular Apelles,
Rubens, and Raphael, inimitable all,
Were not so because of the hue of their paints;
They were made eternal by elegant combination."

The Academies of Siam

Do you know about the academies of Siam? I am well aware that there have never been any academies in Siam, but let's suppose that there were, and that there were four of them, and just listen to my tale.

Chapter I

Upon seeing a cluster of milky-colored fireflies fluttering throughout the night sky, the stars used to claim that they were the sighs of the King of Siam, who was entertaining himself with his three hundred concubines. And winking slyly at each other, they'd ask:

"Oh royal sighs, what is our handsome Kalaphongko up to this night?"

To which the fireflies replied solemnly:

"We are the sublime thoughts of the four academies of Siam. We carry with us all the wisdom of the universe."

One night, there were so many fireflies that the stars took fright and took refuge in alcoves; the fireflies took over the space that was left behind and stayed there forever. They were called the Milky Way.

This enormous ascension of thoughts stemmed from the fact that the four academies wished to answer this curious question: Why are there feminine men and masculine women? It was the temperament of their young king that led them to pose this question. Kalaphongko was practically a lady. Every ounce of his being exuded the most exquisite femininity: he had honeyed eyes, a silvery voice, an effeminate, submissive posture, and true aversion to arms. The warriors of Siam bemoaned their lot, but the rest of the nation lived a merry life, full of dances, comedies, and songs, after the manner of their king, who cared for little else. Thus the stars' misconception.

This went on until, suddenly, one of the academies discovered this solution to the problem:

"Some souls are masculine, others feminine. The anomaly in question is a matter of a soul in the wrong body."

"Not so," cried the other three academies, "the soul is neuter, it has nothing to do with this external contrast."

Nothing more was needed to stain the alleys and canals of Bangkok with academic blood. First came controversy, then disorder, and, finally, an attack. It wasn't all that bad in the early stages of the disorder: the rival groups never hurled a single insult that wasn't scrupulously derived from the Sanskrit, which was the scholarly language, the Latin of Siam. But after that they became shameless. The enmity grew, tousling its hair, putting its hands on its hips, and lowering itself to the mud, resorting to flinging rocks, fisticuffs, and vulgar gestures, until the academy in favor of gendered souls, exasperated, decided to put an end to the three others, and prepared a sinister plan . . . Oh you winds that blow past me, if only you would take these pages with you, so that I'd never have to relate the tragedy of Siam! It pains me—oh, woe is me!—it pains me to describe such extraordinary vengeance. The academics secretly took arms and went out after the others, at the very moment that these other academics, bent in study over the famous question, were sending a cloud of fireflies into the heavens. The former fell upon the latter, seething with rage. Those who managed to escape weren't free for long; pursued and attacked, they died on the banks of the river, aboard barges, and in darkened alleys. All told, there were thirty-eight corpses. They cut off the ear of one of the leaders and used it to make a necklace and some bracelets for the victorious president, the glorious

U-Tong. Drunk with victory, they celebrated their success with a great feast, at which they sang this magnificent hymn: "Glory to us, who are the rice of science and the lantern of the universe."

The city awoke in shock. The multitude was overcome with fear. No one could absolve such a cruel, ugly action; some went so far as to doubt their own eyes . . . Only one person approved of it: the beautiful Kinnara, the jewel of the royal concubines.

Chapter II

Languidly lying at the feet of beautiful Kinnara, the young king asked her for a song.

"I'll sing no other tune but this: I believe that souls have a sex."

"What an absurd belief, Kinnara."

"So, Your Majesty believes that the soul is neuter?"

"That, too, is absurd, Kinnara. No, I don't believe that the soul is neuter, nor that the soul has a sex."

"But what, then, does Your Majesty believe, if you don't believe in either of these?"

"I believe in your eyes, Kinnara, which are the sun and the light of the universe."

"But you must choose: either you believe that souls are neuter, and you punish the lone remaining academy, or you believe that souls have a sex, and you pardon it."

"How delicious your mouth is, my sweet Kinnara! I believe in your mouth; it is the font of all wisdom."

Kinnara got up, agitated. Just as the king was a feminine man, Kinnara was a masculine woman—a buffalo with the feathers of a swan. It was the buffalo who, at this moment, was storming out of the bedroom, but seconds later it was the swan who stopped and leaned her long neck down to her king, requesting and receiving, between caresses, a decree proclaiming that the doctrine of gendered souls was legitimate and orthodox, the other being absurd and perverse. On this same day the decree was sent out to the triumphant academy, and to every pagoda, mandarin, and the entire kingdom. The academy lit its festive lanterns and peace was restored throughout the land.

Chapter III

Meanwhile, beautiful Kinnara had developed an ingenious secret plan. One night, while the king was studying some documents pertaining to the State, she asked him if his subjects paid their taxes on time.

"*Ohimè!*" he exclaimed, repeating a word that had stuck with him after hearing it from an Italian missionary. "Very few taxes have been paid. I didn't want to give the order to cut off the taxpayers' heads . . . No, I could never do it. Bloodshed? Bloodshed? No, I don't want any bloodshed."

"And what if I had a solution to this problem?"

"What is it?"

"Your Majesty decreed that souls are feminine or masculine," began Kinnara, after giving him a kiss. "Suppose that the souls in our two bodies have been switched. All we need to do is return the soul to its rightful body. We can switch bodies . . ."

Kalaphangko laughed loudly at this proposal, and asked her how they'd go about making the switch. She responded that they'd use the method of Mukunda, the king of the Hindus, who entered the corpse of a Brahmin, while a jester entered the vacant body of Mukunda—an old legend that has been passed down to the Turks, Persians, and Christians. Ok, what about the words of the invocation? Kinnara stated that she knew them; an old bonze had discovered a copy of them in the ruins of a temple.

"So, we'll do it?"

"I don't even believe in my own decree," he retorted, laughing, "but why not? If it's really true, let's switch bodies . . . but only for half a year, no longer. At the end of this period we'll switch back."

They decided to do it that very night. While the rest of the city slept, they summoned the royal canoe, got in, and let the current carry it. None of the rowers noticed them. When dawn appeared on the horizon, whipping the resplendent cows that pulled it along, Kinnara proffered the mysterious invocation. Her soul detached from her body and floated above her, waiting for the king's body to become empty as well. Her body fell to the carpeted floor of the canoe.

"Ready?" said Kalaphangko.

"Ready, I'm waiting up here in the air. Please excuse the undignified state of my body, Your Majesty . . ."

But the king's soul didn't hear the rest. Swift and sparkling, it left its physical vessel and entered into Kinnara's body, while her body took possession of that royal reward. Both bodies arose and looked at each other—just imagine their astonishment. It was the same situation as Buoso and the snake, according to what old Dante has to say; but take note of my audacity here. The poet silenced both Ovid and Lucan, believing that his metamorphosis outdid both of theirs. And I silence all three of them. Buoso and the serpent never crossed paths again, while my two heroes, once switched, keep conversing and living together, which is even more obviously Dantesque, and this fact imbues me with modesty.

"Truly," said Kalaphangko, "this business of looking at myself and calling myself 'Your Majesty' is quite odd. Doesn't Your Majesty feel the same way?"

And both of them felt fine, like people who have finally found the perfect house for themselves. Kalaphangko luxuriated in the feminine curves of Kinnara's body. Kinnara, for her part, became stiff in the rigid torso of Kalaphangko. Siam had a king at last.

Chapter IV

The first action taken by Kalaphangko (from here on out the body of the king with Kinnara's soul will go by that name, and the body of the beautiful Siamese woman with Kalaphangko's soul will be called Kinnara) was nothing less than to bestow the highest honors on the gendered academy. He didn't elevate its members to the ranks of mandarins, for these were men of contemplation rather than action or administration, given to philosophy and literature; but he decreed that all must bow in reverence before them, as is customary with mandarins. Furthermore, he presented them with extravagant gifts, things of great rarity or value: stuffed-and-mounted crocodiles, marble chairs, emerald eating utensils, diamonds, and relics. The academy, grateful for all the favor shown, also requested the official right to use the title Light of the World, which was granted to them.

Having done this, Kalaphangko turned his attention to public finances, the justice system, religion, and ceremonial matters. The nation began to feel the "great weight," to borrow a phrase from the sublime Camões, for no fewer than eleven delinquent taxpayers were soon decapitated. All the others, naturally, preferring their heads to their money, made haste to pay their tariffs, and everything got back to normal. The justice system and legislature improved greatly. New pagodas were constructed, and even the religion seemed to gain new life, ever since Kalaphangko, imitating the ancient Spanish techniques, ordered that a dozen poor Christian missionaries who were in the area be burned at the stake; all the bonzes in the kingdom called this the pearl of his reign.

All that lacked was a war. Kalaphangko, under more or less diplomatic pretexts, attacked a neighboring kingdom and carried out the swiftest and most glorious campaign of the century. Upon returning to Bangkok, he was greeted with lavish celebrations. Thirty ships, wrapped in scarlet and blue silks, went out to meet him. Each of these had a golden swan or dragon on its prow and was manned by the city's finest inhabitants. Music and applause thundered through the air. That night, the festivities over, his beautiful concubine whispered in his ear:

"My young warrior, fill this void I felt in your absence, tell me that the greatest celebration of all is your gentle Kinnara."

Kalaphangko responded with a kiss.

"Your lips contain the chill of death or disdain," she sighed.

It was true, the king was distracted and preoccupied; he was contemplating an atrocity. The end of the half-year was approaching and they would have to switch back; he intended to do away with that stipulation by killing the beautiful Siamese woman. He only hesitated because he didn't know if he would also suffer in her death, seeing as the body was his, or if he might even expire as well. This was Kalaphankgo's plan, but the thought of his own death darkened his countenance as he held a flask of poison close to his chest, in imitation of the Borgias.

Suddenly, his thoughts turned to the erudite academy. He could consult with them, not candidly, but hypothetically. He sent for the academics and all of them came, save for the president, the illustrious U-Tang, who was ill. There were thirteen altogether, and they prostrated themselves before the king, saying, after the manner of the Siamese:

"We, worthless weeds, run to attend the call of Kalaphangko."

"Rise up," said the king, benevolently.

"The proper place of dust is on the ground," they insisted, their elbows and knees on the ground.

"Then I shall be the wind that raises the dust," rejoined Kalaphangko. And with a gesture filled with grace and tolerance, he extended his hand to them.

He then began to talk about various subjects right away, so that the subject at hand would come up of its own accord. He spoke of the latest news from the west and the Hindu law of Manu. U-Tong was brought up, and the king asked them if he really was a great sage, as he seemed to be; seeing that they mumbled their response, he ordered them to tell him the whole truth. They confessed, with striking unanimity, that U-Tong was one of the most remarkably stupid people in the entire kingdom, a shallow soul of no worth at all, who knew nothing and was incapable of learning. Kalaphangko was shocked. An idiot?

"It pains us to say so, but it's simply the truth: he's a shallow, hollow soul. He has an excellent heart, and his character is pure and noble."

Kalaphangko, when he came back from the shock to his senses, sent the academics away, without having asked them what he wanted to know. An idiot? It was necessary to remove him from his position without offending him. Three days later, U-Tong showed up in response to the king's summons. The king affectionately asked after his health, and afterwards said that he wanted to send someone to Japan to study some manuscripts, a matter that could only be entrusted to an enlightened individual. Which of his colleagues from the academy did he think would be suitable for such a matter? Make note of the king's clever scheme: he would consider two or three suggested names and conclude that he preferred U-Tong himself to all the others. But U-Tong replied thus:

"My Royal Lord, please forgive the frankness of these words: those thirteen men are all camels, the only difference being that camels are modest, and these men are not. They compare themselves to the sun and the moon. But, in truth, neither the moon nor the sun ever shone on such exceptional imbeciles as these thirteen . . . I understand Your Majesty's surprise, but I would not be worthy of my position if I didn't tell you this in all honesty, albeit in confidence ..."

Kalaphangko's jaw dropped. Thirteen camels? Thirteen, thirteen. U-Tong's only word in their favor was that they all had good hearts, which he declared to be excellent; no one superior when it came to the question of character. Kalaphangko, with a graceful gesture of complacency, dismissed the glorious U-Tong and turned pensive. No one knows the nature of his reflections. It's understood that he sent for the other academics, but each one separately this time, so that what he was doing wouldn't be obvious, and in order to encourage greater candor. The first to arrive, although he was unaware of U-Tong's opinion, confirmed what he said in full, the only correction being that there were twelve camels, or thirteen if you counted U-Tong. The second didn't differ in opinion, nor the third, nor any of the remaining academics. They differed in style alone; some said camels, while others used circumlocutions and metaphors which relayed the same meaning. Nonetheless, there was never any attack made on the moral character of the academics. Kalaphangko was astonished.

But this was not the last shock that the king would receive. Unable to consult the academy, he attempted to deliberate on his own, which he did for two days, at which point the beautiful Kinnara told him, in secret, that she was to be a mother. This news made him recoil from the planned crime. How could he destroy the chosen vessel for the flower that would bloom the coming spring? He swore to heaven and earth that the child would be born and survive. The end of the arranged term arrived and, with it, the time to switch bodies.

Just like the first time, they got into the royal canoe at night, and let themselves be carried downriver, against the will of both of them, feeling empty longing for the body they were going to restore to the other. When the shining cattle of dawn began slowly to tread the sky, they proffered the mysterious incantation, and each soul was returned to its former body. Upon returning to hers, Kinnara felt a maternal sensation, just as she had felt a paternal one while she occupied the body of Kalaphangko. It even seemed to her that she was, at once, both the child's mother and father.

"Father and mother?" repeated the king, restored to his prior form.

They were interrupted by enchanting music, coming from afar. It was some junk or canoe coming upriver, for the music was swiftly approaching. The sun had already flooded the waters and verdant banks with light, lending an undertone of life and rebirth to the scene, which, in some measure, helped the two lovers forget their psychic restoration. And the music kept coming closer, clearer now, until a magnificent boat rounded a bend in the river and appeared before them, adorned with feathers and banners. In it were the fourteen members of the academy (including U-Tong), and in unison they raised their voices to the heavens, singing that old hymn: "Glory to us, who are the rice of science and the light of the world!"

Beautiful Kinnara (formerly Kalaphangko) stared in astonishment, her eyes bulging. She couldn't understand how it was that fourteen men gathered together in an academy could be the light of the world, yet, individually, be a bunch of camels. She consulted Kalaphangko, who could offer no explanation. If someone should happen to find an answer, you could render service to one of the most lovely ladies in the Orient by sending her a sealed letter, or better yet, for added security, a letter sent in care of our consul in Shanghai, China.

THE PRIEST,
OR THE METAPHYSICS OF STYLE

"Come with me from Lebanon, my spouse, with me from Lebanon ... The mandrakes give a smell, and at our gates are all manner of pleasant fruits ..."

"I charge you, O daughters of Jerusalem, if ye find my beloved, that ye tell him, that I am sick with love ..."

It was thus, in the melody of the ancient drama of Judah, that a noun and an adjective sought each other in the head of Padre Matias ... Don't interrupt me, hasty reader; I know that you don't believe anything that I'm going to tell you. I'll tell it all anyway, your lack of faith notwithstanding, for the day of the conversion of all mankind shall come.

On that day—I suppose it will be around the year 2222—this paradox shall remove its wings and put on the cloak of accepted truth. And then shall this page earn more than mere favor; it will attain apotheosis. It will be translated into every tongue. Academies and institutes will turn it into a small volume, made to last for centuries, printed on bronze pages with gilded edges, letters of inlaid opal, and a frosted silver cover. Governments will decree that it should be taught in grammar and secondary schools. Philosophical schools will burn all prior doctrines, even the most conclusive, and embrace the new psychology, the sole truth, and all will be accomplished. Until then, I'll be taken for a fool, as you'll soon see.

Matias, an honorary canon and a practicing preacher, was composing a sermon when he fell into a psychic idyll. He is forty years old and lives among books and more books on the outskirts of the Gamboa neighborhood. He had, of late, been asked to deliver a sermon for an upcoming celebration, but he was engrossed with a book of great spiritual worth that had arrived on the most recent steamship, so he declined the offer. But the sponsors of the celebration insisted so forcefully that he eventually consented.

"Your Reverence could write one in your sleep," said the main sponsor.

Matias smiled meekly and discreetly, as clergymen and diplomats should smile. The celebrants bid farewell with grand gestures of veneration and went to advertise the celebration in the newspapers, with the added announcement that Padre Matias, "a jewel of the Brazilian clergy," would be preaching the gospel. The "jewel of the clergy" part made the priest lose his appetite and skip lunch when he read it in the morning. He only sat down to write the sermon once he began to feel better.

He started off begrudgingly, but after a few minutes he was working with passion. Inspiration, with its eyes in the heavens, and reflection, with its eyes on the ground, are on either side of his chair, whispering a thousand mystical and solemn things in the priest's ear. Matias keeps on writing, now slowly, now swiftly. The lines flow from his hands, lively and polished. Some of them need little or no improvement. Then suddenly, as he goes to write a certain adjective, he freezes; he writes a different one, then scratches it out; then another, which suffers the same fate. This is the crux of his reverie. Let's go up into the priest's head.

Jump! Here we are. It was hard for you, wasn't it, dear reader? We're doing this so that you won't believe those people who climb to the top of Corcovado and claim that the heights are so great that it makes man seem absolutely insignificant. It's a panic-driven opinion, and false as well, as false as Judas and other such diamonds, so don't believe it, beloved reader. Neither Corcovado nor the Himalayas are worth much compared to your own head, which measures their height. And here we are. Take a good look around; this is the priest's head. We can choose between the two cerebral hemispheres, so let's choose this one here, wherein adjectives are born. Adjectives are created on the left side. This is my own discovery, but even so, it's not the principal discovery, just the basis for it, as shall be seen. Yes, good sir, adjectives are born on the left side and nouns on the right, and all manner of words are divided thusly on the basis of sexual difference ...

"*Sexual* difference?"

Yes, my lady, sexual difference. Words have a sex. I'm currently finishing my grand psycholexicological memoir, in which I lay out and prove this discovery. Words have a sex.

"But, then, do they love one another?"

Yes, they love one another. They marry, too. The marriage of two words is what we call style. My dear lady, admit that you don't understand this at all.

"I admit that I don't."

Well then, come with me into the priest's head. They just happen to be whispering right here, on this side. Do you know who it is that's whispering? It's the noun from just a moment earlier, the one that the priest wrote down on the paper just before he froze, pen in the air. It's calling out to a certain adjective, which isn't answering his call: "Come with me from Lebanon, come ..." It talks that way because it's in the head of a priest; if it were in the head of a person from the secular world, it would speak the language of Romeo: "Juliet is the sun ... Arise, fair sun." But in the brain of a clergyman, the language is that of the scriptures. And, at bottom, what does the phrasing matter? Lovers from Verona or Judah all speak the same tongue, as happens with the taler and the dollar, the florin and the pound, which are all the same money.

Therefore, let's dive into the circumvolutions within the priest's brain, following the noun as it searches for the adjective. Silvio calling out for Silvia. Listen: from a distance it sounds like someone else is whispering as well. It's Silvia calling out for Silvio.

They can hear each other, and they start searching. It's a difficult and complex path, this trip through a brain filled with things both old and new. There's a rustling of ideas in here that barely allows the lovers' calls to be heard; let's not lose sight of the ardent Silvio, who continues on, hiking up and down, losing his footing here, leaping over something there. Here, he grabs hold of some Latin roots so he doesn't fall; there, he props himself up with a psalm; in the distance, he climbs atop a pentameter. And he always keeps walking, spurred on by an inner force, which he is unable to resist.

From time to time, other women appear before him—adjectives, like Silvia—and offer him their charms, be they ancient or new. But, by God, they're not the same, they're not the one and only, the one that was destined for this marriage *ab æterno*. And Silvio keeps walking, searching for the one. Pass on by, eyes of every color, bodies of every shape, heads of hair as bright as the sun or as dark as night; die off without echo, tender love songs, wafting from the eternal violin. Silvio isn't just searching for a random, casual, anonymous love, he's searching for a specific love, named and predestined.

Now don't be frightened, reader, it's nothing, just the priest moving around; he's getting up from his chair, going over to the window, and leaning against it, to distract himself from the task at hand. There, see? He's forgetting about the sermon and all that. The parrot beside the window, at the top of its cage, is repeating its customary words and, out in the yard, the peacock is spreading its feathers in the morning sun. The sun itself, recognizing the priest, sends him one of its faithful rays as a greeting. The ray arrives and stops in front of the window: "Illustrious priest, I come to bring you greetings from the sun, my lord and father." All of nature seems to applaud the return of that emissary from the heavens. The priest himself becomes cheerful and looks out at the pure air, letting his eyes roam and get their fill of the fresh, green expanse, to the sound of a songbird and a piano. Then he says a few words to the parrot, calls hello to the gardener, rubs his hands together, and leans against the window once more. He's no longer thinking about Silvio and Silvia.

But Silvio and Silvia are still thinking about each other. While the priest is lost in thought about unrelated things, the two of them are still searching for each other, without him knowing or even suspecting it. But now the way is dark. We're passing over from the conscious mind to the unconscious mind, where ideas emerge in disorder, where reminiscences doze and repose. Herein abounds life without form, the seeds, the debris, the rudiments and sediments of life; it is the immense attic of the spirit. And this is where the two of them ended up, in search of one another, calling out for each other and sighing. Give me your hand, dear lady, my reader; stay close to me, good sir, good reader. Let's trudge along with them.

It's a vast, unknown world. Silvio and Silvia are traipsing through embryos and ruins. Groups of ideas, deduced by way of syllogism, get lost in the tumult of reminiscences from childhood and the seminary. Other ideas, pregnant with even more ideas, trod heavily, helped along by virgin ideas. Men and things, once distinct, become fused together. Plato is wearing the eyeglasses of a scribe of an ecclesiastical court. Mandarins of various ranks are handing out Etruscan and Chilean coins, English books, and pale roses, so pale, in fact, that they no longer resemble the roses that the priest's mother planted when he was a child. Religious memories and family ones cross paths and commingle. Here are the remote voices from his first mass, and the country songs that he used to hear the black women sing back home, scraps of evaporated sensations, a little fear here, a minor pleasure there, and farther on moments of boredom, which, at the time, came one by one, but which now dwell together in that enormous coalescence, murky and impalpable.

"Come with me from Lebanon, my spouse . . ."

"I charge you, O daughters of Jerusalem . . ."

They can hear the other drawing ever closer. They've now arrived at the deepest layers of theology, philosophy, liturgy, geography, and history: ancient lessons and modern notions all jumbled up, both dogma and syntax. Spinoza's pantheistic hand grazes one of them; Doctor Angelicus scratches the other. But none of them are Silvio or Silvia, who keep trudging their way— entranced by an inner force, a secret affinity—past obstacles and over abysses. And there is sorrow as well. Dark sorrows that didn't remain in the priest's heart have made their way here, as have moral blemishes, and, beside those, reflections of yellow or purple light, or whatever is retained from the pain of others and universal suffering. Yet the two of them cut their way through all of this, with the swiftness of love and desire.

Are you wobbling, reader? Don't worry, the world isn't crashing down around you; it's just the priest sitting back down at this very moment. He remained distracted, at his leisure, then turned to face his desk and reread what he had written, getting back to work. Now he grabs the pen and lowers it to the page, to see which adjective he should attach to the noun.

And at this very moment the two desirous lovers are closer than ever. Their voices grow louder, their zeal grows too, and the whole Song of Songs passes through their lips, which burn with fever. Amusing limericks, anecdotes from the sacristy, caricatures, witticisms, nonsense, strange-looking fellows; none of this slows them down, or even makes them crack a smile. They keep going and going, and the distance between them shrinks. Remain where you are, you fools who once made the priest laugh, whom he has now completely forgotten; stay there, you faded disagreements, ancient riddles, rules to outmoded card games . . . and you too, embryos of new ideas, rough drafts of emerging concepts. Abandon hope, for they want nothing to do with you. They are in love and search only for each other.

They search and eventually find each other. At last, Silvio finds Silvia. They stare into each other's eyes and fall into the other's arms, breathless and weary, but their reward was worth it. Then they stand together and, arm in arm, make their way back from the unconscious to the conscious mind, their hearts aflutter.

"Who is this that cometh up from the wilderness, leaning upon her beloved?" asks Silvio, as in the Song of Songs.

And Silvia, with the same erudite lips, replies that it is "the seal upon thine heart," and that "love is strong as death."

At this moment, the priest trembles. His face lights up. The pen, full of emotion and respect, completes the noun by adding the adjective. Silvia will now walk beside Silvio in the sermon that the priest will give in a few days, and together they'll go to the printing press, if he ends up publishing his collected writings, which is unknown.

To Live!

[The end of time. Ahasverus, seated on a rock, stares at length out at the horizon, where two eagles are soaring, crossing paths. He reflects, then begins to daydream. The day is coming to a close.]

AHASVERUS: I have arrived at the end of time; this is the threshold of eternity. The earth is deserted, no one but me breathes the air of life. I am the last; I can die. To die! What a delicious thought! I've lived for centuries and centuries—tired, tormented, ceaselessly walking—yet they have come to an end, and I shall die along with them. Farewell, ancient nature! Blue sky, renascent clouds, roses that bloom today and roses of all other days, perennial waters, inimical earth—which did not consume my bones—farewell to you all! The wanderer shall wander no more. God will forgive me if he will, but death shall console me. That mountain there is as rough-hewn as my pain; those eagles passing overhead must be as famished as my despair. Will you die too, divine eagles?

PROMETHEUS: Mankind has disappeared, it's true: the earth is devoid of men.

AHASVERUS: I can still hear a voice . . . Is it the voice of a man? You pitiless heavens, am I not the last? There he is, approaching . . . Who are you? There is something like the mysterious light of the archangels of Israel in your large eyes. You aren't human . . .

PROMETHEUS: No.

AHASVERUS: A deity?

PROMETHEUS: You have said it.

AHASVERUS: I don't know who you are. But what does that matter? You're not human, so I can die, for I am the last one, and I shall close the gate of life behind me.

PROMETHEUS: Life, like ancient Thebes, has one hundred gates. Close one, and others will open. You're the last of your species? Another, better species shall come, not made of the same clay, but of the same light. Yes, you last among men, the spirits of the rabble shall remain dead forever, but the choicest souls shall return to the earth to rule all things. Time shall be restored; there shall be no evil. The winds will no longer spread the seeds of death nor carry the lamentations of the oppressed; they will only broadcast the song of eternal love and the universal blessing of justice ...

AHASVERUS: What do these posthumous delights matter to the species that shall perish with me? You're immortal, so you'll have to trust me: the purple dyes of Sidon are worthless to the bones that are rotting in the earth. The tale you're telling me is even better than Campanella's dream. There was still crime and illness in the city he imagined; yours eliminates all moral and physical afflictions. May the Lord hear your plea! As for me, just let me die.

PROMETHEUS: Go ahead, go ahead. But why do you wish to bring your days to an end with such haste?

AHASVERUS: It is the haste of a man who has lived for thousands of years. Yes, thousands. Men who only drew breath for a few dozen years invented the concept of boredom, *tedium vitæ*, which they could never truly know—at least not in all its vast, implacable reality—because it's necessary to have walked among every generation, among all ruins, to experience this profound aversion to existence.

PROMETHEUS: Thousands of years?

AHASVERUS: My name is Ahasverus. I lived in Jerusalem at the time when Jesus Christ was to be crucified. When he passed by my doorstep, he struggled beneath the weight of the wood that he carried on his shoulders, and I shoved him, yelling at him, telling him not to stop, not to rest . . . that he had to keep walking until he reached the hill where he would be crucified. And then I heard a voice from the heavens declare that I would walk forever, endlessly, until the end of time. Such was my offense: I didn't show mercy to the man who was marching toward his own death. I'm really not sure why. The Pharisees said that the son of Mary had come to destroy the law, and that he had to be killed. I, a poor, unlearned man, wished to show my zeal, and thence my deed on that day. How many times did I witness that very same thing, in the years after, as I traveled across the ages and cities! Wherever zeal inhabited an inferior soul, it became cruel or ridiculous. Such was my unpardonable offense.

PROMETHEUS: A serious offense, to be sure, but the punishment was benevolent. Other men only read a chapter of life, but you got to read the whole book. What does one chapter know of another? Nothing. But he who has read them all is able to connect one to the next and finish the volume. Are there melancholic pages? Well, there are others that are merry and gay. A tragic moment is followed by a laughable one, life blossoms out of death, storks and swallows migrate from one climate to another, yet they never abandon them for good; in this way all is harmonized and restored. You saw this yourself, not ten times, not a thousand times, but every single time. You've seen the splendor of the earth cure an afflicted soul, and the soul's joy makes up for the desolation all around it. It's the back-and-forth dance of nature, which extends its left hand to Job and its right hand to Sardanapalus.

AHASVERUS: What do you know of my life? Nothing. You know nothing of human existence.

PROMETHEUS: I know nothing of human life? What a laugh! Out with it, you eternal man, explain yourself. Tell me everything. You left Jerusalem and . . .

AHASVERUS: I left Jerusalem. And I began my journey across all the ages. I went everywhere, whatever the race, religion, or language may have been. Sun and snow, peoples both savage and civilized, islands, continents—wherever a man drew breath, I drew breath there too. I never worked again. Work is a refuge, one that wasn't afforded me. I'd awake every morning with the coin for the day in my possession . . . Look, here's the last one. Be gone, for you're no longer needed [*he throws the coin into the distance*]. I never worked, just walked, always walking, walking, walking, one day after another, one year after another, throughout every year, every century. Eternal justice knew what it was doing: it added idleness to eternity. One generation bequeathed me the next. My name is inscribed on the bones of dead languages. As times changed, everything was forgotten. Heroes faded into myth, into the shadows, into the distance, and history crumbled bit by bit, until nothing but two or three of its features remained in the hazy distance. And I saw it all, first one way and then the other. You mentioned chapters? Happy are they who only read one of life's chapters. Those who passed away at the beginning of a new empire died believing in its perpetuity; those who expired as an old empire fell were buried with the hope that it would be rebuilt. But do you know what it means to see the same things over and over, the same fluctuation from prosperity to devastation, from devastation to prosperity, eternal funeral and eternal joy, dawn upon dawn, dusk upon dusk?

PROMETHEUS: But you didn't suffer pain, I believe. That's something, never to suffer.

AHASVERUS: True, but I saw other men suffer, and, toward the end, a joyful sight produced in me the same sensation as a tale told by a madman. The shedding of blood, the rending of flesh, insoluble conflicts; they all passed before my eyes, to such an extent that night made day distasteful to me, that I can no longer distinguish flowers from thorns. Everything gets mixed up in my weary retina.

PROMETHEUS: But you never personally felt pain. What about me, who suffered the consequences of divine wrath countless times?

AHASVERUS: You?

PROMETHEUS: My name is Prometheus.

AHASVERUS: You, Prometheus?

PROMETHEUS: And what was my crime? I made the first humans from clay and water, and afterwards, taking pity on them, I stole fire from the heavens for them. Such was my crime. Jupiter, who ruled Olympia at the time, condemned me to the cruelest torture. Come on, climb up this rock with me.

AHASVERUS: What you're telling me is a myth. I know this ancient Hellenic dream.

PROMETHEUS: You old skeptic! Come up here and see the very chains that bound me. It was an excessive punishment for an offense that wasn't one at all, but that prideful, terrible deity . . . Here we are, look, there are the chains . . .

AHASVERUS: Time, which ravages all, didn't want them?

PROMETHEUS: They were made by divine hands; Vulcan fabricated them. Two divine emissaries came down to chain me to this rock, and an eagle, just like the one soaring across the horizon there, ate my liver without ever devouring it entirely. This lasted for longer than I could count. No, you can't imagine such torture . . .

AHASVERUS: You aren't deceiving me? You're truly Prometheus? So it wasn't just a reverie of the ancient imagination?

PROMETHEUS: Behold me, touch my hands. See for yourself if I really exist.

AHASVERUS: Moses lied to me. You, Prometheus, are the creator of the first humans?

PROMETHEUS: That was my crime.

AHASVERUS: Yes, it was your crime, indeed, you hellish artificer, your unpardonable crime. You should have remained bound here for all time, chained and devoured—you, the origin of all the ills that afflicted me. I lacked pity, it's true; but you, who brought me into existence, you perverse deity, were the original cause of all that exists.

PROMETHEUS: Your impending death is clouding your reason.

AHASVERUS: Yes, it's really you, you have the countenance of an Olympian, you strong, handsome Titan . . . Are these the chains? I see no sign of your tears?

PROMETHEUS: I shed them for your species.

AHASVERUS: My species shed many more tears because of you.

PROMETHEUS: Listen to me, you final man, you final ingrate!

AHASVERUS: Why would I want to hear what you have to say? I want to hear you wail and moan, you perverse deity. Here are the chains. Behold how I hold them in my hands, listen to the irons as they clank together . . . Who set you free so long ago?

PROMETHEUS: Hercules.

AHASVERUS: Hercules . . . See if he won't lend you a hand once more, because you're going to be chained up again.

PROMETHEUS: You've gone mad.

AHASVERUS: The heavens castigated you the first time; now the earth will give you your second and final punishment. Not even Hercules will be able to break these chains. Behold how I wave them about in the air, as if they were feathers; it's because I represent the strength of millennia of despair. All of humanity is present in me. Before I plunge into the abyss, I shall write the epitaph of the world on this rock. And I'll call the eagle, and it will heed my call. I'll tell it that the last man, as he leaves this life, bequeaths it a gift from the gods.

PROMETHEUS: You poor fool, you're rejecting a throne! No, you can't reject it.

AHASVERUS: Now it's you who has gone mad. Come along, lie down here, let me bind your arms. Yes, there we go, you can no longer resist. Lean over that way, alright, now for the legs . . .

PROMETHEUS: Hurry up, hurry up. The passions of the earth have turned against me. But I, who am not a man, don't know ungratefulness first hand. You shall not change your fate one jot, it shall be fulfilled completely: you shall be the new Hercules. I, who sang the praises of the other Hercules, shall sing yours as well. And you shall be no less generous than he.

AHASVERUS: Have you gone mad?

PROMETHEUS: Truths unknown to men sound like the ravings of a madman. Hurry up, get it over with.

AHASVERUS: Glory doesn't pay, and it eventually fades away.

PROMETHEUS: This one shall never fade. Hurry up, go ahead, teach the crooked beak of the eagle how it should devour my entrails, but at least listen . . . No, don't bother, you wouldn't understand it anyway.

AHASVERUS: Tell me, tell me.

PROMETHEUS: The temporal world cannot understand the eternal world. But you shall be the link between the two.

AHASVERUS: Tell me everything.

PROMETHEUS: I'm not going to tell you anything. Go ahead, make it tight around my wrists, so that I can't escape, so that you'll still find me here when you return. You want me to tell you everything? I've already told you that a new race will populate the earth, made up of the choicest spirits from the human race that is now extinct. The multitude of others shall remain dead. This noble family, lucid and powerful, shall be the perfect communion of the divine and the human. There will be new ages, but there must be a link between the old ones and the new. You are that link.

AHASVERUS: Me?

PROMETHEUS: You, indeed. You, the chosen one, the king. Yes, Ahasverus, you shall be king. The wanderer shall rest. The despised of all men shall rule mankind.

AHASVERUS: You crafty Titan, you're tricking me . . . me, a king?

PROMETHEUS: Yes, you, king. Who else could it be? The new world will need to know the traditions of the old one, and no one can speak of one to the other like you. In this way, there will be no interruption between the two human races. Perfection shall arise from imperfection, and your mouth will tell humanity of its origins. You'll tell the new men of their origins, of all the good and evil thereof. In this way you'll be revivified, like a tree that's been pruned of its dry leaves, leaving only the green, flourishing ones. But in this case their green is eternal.

AHASVERUS: Such a beautiful vision! Me, really?

PROMETHEUS: The very same.

AHASVERUS: These eyes . . . these hands . . . a new and better life . . .
what a glorious vision! This is just, Titan. My punishment was just,
and the glorious remission of my sin shall be equally just. I shall live?
Me, really? A new, better life? No, you must be putting one over on
me.

PROMETHEUS: Well, leave me here. You'll come back one day,
once these vast heavens have opened to allow the spirits of the
new world to descend. You'll find me here, at ease. Go.

AHASVERUS: I shall greet the sun once more?

PROMETHEUS: The very sun that is now about to set. The friendly
sun, eye of the ages, shall never again shut its eyelids. Stare at it,
if you're able.

AHASVERUS: I can't.

PROMETHEUS: You'll be able to do it once the conditions of this life
have changed. Then your retina shall stare at the sun without any
danger, because all that is best in nature—be it forceful or subtle,
flashy or simple—shall be concentrated in the man of the future.

AHASVERUS: Swear that you're not lying.

PROMETHEUS: You'll see that I'm not.

AHASVERUS: Go on, keep talking, tell me everything.

PROMETHEUS: The description of this new life can't do justice to
the experience of it, and you'll have that in spades. The bosom of
Abraham from your ancient scripture is nothing less than this
subsequent, perfected world. There you shall see David and the

prophets. There you shall tell tales—to an astonished audience—of not only the great events of the old world, but also of all its evils, which they won't experience firsthand: injury and old age, fraud, selfishness, hypocrisy, loathsome pride, unexpected folly, and all the rest of it. The soul shall be draped in an incorruptible tunic, as shall the earth.

AHASVERUS: I'll still be able to lay eyes on the vast blue sky!

PROMETHEUS: Look how beautiful it is.

AHASVERUS: Beautiful and serene, like eternal justice. Majestic sky, greater still than the tents of Kedar, I shall gaze upon thee now and forever. You shall take in and shelter my thoughts, as before; you shall give me clear days and kindly nights . . .

PROMETHEUS: Dawn upon dawn.

AHASVERUS: Come on, tell me more, tell me everything. Here, let me remove your chains . . .

PROMETHEUS: Remove them, new Hercules, the last man of this world, who shall be first among men in the world to come. It's your fate; neither you nor I, nor anyone else, can change it. You are greater still than your beloved Moses. Nearing death, he saw all the land of Jericho from the heights of Mount Nebo, which would belong to his posterity. And the Lord said unto him: "I have caused thee to see it with thine eyes, but you shall not go over thither." But you shall go over thither, Ahasverus. You shall inhabit Jericho.

AHASVERUS: Put your hand on my head, look at me squarely; instill this reality, this prediction in me. Let me feel some of this new, flawless life . . . King, you say?

PROMETHEUS: The chosen king of a chosen race.

AHASVERUS: It's not excessive compensation to counterbalance the profound scorn I've felt. Where one life covered me in mire, the other shall reward me with a crown. Go on, tell me more . . . tell me more . . . [*He continues to daydream. The two eagles draw up beside each other.*]

ONE EAGLE: Woe, woe, woe unto this last of men, he is dying, yet still he dreams of life.

THE OTHER EAGLE: And he only hated it so much because he loved it so dearly.

EX CATHEDRA

"Godfather, you'll go blind from that, sir."

"What?"

"You're going to go blind. Reading is so sad. No sir, give me that book."

Caetaninha took the book out of his hands. Her godfather paced around and then went into his study, where there was no lack of books. He closed the door behind him and kept reading. That was his vice. He read excessively; he read morning, noon, and night, during lunch and dinner, before going to sleep, after bathing; he read as he walked, read standing up, read in his house and in his barn; he read before reading and he read after reading; he read all sorts of books, but especially books on law (in which he'd received his degree), mathematics, and philosophy. Lately, he'd also been reading up on the natural sciences.

Worse than going blind, he went crazy. It was near the end of 1873, in Tijuca, when he started to show signs of mental disturbance; but, since the episodes were minor and few, his goddaughter only started to notice the difference in March or April of 1874. One day, over lunch, he interrupted his reading to ask her:

"What's my name again?"

"What's your name, Godfather?" she repeated, astonished. "Your name is Fulgencio."

"From this day forth, my name will be Fulgencius."

And, burying his face in the book, he went on reading. Caetaninha mentioned the episode to the slave women, who admitted that they'd had their doubts about him for some time, that he hadn't seemed well. Just imagine how fearful she was;

but her fear soon passed, leaving only compassion behind, which increased her affection for him. His mania was also limited and docile, and was only related to books. Fulgencio lived for the written word, the printed word, doctrines, abstract thought, principles, and formulas. He eventually passed from mere superstition to true hallucination of the theoretical. One of his maxims was that liberty would not die, so long as there was a single piece of paper on which to declare it. So one day, waking up with the idea of improving the condition of the Turks, he wrote a constitution for them and sent it to the British diplomat in Petrópolis as a gift. On another occasion, he set about studying the eyes in anatomy books to verify whether they were really able to see, and concluded that they were.

Tell me, readers, whether, under such conditions, Caetaninha's life could have been a happy one? It's true that she wanted for nothing, because her godfather was rich. He had been the one who'd raised her, from the age of seven, when he lost his wife. He had taught her to read and write, French, and a little bit—so as not to say almost nothing—of history and geography, and had charged the domestic slaves with teaching her embroidery, lace-making, and sewing. There's no denying any of that. But Caetaninha had turned fourteen, and if in the early years her toys and the slaves were enough to entertain her, she was now at an age when toys fall out of favor and slaves hold no interest, when no amount of reading or writing can transform a solitary house in Tijuca into a paradise. She went out sometimes, but rarely, and always in a rush. She never went to the theater or to dances, never made or received visits. Whenever she saw a cavalcade of men and women on horseback out in the street, her soul would ride pillion on one of the horses and ride off with them, leaving only her body behind, right next to her godfather, who kept on reading.

One day, while she was out by the barn, she saw a young man

mounted on a little mule approach the gate, and heard him ask her if this was the house of Doctor Fulgencio.

"Yes, sir, this is."

"May I speak with him?"

Caetaninha replied that she would see about it. She walked into the house and went to the study, where she found her godfather contemplating, with the most delighted, beatific expression on his face, a chapter of Hegel.

"A young man? What young man?"

Caetaninha told him that the young man was in mourning clothes.

"Mourning clothes?" repeated the old doctor of law, hastily closing his book. "It must be him."

I forgot to mention (although there's time enough for everything here) that three months earlier, Fulgencio's brother had passed away up north, leaving behind a son. A few days before he died, the brother wrote him, entrusting him with the orphan he would soon leave alone, and Fulgencio replied that he should come down to Rio de Janeiro. When he heard that there was a young man in mourner's garb at his gate, he assumed that it must be his nephew, and he was right to do so. It was the nephew indeed.

It seems that, up to this point, there has been nothing in this story that departs in any way from a naively romantic tale: we have an old lunatic, a lonely, sighing maiden, and we've just seen a nephew suddenly arrive on the scene. So that we don't come down from the poetic region in which we currently find ourselves, let me merely mention that the mule on which Raimundo arrived was led to the stables by one of the blacks; I'll also gloss over the circumstances pertaining to the young man's accommodations, limiting myself to mentioning that, since his uncle had completely forgotten that he'd told him to come—by dint of spending all his waking hours reading—nothing was ready for him at the house.

But it was a big, affluent house, and, an hour later, the young man was set up in a gorgeous bedroom, from which he could see the barn, the old well, the wash basins, plenty of green leaves, and the vast blue sky.

I believe I haven't yet mentioned the young guest's age. He has fifteen years under his belt and a hint of fluff on his upper lip; he's nearly a child. Now, if this made our dear Caetaninha restless, and if the slave women went from one end of the house to the other eavesdropping and talking about "ole massa's nephew from out of town," it was only because there was nothing else going on in their lives there, not because he was a dashing, grown man. The man of the house had this same impression, but there's a difference here. The goddaughter didn't realize that the purpose of upper-lip fluff is to one day become a mustache, or if she did think about this, she only did so in passing, and it's not worth writing it down here. Not so with old Fulgencio. He understood that he had before him the makings of a husband, and he resolved to get them to marry. But he also saw that, short of taking them by the hand and ordering them to love each other, chance and circumstance could lead these things down a different path.

One idea begets another. The idea of getting them to marry each other somehow fused together with one of his recent opinions. It went like this: in matters of the heart, calamities or simple displeasures stemmed from the fact that love was conducted in empirical fashion and lacked a scientific basis. A man and a woman who understood the physical and metaphysical reasons for this feeling would be more apt to receive it and nurture it effectively than another man and woman who knew nothing of the phenomenon.

"My little ones are yet green," he said to himself, "I have three or four years ahead of me, and I can start preparing them now. We'll proceed logically: first the foundations, then the walls, then the ceiling ... instead of starting with the ceiling straight away .."

. A day will come when people learn to love the way they learn to read . . . and on that day . . ."

He was stunned, dazzled, delirious. He went over to the bookshelves, pulled down a few volumes—astronomy, geology, physiology, anatomy, jurisprudence, political science, linguistics— and opened them, leafed through them, compared them, copying down a little from this one and little from that one, until he had a program of study. It was composed of twenty chapters, in which he put forth general concepts about the universe, a definition of life, a demonstration of the existence of man and woman, the organization of societies, the definition and analysis of the passions, a definition and analysis of love, as well as its causes, necessities, and effects. To tell the truth, the subjects were daunting, but he intended to make them more amenable, discussing them with simple, common language, giving them a purely familiar tone, like Fontenelle's astronomy. And he stated emphatically that the essential part of the fruit was the pulp, not the peel.

All of this was ingenious, but here's the most ingenious part: he didn't invite them to learn. One night, gazing up at the sky, he said that the stars were shining brightly. And what were stars, after all? Did they, perchance, know what stars really were?

"No, sir."

It was only a small step from this point to the beginning of a description of the universe. Fulgencio took this step so nimbly and naturally that they were enchanted, and asked for the entire journey.

"No," said the old man, "let's not exhaust it all today. This can't be understood well if it isn't learned slowly. Maybe tomorrow or the day after . . ."

In this shrewd manner, he began to execute his plan. The two students, astonished by the world of astronomy, asked him to continue his lessons day after day, and although Caetaninha was a little confused at the end of this first chapter, she still wanted to hear all the other things her godfather had promised to explain.

I'll say nothing of the familiarity between the two students, since it should be obvious. There's such a tiny difference between fourteen and fifteen year-olds, that all they have to do to bridge the gap is hold out their hands to each other. And that is what happened.

At the end of three weeks, it seemed as if they'd been brought up together. This alone was enough to change Caetaninha's life dramatically, but Raimundo gave her even more. Not ten minutes ago we saw her watch longingly as a cavalcade of men and women passed by in the street. Raimundo quenched this longing, teaching her to ride despite the reluctance of the old man, who was afraid some disaster would befall her. He eventually agreed and readied two horses for them. Caetaninha ordered a custom-tailored riding outfit, and Raimundo went into town to buy her gloves and a whip—with his uncle's money, of course, which also provided him with boots and the rest of the men's riding gear he needed. It was soon a pleasure to see the two of them, graceful and daring, riding up and down the mountainside.

At home, they were always together, playing checkers and cards, tending to the birds and plants. They argued a lot, but according to the slave women, they were play-fights, which they only got into so they could make up later. And that was the extent of their quarreling. Raimundo would go into town sometimes at his uncle's request, and Caetaninha would wait at the gate for him, anxiously scanning the horizon. When he arrived they'd always argue, because she'd want to take in the heaviest packages, saying that he must be tired, and he would try to give her the lightest ones, claiming that she was too dainty.

At the end of four months, life in the house had changed completely. You could even say that only then did Caetaninha start to wear flowers in her hair. Previously, she would often show up at the lunch-table with her hair uncombed. Now, not only did she comb her hair first thing in the morning, but she even, as I mentioned, wore a flower or two in her hair. The flowers were gathered either the night before—by her—and put in water, or the next morning—by him—and he would take them to her window. The window was high off the ground, but Raimundo was still able, by standing on his tiptoes and extending his arm, to hand the flowers to her. It was around this time that he developed the habit of teasing out the fluff on his upper lip, tugging it to one side and the other. Caetaninha even started to slap his hand away, to rid him of such a bad habit.

Meanwhile, the lessons continued regularly. They already had a general idea of the universe and a definition of life, which neither of them understood. Thus they entered the fifth month of instruction. In the sixth, the old man began to demonstrate the existence of man. Caetaninha couldn't contain her laughter when her godfather, explaining the subject at hand, asked them if they knew that they existed, and why. But she quickly became serious again, and answered that she didn't.

"You either?"

"No, me either, sir," said the nephew in agreement.

Fulgencio began his general, profoundly Cartesian demonstration of this fact. The following lesson took place in the barn. It had rained a lot in the previous days, but now the light from the sun flooded everywhere, and the barn looked like a beautiful widow who has traded her widow's veil for that of a bride. Raimundo, as if wishing to imitate the sun (the great ones naturally copy each other), shot a wide, long look from his pupils, which Caetaninha received from him, quivering like the barn itself. Fusion, transfusion, diffusion, confusion, and profusion of beings and objects.

While the old man spoke—impartially, logically, deliberately, making extensive use of formulas, his eyes staring out at nothing in particular—the two students made thirty thousand efforts to listen to him; but there were also thirty thousand things to distract them. At first it was a pair of butterflies frolicking in the air. Would you please explain to me what's so extraordinary about a couple of butterflies? I'll concede that they were yellow ones, but this detail doesn't serve to explain the distraction. The fact that they were chasing each other—now flitting to the right, now to the left, now down, now up—isn't the reason for their sidetracked attention either, since butterflies never fly in a straight line, like columns of soldiers.

"The understanding," said the old man, "the understanding, as I've already explained ..."

Raimundo looked at Caetaninha, and found her looking over at him. Both one and the other seemed embarrassed and bashful. She was the first to lower her eyes to her feet. She then raised them in order to look somewhere else, somewhere farther off, at one of the walls of the barn. Since they passed by Raimundo's eyes as they made their journey, she glanced at them and looked away as quickly as she could. Fortunately, the wall presented a spectacle that filled her with admiration: a couple of swallows (it was a day for couples, it seems) were flitting about it, with that grace peculiar to winged beings. They chirped as they cavorted, saying things to one another—who knows what they said, maybe this: that it was a very good thing that there was no philosophy on the walls of barns. Suddenly, one of them flew off—probably the lady—and the other—the gentleman, of course—wouldn't let himself get left behind; he spread his wings and followed the same route. Caetaninha lowered her eyes to the straw on the ground.

When the lesson ended a few minutes later, she asked her godfather to keep going, and, since he declined, took his arm and invited him to take a stroll around the barn with her.

"It's too sunny," replied the old man.

"We'll walk in the shade."

"It's too hot."

Caetaninha proposed that they continue the lesson on the porch, but her godfather mysteriously told her that Rome wasn't built in a day, and then stated that they would only continue the lesson two days later. Caetaninha retired to her room, where she remained for three quarters of an hour with the door closed, sitting, standing by the window, pacing from one side to the other, looking high and low for things that she was already holding in her hands, and even going so far as to see herself on horseback, trotting up the street next to Raimundo. Suddenly, she thought she saw the young man out by the wall of the barn, but upon closer inspection she realized it was just a couple of beetles, buzzing about in the air. And one beetle said to the other:

"You are the flower of our species, the flower of the air, the flower of flowers, the sun and the moon of my life."

To which the other replied:

"No one is your equal in beauty and grace, your buzzing is the echo of divine tongues. But leave me . . . leave me . . ."

"But why should I leave you, you, the soul of the thicket?"

"I have spoken, king of these pure breezes. Leave me."

"Don't say that, you jewel and charm of the forest. Everything above and around us implores you not to say that. Do you know the song of the blue mysteries?"

"Let's go listen to it among the green leaves of the orange tree."

"The leaves of the mango tree are more lovely."

"You are more lovely than both."

"And you, sun of my life?"

"Moon of my being, I am whatever you want me to be . . ."

This was what the two beetles were saying. She listened to them as she daydreamed. When the beetles flew off, she turned away from the window, noticed the time, and left her bedroom. Raimundo had gone into town, and she waited for him at the gate:

ten, twenty, thirty, forty, fifty minutes. When he got back they said very little, spending time together and then going separate ways two or three times. The last time they were together, she had brought him out on the porch to show him a bauble that she had thought was lost, but had just found. Reader, show her the courtesy of believing that it was a complete fabrication. Meanwhile, Fulgencio moved up their lesson, teaching it the following day between lunch and dinner. Never had he spoken such lucid, unadorned words. And that's how it should be; it was the chapter on the existence of man, a profoundly metaphysical lesson, in which it was necessary to take everything into consideration and examine it from all sides.

"Are you getting all this?" he asked.

"Perfectly."

The old man continued until he came to the end of the lesson. When it was over, the same thing happened as on the day before: Caetaninha was afraid of being alone and asked him to continue his lesson or go for a walk. The old man said no to both, patted her head paternally, and locked himself up in his study.

"Next week," thought the old doctor, as he turned the key, "next week I'll start the lesson on the organization of societies, then spend all next month and the one after that on the definition and classification of the passions. Then in May, we'll turn to love . . . the time will be right for . . ."

While he was saying this to himself and locking the door, there was a sound out by the porch—a thunderous roar of kisses, according to the caterpillars out by the barn. But, then again, any little noise sounds like thunder to a caterpillar. As for the true authors of the noise, nothing is known for sure. It seems that a wasp, who saw Caetaninha and Raimundo together at that very moment, inferred consequence from coincidence and assumed it was they who made the sound; but an old grasshopper demonstrated the inanity of the foundation of his argument, pointing out that he had heard plenty of kisses in his time, in places where neither Raimundo nor Caetaninha had ever set foot. We can all agree that this second argument is absolutely worthless. But such is the influence of a good reputation, that the grasshopper was applauded for having defended, once again, truth and reason. And maybe that's the case. But a thunderous roar of kisses? Let's suppose there were just two, or perhaps three or four.

VOYAGE AROUND MYSELF

Chapter I

When I opened my eyes, it was almost nine in the morning. I had dreamt that the sun, wearing only knickers and stockings, was doffing his hat to me with grand gestures, yelling at me that it was time, that I should get up, that I should go to Henriqueta and tell her everything that was in my heart. Twenty-one years have passed since then! This was in 1864, toward the end of November. I was twenty-five years old at the time, two years her junior. Henriqueta had been widowed in 1862 and, according to everyone around her, had sworn to herself that she would never marry again. I first saw her a few weeks after I arrived from the provinces in July—newly minted bachelor's degree in hand—and I was immediately smitten.

I was determined to marry her, as certain that it would happen as two and three make five. You can't imagine my confidence in the future back then. I had been recommended for a position as a magistrate in the interior of the state by one of the ministers in Furtado's cabinet, and received a warm welcome from him upon arriving in Rio. But my first gulps of water from the Carioca River in Rio left me intoxicated, so much so that I resolved to forsake the position and never leave the capital. I went over to the window of life, my eyes on the river that flowed below me, the river of time, not merely to contemplate the perpetual course of the water, but to wait for a ship to emerge into view upriver or down, a ship made of gold and sandalwood, with sails of silk, which would take me away to an eternal, enchanted isle. That was what my heart was telling me.

The ship came, and it was called Henriqueta. Amid all the opinions that divided the capital, everyone agreed that she was the most beautiful woman that year. Her only flaw was that she didn't wish to remarry, but to me this was more like a peak to be ascended, an obstacle that would make victory even more valuable—a victory that I would not fail to attain, whatever the cost, though it wouldn't take much effort at all.

Around this time I had opened a law firm with another lawyer and was living in a boarding house. During the legislative session, I would sit in on sessions at the Chamber of Deputies, where, while they hadn't offered me a position as a minister—which I always assumed was just a matter of time—they at least offered me news and handshakes. I didn't make much money, but I didn't spend much either. My biggest expenditures were all imaginary ones. The realm of dreams was my personal mint.

I don't dare say whether or not Henriqueta was willing to break her widow's vow with me, but I believe that she had a certain inclination toward me, that she saw something in me that was different from all her other suitors, who were all diluted in the same ballroom pond. She saw me as an unaffected, enchanting sort of guy. To use of a figure of speech that will serve to illustrate our respective positions, she was a star that deigned to descend to the eaves of my house. All I had to do was climb up onto the roof and bring her inside. But that was precisely what I couldn't bring myself to do, waiting instead for her to descend and set foot on my windowsill. Out of pride? No, no, out of timidity and apathy. I even started to believe that such a descent was customary of all stars. After all, the sun didn't hesitate to do so on that noteworthy morning. After it appeared to me—as I mentioned, in knickers and stockings—it took off its clothes and entered my bedroom, its rays nude and crude, brazen November rays, oozing summer. It came in through every slit in the shutters, singing gaily the same refrain from my dream: "Come on, Plácido! Wake up! Open your heart! Get up! Get up!"

I got up, full of resolve, ate, and left for the office. At the office, I didn't work on anything—let's say I refrained from work in honor of love—didn't draft a single plea or petition. Instead, I drafted, in my head, a plan for a new and magnificent life and, since I had a pen in my hand, I even seemed to be writing. In reality I was just doodling: noses, pigs' heads, Latin phrases, juridical dictums, literary quotes. I left a little before three in the afternoon and headed to Henriqueta's house.

She was alone. Perhaps she had been thinking of me, or maybe she'd even been thinking about breaking her oath. Most likely, in this case, it was her pride that gave safe passage to my desire; refusing me entry would have made her seem fearful, so she let me in. What's certain, however, is that her eyes looked ice-cold. Perhaps her blood was less so, since I saw traces of it coloring her cheeks.

I felt impassioned as I entered her house. It wasn't the first time we'd been alone together (it was the second), but my determination on this occasion intensified my emotional state. When there were other people around—whether in her house or someone else's—I could always fall back on the strategy of staring at her from afar if we weren't conversing, from some spot where her eyes would often meet mine. Now, however, we were alone. Henriqueta greeted me warmly, extending her hand to me and saying:

"I thought you were going to let me leave for Petropolis without coming to see me."

I stammered out some excuse. It's true, the heat was becoming oppressive and it was about time to retreat up into the mountains of Petropolis. When was she leaving? She replied that she was going on the twentieth or twenty-first of December and, at my request, gave me a description of the city. I listened to her and said something else in turn, then asked her if she was going to attend such-and-such ball in the Engenho Novo neighborhood; after that we talked a little more about this or that. The thing I feared the most were pauses in conversation. I didn't know where to look, and if I was the one to restart the conversation, I always made a great show of it, making a big deal out of some odd or irrelevant thing, so that she wouldn't think that I had been thinking about her. At times, Henriqueta seemed bored with me; at others, she spoke with real interest. Certain of eventual victory, I thought about charging into battle, especially when she was at her most expansive. But I didn't dare march forward. The minutes flew by; the clock struck four, then four-thirty.

"Come on," I said to myself, "now or never."

I looked at her, she looked back at me. And then, either casually or because she feared that I was going to say something that she didn't want to hear, she mentioned some recent anecdote or another. Blessed anecdote! Gift from the heavens! I latched onto it, glad to escape from my own intentions. What was the anecdote about? Who knows, I don't remember what it was. I do remember that I told it with all its variants, analyzed it, and carefully revised it until five o'clock, which is when I took my leave, disgusted, irritated, disconsolate . . .

Chapter II

Cranz, quoted in Tylor, discovered among Greenlanders the belief that there are two equal people in a single man, and that they sometimes separate, as happens in sleep, wherein one of them sleeps while the other goes out to hunt and walk around. Thompson et al., referenced in Spencer, affirm that they found this same belief among many different peoples and races. The Egyptian version (ancient Egypt), according to Maspero, is more complicated; the Egyptians believed that, in addition to various spiritual souls that a man possessed, there was also one that was completely physical, a reproduction of every shape and feature of the body, a perfect facsimile.

I don't want to go into all the beliefs professed in our own language and traditions, so I'll mention just two: the miracle of Saint Anthony, who, in the middle of a sermon—and without interrupting his preaching or leaving the pulpit—went to another city to save his father from the gallows, and these melodious lines from Camões:

> I know not what occurred
> Between myself and me
> To make me my own enemy

It's possible that the meaning of these lines is merely figurative, but there is no proof that it isn't literal, and that "myself and me" aren't really two separate, tangible, visible people, standing face-to-face.

For my own part, be it hallucination or reality, something of this nature happened to me when I was a child. I had snuck into a neighbor's backyard to steal fruit from his trees. My father scolded me for it, and, that night, as I lay in bed—either sleeping or awake, although I'm pretty sure I was awake—I saw my own person appear before me, reprimanding me severely. I lived in fear for a few days, and only much later on did I start sleeping well again. I was afraid of everything. They were childish fears, it's true; ardent, ephemeral impressions. Two months later, spurred on by the same group of youngsters who were my co-conspirators in the first adventure, my soul felt stirred by the same impulses, and I once again stole fruit from my neighbor.

These memories came flooding back when I left Henriqueta's house, mocking me, and I had a strong urge to punch myself right in the face. I felt like I was two separate people: one who made accusations and another who made excuses. Names that I would never allow other people even to think in regard to me I spoke aloud and acknowledged, without incurring my own wrath, as I walked home through the streets and as I ate dinner. That night, I went to the theater to take my mind off things, but the same duel would start up again during the intermissions, although a little less vehemently. By the end of the night I had patched things up with myself, by means of a promise I made not to let Henriqueta leave for Petropolis without confessing everything. I would either marry her or move back to the provinces.

"Yes," I told myself, "she owes me for what she made me do to Veiga."

Veiga was a member of the Chamber of Deputies who lived in my boarding house along with three other deputies, and of all the people in the legislature, he was the one who had showed me the most kindness. He was a member of the opposition party, but he promised that he would pull some strings for me as soon as the current administration lost power. One day he did me a very generous favor. Knowing that I had lately been worried about a certain debt, he found a way to pay it through back channels. I went to see him as soon as I uncovered the identity of the author of this good deed, thanking him with tears in my eyes. Veiga tried to deny it, and ended up telling me not to run myself ragged trying to pay him back, that I could pay him once the legislative session ended and he had to leave the capital, or even in May, if need be.

Not long afterwards, I saw Henriqueta for the first time and was immediately enamored. We ran into each other a few times after that, and then one day I received an invitation to a soirée at the house of a third party who knew of my feelings and was resolved to do whatever possible to get us together. The day of the soirée arrived, but in the evening, as I went to have dinner, I was met with unexpected news: Veiga, who had complained of headaches and chills the night before, had awoken with a fever which had turned violent by the afternoon. That was already bad news, but here comes the worst of it: the three deputies, friends of his, had to go to a political meeting, and had decided that I should stay with the sick man, along with a servant, until they got back, which wouldn't be too late.

"Stay here," they told me, "and we'll be back before midnight."

I tried to sputter out some excuse, but my tongue refused to obey my command, and the three deputies wouldn't have heard a word of it anyway, since they'd already turned to leave. I told them to go to hell under my breath, them and their parliaments. After dinner I went to get dressed so that I'd be ready to leave, putting a robe on over my clothes rather than a suit coat, then went to Veiga's room. He was burning up with fever, but, as I approached his bedside, he saw my white tie and vest and told me not to worry about it, that it wasn't necessary for me to stay.

"No, I won't leave."

"Go, sir, João will stay with me. The others will be back soon."

"They'll be back around eleven."

"So be it, eleven. Go, go."

I wavered between going and staying. Duty bound my feet; love spread my wings. I stared for a few moments at the sick man languishing on his bed, his eyes closed, his breathing labored. The others wouldn't be back until midnight—I'd told him eleven, but they themselves had told me midnight—and to have no one but a servant until then . . .

"Go, sir."

"Did you take your medicine yet?" I asked.

"I'll take the second dose at nine-thirty."

I put my hand on his forehead; it was a live coal. I took his pulse; it was at a full gallop. While I was still hesitating, I straightened his bed sheets, then went around tidying up things in the room. Finally, I turned to the sick man to tell him that I was going to leave, but that I'd be back early. He only half opened his eyes and responded with a gesture. I squeezed his hand. "I'm sure it's nothing, you'll be fine tomorrow," I said as I left. I ran to put on my suit coat and headed out to the house where I would find the beautiful Henriqueta. I didn't find her there; she arrived fifteen minutes later.

That night was one of the best of that era for me. Oh sensations, you fugitive butterflies who fly from me, would that I could gather you all up and pin you to this page for the entertainment of those who read me! All would see that there have never been butterflies so beautiful, nor in such abundance, nor so spirited and sprightly. Henriqueta had more than one would-be suitor in attendance, but I don't know if she treated the others the way she treated me, shooting a look my way every now and then. Her friends said that she lived by the maxim that the glances of women, like the doffing of a man's hat, were acts of courtesy and thus insignificant, but I always viewed this as pure gossip. She only danced one waltz, and it was with me. I asked her to dance a quadrille with me, but she refused, saying that she would rather just talk. What it is we talked about, I don't rightly remember; it was twenty-one years ago. I only recall that I spoke less than she did, that for most of the time I just leaned back and watched as a flood of various things streamed from her mouth . . . Twice I thought of Veiga, but I purposely abstained from checking my watch, out of fear.

"You are absolutely giddy," a friend said to me.

I think I smiled, or shrugged my shoulders. I did something, but didn't say anything, because it was true that I was giddy, and dizzyingly so. I only came to my senses when I heard the door to Henriqueta's carriage shut. The horses soon trotted off, and I, standing at the door, pulled out my watch to check the time: it was two in the morning. I thought of the sick man and shuddered. I ran to get my overcoat and flew home, terribly distressed, fearing some disaster. As I walked, I couldn't help but allow the figure of Henriqueta to plant herself between me and the sick man. One idea influences another, and, without noticing it, I would start to slacken my pace, only coming back to my senses once I was at her heels or in front of her, at her feet.

I arrived at the boarding house and ran to Veiga's room. He was in bad shape. One of the three deputies was watching over him, while the others had gone to get some rest. They had come back from their meeting a little before one, and found the sick man delirious. The servant had fallen asleep. They didn't know how long the patient had been left alone, and they'd already called for the doctor.

I was silent and anguished as I heard this. Then I went to change clothes so I could keep watch for the rest of the night. Once in my room, all alone with myself, I called myself an ingrate and a fool; I had left a friend who was battling grave illness in order to chase after a pair of beautiful eyes that could be put off until tomorrow. I slunk down into the armchair. I didn't physically split into two, as it seemed I did as I child, but I became morally separated into two people, one who cursed me, one who lamented. After a few minutes, I changed and went to the sick man's room, where I stayed until morning.

Very well. But this isn't what left me with a twinge of resentment toward Henriqueta; it was the repetition of this situation. Four days later, I was to go to a dinner where she would also be in attendance. A dinner isn't a ball, I told myself; I'll go, but then come back early. I went and came back late, very late. One of the deputies told me, when I left, that our friend might be dead by the time I got back; such was the opinion of the attending physician. I replied ardently that he wouldn't be; such was the feeling of other doctors who had been consulted.

I came back late, as I said. It wasn't the food, which was splendid, nor the wine, which was worthy of Horace. It was her, and her alone. I didn't feel the time pass, I didn't feel anything. When I got to the boarding house it was almost midnight. Veiga hadn't died, and seemed to be out of danger, but I was so ashamed when I came in that I feigned illness and went straight to bed. I couldn't fall asleep until quite late, and slept poorly, very poorly.

Chapter III

I wasn't going to let the same thing happen to me this time. Sure, I was a child when I stole the neighbor's fruit on two separate occasions, but the repetition of the situation with Veiga was intolerable, and repeating my inaction with Henriqueta would be ridiculous.

I thought about writing a letter—long or short, either way—requesting her hand in marriage. I even went so far as to put pen to paper and start a few drafts. Then I realized that this was cowardly and resolved to do it in person. This resolution could have also been another sophism, to avoid the blank page of the letter. It was already nighttime, so I swore to go the next day. Then I left the house and went for a long walk, thinking and imagining; when I got back my legs were worn out, and I slept the sleep of the ambitious.

When I awoke, my mind was still on the task at hand, and I constructed, in my mind, the wedding ceremony, grandiose and exquisite, even going so far as to transform everything that lay around me. I turned a dingy, everyday boarding house bedroom into a lavish *boudoir*, with her inside it, speaking to me of eternity.

"Plácido!"

"Henriqueta!"

I didn't go to her house until that evening. I won't say that the hours passed very slowly on that day, because they do that as a rule when our hopes are in bloom. I battled Henriqueta in my mind. Around this time I was sure that I would be given a deputy's seat, and I often mentally acted out the role of a great politician; in this same way, I mentally vanquished my lady, who surrendered her whole life and person to me. Over dinner, I casually picked up *The Three Musketeers* and read five or six chapters, which did me good and filled me with ideas of bravery, which were like a bunch of smaller precious stones surrounding this central medallion: women belong to the most daring. I drew a fearless breath and marched ahead.

Henriqueta was about to leave, but she invited me in for a moment. Dressed in black, wearing neither cloak nor shawl, her smooth, round bust exposed, and her hair done up in a style—a combination of what was then in vogue and her own invention—that was particular to her, I don't hesitate to say that she mesmerized me.

"I'm going to visit some cousins who've arrived from São Paulo," she told me. "Come sit down for a bit. Did you go the theater last night?"

I first told her that I hadn't, then, correcting myself, said that I had, which was the truth. Now that this episode is long past, I don't think she smirked at this, but at the time the opposite seemed true, and I felt embarrassed. She told me that she hadn't gone to the theater because of a migraine, a horrible illness that she described as she straightened her bracelets and adjusted the position of the watch at her waist pocket. Leaning back in her armchair, with the end of her foot just visible, she seemed to call for me to kneel before her. That was my idea, but then I dismissed it as too grotesque. No, my gaze and my words would suffice. But the gaze isn't always enough, sometimes it gets timid, and other times it doesn't know where to alight. But the words would conquer all.

In the meantime, Henriqueta went on talking and smiling. At times it seemed that she felt the same moral dilemma I did, and the expression in her eyes was kindly. At others, I noticed a sliver of disdain and boredom. My heart was pounding, my fingers trembling. I summoned forth all my earlier thoughts of bravery, and they were all there, but they didn't descend to take root in my heart, they remained in my head, listless, dozing off . . .

All of a sudden we both fell silent, for three or five or ten minutes, I don't know. All I remember is that Henriqueta looked at her watch; I understood that it was time to go, and I asked her leave. She quickly stood up and extended her hand. I shook it and looked at her, with the intention of saying something, but her eyes looked incredibly wrathful or annoyed—I'm not sure which, this was many years ago . . .

I left. When I got to the porch, I swiped at the air with my hat and called myself an ugly name, a name so ugly that I won't set it down here. Her carriage was at the door, and I went off a ways so I could watch her get in. I didn't have to wait long. She came out of the house, stood in front of the door for a moment, got in, and the coach took off. I didn't know what to do with myself, so I set off walking. An hour later, or a little less than an hour, I happened upon a friend, a colleague from the courthouse, who was heading home. We walked together, but after ten minutes he said:

"You seemed preoccupied. What's wrong?"

"I lost a case."

"Well it couldn't be worse than mine. Did I already tell you about the Matos inventory?"

He told me all about the Matos inventory, not sparing a single detail: appeals, appraisals, seizures of goods, pleas, counterpleas, and the final verdict, which was absurd and unjust. While he was talking, I kept thinking of the beautiful Henriqueta. I had lost her for the second time; then I thought of the incident with Veiga, in which my plans had failed in a similar manner, and the matter with the fruits when I was little. As I thought about the fruits, I also thought of the mysterious doubling of my person, and I hallucinated.

Yes, dear sir, it's true. It seemed to me that the colleague who was walking next me was actually me, and that I was shaking my fists in my face, furious at myself, and kept calling myself the name I'd said on the porch, which I didn't write then and I won't write now. I stopped in my tracks, frightened, and realized I was mistaken. I then heard a laugh in the air above me and raised my eyes. It was the stars, those distant observers of life, and they were laughing at my plans and delusions, with such force that I think buttons popped off their shirts, while my colleague vehemently concluded that business about the Matos inventory:

"... a scandal!"

A Lady

I never run into this lady without remembering the prophecy a lizard made to the poet Heine as he was climbing the Apennines: "One day the stones will become plants, the plants animals, the animals human beings, and the human beings gods." And it makes me want to say to her: "Dear lady, Dona Camila, you loved youthfulness and beauty so much that you turned back your clock to see if you could hold on to those two crystalline minutes. Don't get upset about it, Dona Camila. On the day that the lizard speaks of, you, dear lady, shall become Hebe, goddess of youth. You shall let us drink the nectar of perpetuity from your eternally youthful hands."

The first time I saw her she was thirty-six years old, although she only looked thirty-two, and hadn't yet left the house of twenty-nine. "House" is just a figure of speech here. There isn't a castle in the world more immense than the home of these fair friends, these twenty-nine years, nor is there more courteous hospitality than the kind they offered to their guests. Every time Dona Camila wanted to leave, they would beg her to stay, and she'd stay. And then there would be fresh entertainment, games, music, dancing, a whole series of lovely things, contrived with the sole aim of keeping this lady from getting on her way.

"Mommy, mommy," her growing daughter would say, "let's go, we can't stay here forever."

Dona Camila would look at her, mortified, and then smile, give her a kiss, and tell her to go play with the other children. What other children? Ernestina was between fourteen and fifteen years old at this time, fully developed, very patient, and already had some of the natural qualities of a lady. So she probably wasn't playing with the little girls of eight or nine; but no matter, as long as she left her mother in peace, it didn't matter whether she was happy or bored. But, o, such woe! Everything has its limits, even the age of twenty-nine. Dona Camila finally resolved to bid farewell to her esteemed hosts, and did so, saddened by fond remembrance. They still urged her to give them five or six months of reprieve, but the beautiful woman told them it was impossible and, mounting the sorrel horse of time, went to take up residence in the house of thirty.

She was, nevertheless, of that breed of women who laugh in the faces of sunrises and almanacs. Fresh-faced and unchanging, with milky-white skin, she left the task of aging to other women. She only took up the task of existing. Black hair and warm, chestnut brown eyes. Her shoulders and bosom seemed made specifically for the wearing of low-cut dresses, and her arms as well—which I won't say were the arms of the Venus de Milo, to avoid the cliché, but they were probably nothing less. Dona Camila knew this. She knew she was beautiful, not just because the sidelong glances of other women told her so, but because of a certain instinct that beauty possesses, as do talent and genius. It remains to be said that she was married, that her husband was a redhead, and that the two of them loved each other like newlyweds. And, finally, that she was faithful. But take note that she wasn't faithful by disposition alone, but on principle, out of love for her husband, and I think a little bit out of pride.

No faults, then, except for slowing down time. But is this a fault? In some page or another of the scriptures—I can't remember which, but it's one of the books of the prophets, naturally—a comparison is made between the days that pass and the waters of a river, which never return. Dona Camila wished to make a dam for her own personal use. Amid the tumult of this continual march from birth to death, she latched onto the illusion of stability. One could only ask of her that she not be ridiculous, and she wasn't.

You, dear reader, will tell me that beauty is justified in and of itself, and that her preoccupation with the calendar proves that this lady lived with her eyes principally focused on the opinions of others. It's true, but how else do you expect the women of our day and age to live?

Dona Camila entered the house of thirty and the transition wasn't painful. Evidently the widespread fear of that age was just a superstition. Two or three of her close friends, well trained in arithmetic, continued to say that she seemed to have lost count of the years. They didn't add that nature seemed to be her accomplice in this accounting error, and that at age forty (her actual age), Dona Camila had the looks of someone in her early thirties. They still had one last resort: spot her first gray hair, a tiny strand, if need be, but gray. They watched for it in vain; her damned hair just seemed to get blacker and blacker.

But they were mistaken. The gray hair was there, alright: it was Dona Camila's daughter, who was turning nineteen and was, even worse, pretty. Dona Camila kept her in children's dresses and enrolled in school for as long as she could, doing everything in her power to give her the appearance of a child. Nature, however, is not only immoral, but also illogical; while it reined in the passing years of one, it slackened the reins on the years of the other, and Ernestina, a young woman in full, looked radiant when she arrived at her first ball. She was a revelation. Dona Camila adored her daughter and savored her glory in slow draughts. At the bottom of the cup she encountered a few bitter drops and grimaced. She even thought about giving up entirely, but a flood of pre-formed phrases informed her that she looked like the girl's older sister, and the idea was abandoned. From that night forward, Dona Camila began to tell everyone that she married very young.

One day, a few months later, Ernestina's first boyfriend appeared on the horizon. Dona Camila had thought vaguely about this calamity without really facing it, without girding her loins for her defense. When she least expected it, she discovered a suitor at her doorstep. She questioned her daughter about it and sensed an indefinable enthusiasm in her, a certain disposition typical of twenty year olds, and she was devastated. Marrying off her daughter was the least of it. For if human beings are like the waters described in the scriptures, which never return, it is only because there are others who come after them, the same way that new waters flow after the waters before them. In order to define these successive waves of people, man invented the name "grandchildren." Dona Camila knew that the arrival of her first grandchild was imminent and was determined to delay it. It's obvious that she didn't consciously formulate this resolution, just as she hadn't consciously formulated her thoughts about the danger she was in. The soul understands itself implicitly; a feeling is worth as much as a rational argument. The feelings she had were swift, hazy, and occurred in the most intimate part of her being, from which she never retrieved them, so that she wouldn't be forced to analyze them.

"But what is it that you don't like about Ribeiro?" her husband asked her one night, as he stared out the window.

Dona Camila shrugged her shoulders.

"His nose is crooked," she said.

"That's mean! You're on edge, let's talk about something else," replied her husband. And after looking out onto the street for a couple of minutes, humming to himself, he again brought up the subject of Ribeiro, whom he thought to be an acceptable son-in-law. If Ribeiro asked for permission to marry Ernestina, her husband thought they should grant it. He was intelligent and polite. He was also the likely heir to an aunt who lived in Cantagalo. And, furthermore, he had a heart of gold. People said really lovely things about him. When he was at college, for example . . . Dona Camila listened to the rest of it, tapping her foot on the ground and drumming a sonata of impatience with her fingers. But when her husband said that Ribeiro was expecting a position in the Foreign Service, somewhere in the United States, she couldn't contain herself and cut him off:

"What? And take my daughter away from me? No, sir."

Determining the respective amounts of maternal love and personal consideration involved in this rebuke is a difficult question to resolve, especially now, so far removed from the events and people involved. Let's suppose they were present in equal parts. The truth is that the husband didn't know what to say to defend the Foreign Service, diplomatic necessities, and the inevitability of the marriage. And since he couldn't find the words to say, he went to sleep. Two days later, Ribeiro's appointment came down. On the third day, Ernestina told him not to ask her father's permission, because she didn't want to be separated from her family. It was the same as saying: I prefer my family to you. It's true that her voice was tremulous and faint, marked by a profound air of despair. But Ribeiro only took note of the rejection, and departed. Thus ended the first adventure.

Her daughter's grief weighed on her, but Dona Camila quickly found a way to console herself. There's no lack of potential fiancés, she reflected. To console her daughter, she took her out on long walks all around the city. They were both beautiful, and Ernestina possessed the freshness of youth; but the mother's beauty was perfect and, despite her age, surpassed the beauty of her daughter. Let's not go so far as to believe that this feeling of superiority was what encouraged Dona Camila to prolong and repeat these walks. No, her maternal love, all by itself, explains everything. But let's concede that it encouraged her a little bit. What's wrong with that? Is there anything wrong with a courageous colonel nobly defending his fatherland, while wearing insignia and epaulettes all the while? It doesn't render the love of country or motherly love meaningless.

Months later, signs of a second boyfriend began to appear. This time it was a widow, a lawyer, twenty-seven years old. Ernestina didn't have the same feelings for him that Ribeiro had inspired in her; she merely accepted him. Dona Camila quickly sniffed out this new candidate. She couldn't find anything wrong with him, his nose was as undeviating as his conscience, as was his profound aversion to diplomatic life. But there must be other defects, there had to be. Dona Camila made a spirited search for them, prying into his family life, his habits, his past. She managed to find a few tiny things, a mere sliver of human imperfection: occasional mood swings, the absence of intellectual charms, and, finally, a major excess of self-regard. This last detail is what allowed the beautiful lady to ensnare him. She slowly began to construct the wall of silence. First, she put down a layer of pauses, of medium length. Then came short statements, and then monosyllabic responses, distractions, absorption in other things, complacent glares, resigned attention, feigned yawns behind her fan. He didn't understand it right away, but when he realized that her boredom always coincided with the moments when her daughter left the room, he figured he was visiting too often, and retreated. If he was a man of war, he would have scaled this wall of silence, but he was prideful and weak. Dona Camila gave thanks to the gods.

There was a three-month period of respite. Then a few suitors appeared, all on the same night, sickly little pests who didn't even leave us a story. Dona Camila understood that their ranks were only going to multiply until a decisive one appeared and forced her to surrender. But at the very least, she told herself, she wanted a son-in-law who would provide her daughter with the same happiness that her husband gave to her. Once, either to strengthen this stated desire or for some unknown motive, she repeated this idea aloud, even though she was the only one around to hear it. Reader, you subtle psychologist, you can go on thinking that she said it aloud in order to convince herself of it. I prefer to relate what happened to her in eighteen sixty-something . . .

It took place in the morning. She was at the mirror and her window was open, the yard outside was green and filled with the sounds of cicadas and songbirds. She felt within her a sense of harmony that connected her to the outside world. Only intellectual graces are independent and superior; physical grace is a sister to the landscape. Dona Camila relished this secret, intimate sisterhood, this feeling of oneness, a recollection of a previous life together in the same divine womb. Not an unpleasant memory or incident disturbed this mysterious, expansive feeling. On the contrary, everything seemed to instill in her a feeling of eternity, and the forty-two years she carried with her seemed to weigh no more than forty-two rose petals. She looked outside, then back at the mirror. Suddenly, as if a snake had struck at her, she lurched back in terror. She had spotted, on her left temple, a small, gray hair. For a moment she thought it might be her husband's, but she quickly realized that it wasn't, it was hers alright, a telegram from old age, which was heading her way on a forced march. Her first feeling was one of defeat. Dona Camila felt that everything was faltering, everything, and thought she'd be gray-haired and elderly by the end of the week.

"Mommy, mommy," shrieked Ernestina, as she entered the room, "the box-seat tickets that daddy ordered have arrived."

Dona Camila started, out of shame, and instinctively turned to her daughter, presenting her the side that didn't have the gray hair. Never before had her daughter seemed so lovely and spry. She looked at her with longing. She also looked at her with envy, and to repress that bad feeling she grabbed the tickets; they were for that very night. One thought expels the other, and Dona Camila envisioned herself amid all the lights and people, and her spirits were immediately raised. Once she was alone again, she turned to the mirror, courageously yanked out the gray hair, and dropped it out the window. "Out damned spot! Out!" Our lady was more fortunate than that other one, Lady Macbeth, and watched her blemish disappear in the air; to her mind, old age was a disgrace, and ugliness was a crime. Out, damned spot! Out!

But if our disgraces return to haunt us, why wouldn't gray hairs do the same? A month later, Dona Camila discovered another one lurking in her thick, gorgeous black locks, and she amputated it mercilessly. Five or six weeks later, another one. This third one coincided with the appearance of a third candidate for her daughter's hand, and both of them encountered Dona Camila at a moment of weakness. Her beauty, which had taken the place of her youthfulness, seemed like it was on its way out as well, like one dove taking off in search of another. Days were flying by. Children she had seen in their mothers' arms or pushed around in strollers by their nursemaids were now dancing at balls. The males were now smoking; the females sang tunes at the piano. Some of these even showed off their own chubby little babies to her, another generation that suckled at their mothers' breasts, soon to dance at balls as well, singing or smoking, soon to show off other babies to other people, and so forth.

Dona Camila only quibbled a little, and ended up giving in. What choice did she have but to accept a son-in-law eventually? But since old habits don't die from one day to the next, Dona Camila saw that, parallel to that celebration of love, there was a stage, a grand stage for herself. She prepared for it spiritedly, and the outcome matched her efforts. At church, in the midst of the other women, or in her living room, seated on the sofa (the upholstery on this piece of furniture, as well as the wallpaper, was always dark, to accentuate Dona Camila's fair complexion), she dressed in the latest fashions, lacking the added refinement of extreme youth, but also lacking matronly severity, merely a happy medium destined to show off her autumnal charms in high relief, smiling, happy. In short, the new mother-in-law met with the highest approval. It was clear that a scrap of the royal purple still hung from her shoulders.

Purple implies dynasty. Dynasties require grandchildren. All that remained was for the Lord to bless this union, and bless it he did, the following year. Dona Camila had grown accustomed to the idea, but it was so painful to abdicate her throne that she awaited the arrival of her grandchild with both love and repugnance. Was this annoying embryo, so presumptuous and curious about life, really needed on earth? Obviously not. But it arrived one day nevertheless, along with the flowers of September. In the crisis of labor, Dona Camila only had to think about her daughter; after, her thoughts were turned to both her daughter and her grandchild. Only days later did she start to think about herself again. A grandmother, at last. There was no doubting it, she was a grandmother. Neither her physical features, which were still supple, nor her hair, which was still black (save for half a dozen discarded strands), could contradict reality by themselves. Reality existed, and she was, finally, a grandmother.

She wanted to withdraw from society and, in order to be closer to her grandchild, she'd ask her daughter to visit her. But her house wasn't a convent, and the streets and newspapers, with their constant rumblings, awoke in her echoes of a bygone era. Dona Camila ripped her proclamation of abdication to shreds and once again took her place in the tumult.

One day, I saw her walking beside a black servant, who was holding a five- or six-month-old child in her arms. Dona Camila was holding her wide-brimmed sun hat over the child to give it shade. I ran into her a week later with the same child, the same black servant, and the same sun hat. Twenty days later, and again thirty days later, I saw her getting on the trolley with the black servant and the child.

"Did you already feed him?" she asked the servant. "This sun! It's never going to set. Don't squeeze the baby too hard. Is he awake? Don't bother him. Cover his face. etc., etc."

He was her grandson. She, however, stayed so close to him and paid him such careful attention, and did this so frequently, without any other lady around, that she seemed more like a mother than a grandmother. And a lot of people thought she was the mother. I won't swear to it that this was Dona Camila's intention ("Swear not at all" Matthew 5:34). I'll limit myself to saying that no mother could be more attentive than Dona Camila was with her grandson. To assume that the child was hers was the easiest thing in the world.

TRIO IN A MINOR

I. Adagio Cantabile

Maria Regina accompanied her grandmother to her bedroom, bid her goodnight, then retired to her own room. The slave woman who waited on her, despite the familiarity that existed between them, couldn't get a word out of her and left, half an hour later, saying that Miss was in a very serious mood. As soon as she was alone, she sat at the foot of the bed, her legs outstretched and crossed at the ankles, thinking.

Truth dictates that I tell you that the young woman was thinking amorously about two men at the same time. One of them, Maciel, was twenty-seven; the other, Miranda, was fifty. I agree that it's repulsive, but I can't change the way things were, I can't deny that if the two men were enamored of her, she was no less enamored of both of them. In short, she's an odd one. Or to tell it the way her friends at school did: she was a birdbrain. No one will deny that she had an excellent heart and a pure spirit. It was her imagination that was the problem: sterile and greedy, and, above all else, insatiable, averse to reality, superimposing things of her own invention on top of the reality of life. As a result of this: incurable oddities.

The visit of these two men (who had been courting her for a short time) lasted about an hour. Maria Regina conversed light-heartedly with them and played a classical piece on the piano, a sonata, which made her grandmother nod off a little. Toward the end, they discussed music. Miranda made some insightful observations about modern music and ancient music; the grandmother professed the religion of Bellini and his *Norma*, and spoke of the melodies from her day, which were pleasant, heartfelt, and—principally—clear. Her granddaughter sided with the opinions of Miranda; Maciel politely agreed with everyone.

Now, at the foot of her bed, Maria Regina reconstructed all of this: the visit, the conversation, the music, the debate, the character of one and the other, the words of Miranda, and the beautiful eyes of Maciel. It was eleven o'clock, and the only light in the room came from a small night lamp; all around her welcomed dream and reverie. As she recomposed the evening, she saw the two men there beside her, heard them speak, and conversed with them for a short while, thirty or forty minutes, to the sound of the very same sonata she'd played earlier: la, la, la . . .

II. Allegro Ma Non Troppo

The next day, the grandmother and her granddaughter went to visit a friend in Tijuca. On the way back, their carriage struck a little boy who was running across the street. Someone saw what had happened, threw himself in front of the horses, and, at great risk of personal injury, managed to stop them and save the child, who was unconscious and only slightly hurt. Hordes of people, a great commotion, the child's mother running over, in tears. Maria Regina got out of the carriage and accompanied the wounded child back to his mother's house, which was close by.

Those who are familiar with destiny's techniques will immediately predict that the person who saved the little boy was one of the men from the other night. It was Maciel. Once first aid had been rendered, Maciel accompanied the young lady to the carriage, and accepted the grandmother's offer to take him into town. They were then in the Engenho Velho neighborhood. Once in the carriage, Maria Regina noticed that the young man's hand was bleeding. The grandmother asked over and over again if the little boy was gravely injured, if he would survive, and Maciel told her that his wounds were minor. Then he told the story of the accident. He was on the sidewalk, waiting for a tilbury to pass, when he saw the little boy run into the street, right in front of the horses. He perceived the danger the boy was in and attempted to save him from it, or at least lessen the severity of it.

"But you're hurt," said the old woman.

"It's nothing."

"No it's not, no it's not," said the young woman, offering her help. "We should have treated your wound as well."

"It's nothing, really," he insisted, "it's just a scratch. I can wipe this up with a handkerchief."

But he didn't have time to take out his handkerchief; Maria Regina had already offered him hers. Maciel, touched by the offer, took it from her, but was wary of staining it.

"Go ahead, go ahead," she said. And seeing that he was too timid, grabbed it from him and started to wipe the blood from his hand herself.

His hand was handsome, as handsome as its owner. But it seems that he was less worried about his wound than the wrinkled cuffs of his shirt. As he conversed with them, he snuck looks at his cuffs and tried to hide them. Maria Regina didn't notice a thing. She only saw him, and, above all, the action that he had just performed, which seemed to have bathed him in light. She understood that his generous nature had overcome his habitually reserved, elegant temperament, in order to save a child he didn't even know from certain death. They spoke of the incident until they arrived at the door to the women's house. Maciel refused the carriage they offered to take him home, but thanked them anyway and bid them farewell until that evening.

"Until this evening!" repeated Maria Regina.

She anxiously awaited his arrival. He got there around eight o'clock, with a black bandage wrapped around his hand, and begged their pardon for showing up in that state; he'd been told that it was best to dress the wound and had followed the advice.

"Yes, it's for the best!"

"I'm fine, it was nothing."

"Come here, come here," said the grandmother from the other side of the room. "Sit here beside me. You, sir, are a hero."

Maciel smiled as he heard this. The moment of impulsive generosity had passed, and now he was reaping the rewards of his sacrifice. The greatest of these was Maria Regina's admiration, which was so sincere and of such proportions, that everything else, her grandmother and the room itself, disappeared for him. Maciel had sat down beside the old woman, and Maria Regina had taken a seat in front of them both. While the grandmother, fully recovered from her earlier fright, recounted the commotion she suffered through—at first not knowing what had happened, then thinking that the child had died—the two others stared at one another, discreetly at first, then with abandon. Maria Regina asked herself where she would ever find a better suitor. The grandmother, who wasn't nearsighted, found their glances to be excessive and changed the subject, asking Maciel for the latest society gossip.

III. Allegro Appassionato

Maciel was a man who was, as he himself said in French, *trés répandu*, and he pulled from his pocket a large helping of interesting tidbits. The biggest of these was that the wedding of a certain widow had been called off.

"You don't say!" exclaimed the grandmother, "How is she?"

"It seems that she was the one who called it off. But I can say, with certainty, that she was at the ball the night before last, and danced and chatted vivaciously. Oh! Aside from that news, the thing that made the biggest impression on me was the necklace she wore, a magnificent . . ."

"The cross made out of diamonds?" asked the old woman. "I know that one, it's very beautiful."

"No, not that one."

Maciel knew of the cross necklace, which she had once worn to a get-together at the house of a certain Mascarenhas, but this wasn't it. This new one had only recently been purchased at Resende's shop, and it was a thing of beauty. He described it in detail, including the number, position, and cut of the jewels, and concluded by saying that it was the prized jewel of the evening.

"If she has such luxurious tastes, she should get married," the grandmother commented, maliciously.

"I agree that her fortune doesn't allow for such expenditures. Oh, wait! I'll stop by Resende's shop tomorrow, out of curiosity, and ask how much he sold it for. It wasn't cheap, there's no way it came cheap."

"But why did she call off the wedding?"

"I couldn't find out, but I'm going to dinner on Saturday at Venancinho Correia's house, and he'll tell me everything. Did you know that he's related to her? He's a good man, although he's completely at odds with the baron these days . . ."

The grandmother hadn't heard about their disagreement. Maciel recounted it from start to finish, with all the motives and aggravating circumstances. The final straw was something that was said during a card game, an allusion to one of Venancinho's shortcomings: he was left-handed. Someone told him what was said, and he completely cut ties with the baron. The best part was that the baron's fellow card-players were all accusing each other of revealing what the baron had said. Maciel declared that it was a personal rule of his never to repeat what was heard at the card table, since it's a place where people speak openly.

Then he gave a rundown of the Rua do Ouvidor the day before, between one and four in the afternoon. He knew the names of all the fabrics and the modern colors. He made mention of all the principal *toilettes* of the day. First was Mme. Pena Maia, a distinguished lady from Bahia who was *trés pschutt*. Then came Mlle. Pedrosa, the daughter of a high court judge in São Paulo, who looked *trés adorable*. He mentioned three others, then compared all five of them, weighed the facts, and drew a final conclusion. At times he forgot himself and started speaking French. Or it could be that he did it on purpose; he knew the language well, expressed himself with ease, and one day formulated this ethnological axiom: "There are Parisians everywhere." Then he launched into an explanation of a whist problem.

"You have five trump cards of the spadille and manille variety, and the king and queen of hearts . . ."

Maria Regina was quickly descending from admiration into boredom. She tried to hold onto something here or there, contemplating Maciel's youthful appearance, recalling his generous actions earlier that day, but she kept sliding down, and boredom soon consumed her. There was no stopping it. But then she resorted to a remarkable solution. She attempted to combine the two men, the present one and the absent one, looking at one, but listening to the other in her mind. It was a violent and dolorous solution, but it was so effective that she was able, for some time, to admire a perfect, unique being.

Then Miranda himself arrived, in the flesh. The two men greeted each other coldly; Maciel stuck around for about ten minutes, then left.

Miranda stayed on. He was tall and skinny, with an icy, severe countenance. He had a tired face, and his fifty years were on clear display in his gray hair, his wrinkles, his aged skin. His eyes alone possessed a quality that wasn't age-worn. They were small and hidden beneath the enormous arcade of his brow; but there in the back, when they weren't pensive, his eyes sparkled with youthfulness. The grandmother asked him as soon as Maciel left if he'd heard about the accident in Engenho Velho, and then related it to him, exaggerating greatly, but Miranda was neither astonished nor envious as he listened.

"Don't you find it sublime?" she asked, once the story ended.

"I think he may have saved the life of some soulless wretch who one day, without recognizing him, could very well stick a knife in his gut."

"Oh!" cried the grandmother, objecting.

"Or even if he does recognize him," he added.

"Don't be so bad," said Maria Regina, coming to his aid, "you most likely would have done the same thing, had you been there."

Miranda smiled sardonically. The smile accentuated the rigidity of his face. Egotistical and ill-natured, Miranda excelled in one area alone: intellectually, he was perfect. Maria Regina saw him as the marvelous and faithful translator of many ideas that writhed inside her, vaguely, lacking form and expression. He was inventive, shrewd, and even profound, and all without being pedantic, all without meandering off into dense jungles of subject matter, almost always staying, instead, on the level ground of ordinary conversation, so certain it is that things are only as valuable as the ideas they inspire in us. They also had the same taste for the arts; Miranda had studied law to obey his father, but his true vocation was music.

The grandmother, anticipating the sonata, readied her soul for a few winks of shut-eye. What's more, she was unable to let such a man into her heart; she found him tiresome and unlikeable. She just kept quiet after a few minutes of conversation. Then came the sonata, right in the middle of a conversation that Maria Regina found delightful, and the only reason she started playing was because he asked her to, saying that he really wanted to hear her.

"Grandma," she said, "you'll have to be patient now . . ."

Miranda went over to the piano. Standing right beside the lamplight, his head revealed all the weariness of his fifty years and the expression on his face was harsher than stone and bile. Maria Regina noticed the exaggerated features and played without looking at him. This was difficult though, since whenever he spoke, the words penetrated her soul and she would raise her eyes to him without thinking, only to encounter an atrocious old man. And then her thoughts turned to Maciel—in the flower of youth, with a countenance that was sincere, tender, and kind— and to his actions from earlier that day. The comparison was cruel to Miranda, just as the comparison of intellectual virtues was for Maciel. And the young woman resorted to the same recourse. She completed one with the other, listened to this one with her thoughts on that one. The music bolstered the fiction, which wavered at first, but was soon intense and well-wrought. Thus Titania, enamored of the weaver's song, admired his lovely features, unaware he had the head of an ass.

IV. Minuetto

Ten, twenty, thirty days passed after that night, then another twenty, and another thirty more. The chronology of all this is uncertain, so it's better to remain vague about it. The situation remained the same. The same individual deficiency of the two men, the same ideal harmonization of the two on her part, which resulted in a third man, perfect and unknown to her.

Maciel and Miranda distrusted each other and detested each other more and more, and suffered because of this, especially Miranda, since his was a passion of the eleventh hour. The young woman eventually got bored with them and watched them retreat little by little. Hope made them backslide a few times, but everything dies, even hope, and they eventually departed, never to return. Night after night passed . . . Maria Regina understood that it was all over.

The night that she finally convinced herself of this completely was one of the most beautiful that year, clear, cool, and bright. The moon wasn't visible, but our friend abhorred the moon. It's not really known why; either because it shines with borrowed light or because everybody else loves it, or for both of these reasons. It was one of her quirks. Here's another:

That morning, she had read in the newspaper that there are double stars that appear to us a single star. Instead of going to sleep that night, she sat next to the window, looking at the sky to see if she could find one of them. But her efforts were in vain. Since she couldn't find one in the sky, she searched for one inside herself, closing her eyes in order to imagine the phenomenon—a cheap and easy form of astronomy, but not without risks. The worst part of it is that it places the stars within reach, and so when a person opens her eyes and sees that the stars are still sparkling way up in the heavens, the feeling of depression is great and blasphemous thoughts are inevitable. Which is what happened here. Maria Regina saw this double-yet-singular star inside her. Each star was of great worth on its own, but together they formed one magnificent star. And this magnificent star was what she wanted. When she opened her eyes and saw that the heavens were as high as ever, she concluded that all of creation was but a flawed, error-ridden book, and lost hope.

She didn't fall asleep right away, because of the two opal roundels that were hanging on her wall. Realizing this was just another illusion, she closed her eyes and slept. She dreamed that she had died, and that her soul, floating in the air, was flying toward that beautiful double star. The star then separated into two, and she flew toward one of the two pieces. Not finding that original sensation there, she hurled herself toward the other, with the same result, then the same return trip back to the first. And there she was, going back and forth between the two separate stars. Then voices emerged from the abyss, saying words she didn't understand:

"This is your punishment, you soul in search of perfection. You are condemned to waver for all eternity between two incomplete stars, to the sound of the old sonata of the absolute: la, la, la . . ."

WEDDING SONG

Imagine, reader, that you are in 1813, in the Church of the Carmo, at one of those grand old celebrations that were the height of public recreation and the height of musical artistry. You know what a sung mass is; you can imagine what a sung mass of that remote era would have been. I won't call your attention to the priests or the sacristans, nor to the sermon, nor to the eyes of the young Carioca girls, which were already beautiful in this era, nor to the veils of the serious women, the trousers, the wigs, the decorative borders, the lights, the incense, none of it. I don't even speak of the orchestra, which is excellent. I'll limit myself to showing you one white head, the head of that old man who leads the orchestra with soul and devotion.

His name is Romão Pires. He is around seventy years old, no less, and he was born in Valongo, or around those parts. He is a good musician and a good man; all the musicians like him. Maestro Romão is his nickname, and for a person's nickname and stage name to be the same was common in such an environment at that time. "Maestro Romão is conducting the mass" was the equivalent of this other form of announcement years later: "The actor João Caetano enters the scene" or: "The actor Martinho will sing one of his best arias." It was just the right seasoning, the delicate and popular lure. Maestro Romão conducts the mass! Who didn't know Maestro Romão with his serious manner, eyes on the ground, sad laugh, and unhurried step? All of that disappeared in front of the orchestra. There, life poured out from the maestro's entire body and every gesture; his gaze was inflamed, his laugh was illuminated. He was another person. Not that the mass was his; this one, for example, that he is conducting now at the Carmo is by José Maurício; but he conducts it with the same love that he would employ if the mass were his.

The celebration ended; it was as if an intense brightness had ended, leaving the face illuminated solely by ordinary light. There he was coming down from the choir, helped along by a cane; he went to the sacristy to kiss the hands of the priests and accepted a seat at the dinner table. All of this indifferently and quietly. He ate, left, and walked toward the Rua da Mãe dos Homens, where he lived with an old black slave, Papa José, who cared for him like a mother, and who was at that moment conversing with a neighbor woman.

"Here comes Maestro Romão, Papa José," said the neighbor woman.

"Yep! Yep! Good-bye, ma'am, see you soon."

Papa José started a little, entered the house, and waited for the elderly gentleman, who a little later entered with his customary look. Naturally, the house was neither rich nor cheerful. It did not have even the slightest trace of a woman, old or young, nor birds that sing, nor flowers, nor lively or pleasant colors. A somber and bare house. The most cheerful thing was a harpsichord where the maestro would sometimes play, practicing. On a chair at the foot of it, some sheet music, none of it his own.

Ah! If Maestro Romão were able, he would be a great composer. It seems that there are two kinds of vocations: those that have a voice and those that do not. The former are fulfilled; the latter represent a constant and sterile struggle between the inner impulse and the absence of a mode of communication with mankind. Romão was of this kind. He had an intimate vocation for music; he had within him many operas and masses, a world of new and original harmonies that he could not manage to express and put onto paper. This was the sole cause of Maestro Romão's sadness. Naturally, people never knew what was wrong. Some said this, others that: sickness, lack of money, some old sorrow.

But, in truth, the cause of Maestro Romão's melancholy was not being able to compose, not possessing a way to translate what he felt. It isn't that he hadn't scribbled notes onto many sheets of paper or hadn't interrogated the harpsichord for hours; but everything came out of him shapelessly, without idea or harmony. In these latter days he was even shy of his neighbors, and no longer attempted anything.

And nonetheless, if he could, he would finish at least one certain piece, a wedding song, begun three days after he married in 1779. The woman, who was then twenty years old and died at twenty-three, was not very pretty, but extremely warm-hearted, and she loved him as much as he did her. Three days after they married, Maestro Romão felt inside him something akin to inspiration. Thus, he came up with the idea of the wedding song and wanted to compose it, but the inspiration could not find a way out. Like a bird that has just been confined and strives to escape the walls of the cage, flitting up and down, impatient and terrified, thus beat the inspiration of our musician, locked up inside him with no way out, unable to find a door, nothing. A few notes ended up coming together, he wrote them down, resulting in a single sheet of paper, nothing more. He kept on the following day, ten days later, twenty times during his marriage. When his wife died he reread those first conjugal notes and became even sadder for not being able to fix onto paper that feeling of happiness that was now extinct.

"Papa José," he said as he entered, "I'm feeling sick today."

"Did you eat something that made you feel bad, sir ..."

"No, I wasn't feeling well this morning either. Go to the drugstore ..."

The pharmacist sent him something, which he took that night; on the following day Maestro Romão did not feel any better. It is necessary to mention here that he had a bad heart: a serious and chronic illness. Papa José was terrified when he saw that the sickness did not yield to the medicine, nor to repose, and he wanted to call the doctor.

"For what?" said the maestro. "This will pass."

The day ended with the patient no worse, and he held up well during the night, unlike the black man, who was barely able to sleep two hours. The neighbors, as soon as they heard of the illness, needed no other reason for a chat; those that maintained relations with the maestro went to visit him. One jokingly added that it was just a ruse to avoid the whippings that the pharmacist gave him in their backgammon games, another held that he was in love. Maestro Romão smiled, but said to himself that this was the end.

"It is over," he thought.

One morning, five days after the celebration, the doctor found him really sick; he could see this in the doctor's face, behind his deceitful words:

"This is nothing; you need to stop thinking about music . . ."

About music! It was exactly this word from the doctor that gave the maestro an idea. As soon as he was alone with the slave he opened the drawer wherein he'd kept, since 1779, the wedding song he'd started. He reread those notes that had been wrenched out of him with such difficulty and never concluded. And then he had a remarkable idea: to finish up the piece now, be it what it may. Anything would work, as long as he left a piece of his soul on earth.

Who knows? In 1880, maybe they will play this, and say that a certain Maestro Romão . . .

The beginning of the song ended with a certain *la*; this *la*, which fit perfectly in its spot, was the last note he had written. Maestro Romão insisted that they move his harpsichord out to the room in the back of the house that looked onto the backyard: he needed air. Through his window he could see into the window of the back of a neighboring house, where he spied two newlyweds, eight days wed, locked in an embrace with their arms on each other's shoulders and hands locked together. Maestro Romão smiled with sadness.

"They are arriving," he said, "I am leaving. I will compose at least this one song that they can play . . ."

He sat down at the harpsichord, reproduced the notes, and arrived at the *la* . . .

"*La, la, la* . . ."

Nothing, it didn't go anywhere. And, notwithstanding, he knew music like nobody's business.

La, do . . . la, mi . . . la, si, do, re . . . re . . . re . . .

Impossible! No inspiration. He did not demand a profoundly original piece, but at least something, something that did not belong to someone else and that was linked to the idea that he had already started. He returned to the beginning, repeated the notes, and endeavored to recover those long extinct feelings, remembering his wife and those first days together. To complete the illusion he glanced at the window in which stood the newlyweds. They continued where they were, their hands locked and their arms on one another's shoulders; the difference was that now they were looking at each other, instead of looking down. Maestro Romão, breathless from the illness and impatience, turned to the harpsichord, but the sight of the couple did not provide him with inspiration, and the subsequent notes did not sound.

La . . . la . . . la . . .

Hopeless, he rose from the harpsichord, grabbed the paper, and ripped it. At this very moment, the young woman, absorbed in her husband's gaze, began to hum at random, unconsciously, something never before sung or known, in which a certain *la* was followed by a lovely musical phrase, the exact one that Maestro Romão had sought for years without ever finding. The maestro heard it with sadness, shook his head, and passed away that night.

A VISIT FROM ALCIBIADES

A letter from High Court Judge X to
the Chief of Police of Rio de Janeiro
Rio, 20 September 1875

Your Excellency, please excuse my shaky handwriting and twisted
style: you will understand them soon enough.

Today, in the afternoon, having already finished dinner, I
stretched out on the sofa and opened a volume of Plutarch while
I waited until it was time to go to the club. Your Excellency, who
was my classmate, surely remembers that ever since I was a boy
I suffered from a devotion to Greek; a devotion or mania—the
latter is the name Your Excellency gave it—so intense that it
made me fail all my other subjects. I opened the volume and there
transpired what always transpires when I read something ancient:
I transported myself back to the time and milieu of the action of
the piece. It's excellent after dinner. In no time at all one is on a
Roman road, at the foot of a Greek portico, or in a grammarian's
workshop. The modern era disappears: the insurrection of
Herzegovina,[2] the Carlist Wars,[3] Rua do Ouvidor,[4] the Chiarini
circus.[5] Fifteen or twenty minutes of ancient life, and all for free.
A true literary digestion.

2. Uprisings by Bosnia and Herzegovina against the Ottoman Empire in
1875 and 1876.

3. A series of wars in Spain between 1833 and 1876 that pit supporters of a
traditionalist pretender to the throne—Charles V—against the forces of liberal-
ism represented by the infant queen Isabella II.

4. Many publishing houses were located on this street in the nineteenth
century, a major commercial thoroughfare in downtown Rio de Janeiro.

5. One of the earliest traveling circuses. Founded by the Italian equestrian
Giuseppe Chiarini, the circus toured Brazil in 1874.

That is how it happened today. The book happened to open up at the life of Alcibiades. I let myself savor the Attic language; soon enough I was entering the Olympic games, admiring the most beautiful of Athenian men as he magnificently steered the chariot with the same steadfastness and grace with which he led battles, citizens, and his own intellectual faculties. Your Excellency, imagine how I came alive! But then the servant entered and lit the lamps, and nothing more was needed to make all the archaeology of my imagination fly away. Athens returned to history while my eyes came back down from the clouds; that is, my eyes came back down to my white cotton pants, an alpaca suit coat, and my cordovan shoes. I then reflected to myself:

"What impression would our modern dress make on the illustrious Athenian?"

I have been a Spiritualist for a few months. Convinced that all systems are pure nihilities, I resolved to adopt the most recreational of them all. There will come a time when this one is not merely recreational, but also useful for the solution of historical problems: it is more efficient to evoke the spirits of the dead than to waste our critical forces, and to waste them in a pure loss, since there is no document that explains the intention of an act better than the author of the act himself. And such was my case this night. To conjecture about Alcibiades's impressions was to waste time, without any benefit other than the pleasure of admiring my own ability. I therefore decided to evoke the Athenian; I asked him to appear in my house immediately, without delay.

And here begins the extraordinary part of the adventure. Alcibiades wasted no time in heeding my call; two minutes later he was there, in my room, close to the wall. But it was not the impalpable shadow that I believed I had evoked using the methods of our school: it was the actual Alcibiades, flesh and bone, the man himself, the authentic Greek, dressed as an ancient, full of that kindness and elegance with which he used to harangue the great assemblies of Athens, as well as harangue, to some extent, his foolish subordinates. Your Excellency, who is so knowledgeable about history, cannot overlook the fact that there were also fools in Athens. Yes, Athens also possessed them, and this precedent provides an excuse. I swear to Your Excellency that I was in disbelief; as faithful as the testimony of my senses was, I could not begin to believe that there, in my house, was—not just the shadow of Alcibiades—but Alcibiades himself, come back to life. I still harbored the hope that all of it was nothing more than an effect of indigestion, a simple over-release of gastric juices, transformed through the lens of Plutarch. So I rubbed my eyes, fixed them on him, and ...

"What do you want with me?" he asked.

My flesh shivered when I heard this. The figure spoke, and spoke Greek—of the purest Attic variety. It was he! There was no doubt that it was he, a dead man for twenty centuries, restored to life, as completely as if he had just now come from cutting that famous dog's tail. It was clear that, without even meaning to do it, I had just taken a great stride in the history of Spiritualism. But woe unto me! I didn't understand this at once, and I was completely astonished. He repeated the question, looked about, and seated himself in an armchair. I was cold and trembling (as I still am this very moment). He perceived this and spoke to me with much tenderness, laughing and making jokes in order to restore my calm and trust. As clever as before! What more can I tell Your Excellency? Within a few minutes we were conversing in ancient Greek, he lounging in his chair and totally at ease, while I was begging all the saints in heaven for the presence of a servant, of a visitor, of a patrolman, or, if it were necessary—a fire.

It goes without saying, Your Excellency, that I had let go of the idea of consulting him in regard to our modern dress; I had asked for a specter, not a "real man," as the children say. I limited myself to answering what he wanted; he asked for news from Athens, and I gave it to him. I told him that Athens was now, after all this time, the head of a unified Greece; I narrated the Muslim domination, the independence, Botzaris,[6] Lord Byron. The great man had his eyes glued to my mouth and, telling him that I was surprised that the dead hadn't told him anything, he explained to me that at the door to the other world they really let go of their interest in this one. He had seen neither Botzaris nor Lord Byron—in the first place, because the multitude of spirits is so very, staggeringly large that they naturally would become lost in it. In the second place, because there they group themselves not by nationality or any other established order, but by categories of temperament, custom, and profession: that is why he, Alcibiades, keeps company with a group of elegant politicians and bachelors, with the Duke of Buckingham, Garret,[7] our own Maciel Monteiro,[8] etc. After this he asked me for current news. I told him what I knew, in summary. I told him of the Hellenic parliament and the alternative method with which Bulgaris[9] and Koumoundouros[10]—statesmen and also his compatriots— imitate Disraeli and Gladstone, taking turns in power and thus, like them, taking turns at discursive attacks. He, the magnificent orator, interrupted me:

"Bravo, Athenians!"

If I am going into minute details it is in order to omit nothing which could give Your Excellency an exact knowledge of the extraordinary case that I am narrating. I have already said that

6. Markos Botsaris (1788–1823): martyr in the war of Greek Independence from the Turks.

7. Almeida Garret (1799–1854): Portuguese orator, writer, and dramatist.

8. Maciel Monteiro (1804–1868): Brazilian politician, orator, journalist, and diplomat.

9. Demetrius Bulgaris (1803–1878): Greek statesman, member of the senate, and member of various cabinets.

10. Alexandros Koumoundouros (1817–1883): Greek statesman and Prime Minister of Greece in various terms from 1865 to 1882.

Alcibiades listened to me with utmost attention; I shall add that he was clever and shrewd. He understood things without a great expenditure of words. He was also sarcastic, at least he seemed that way to me at one or two points in our conversation, but in general he showed himself to be simple, attentive, polite, sensible, and dignified. And dandified, Your Excellency will note, as dandified as while alive; he looked sideways at the mirror, as do our women and other women of this century, gazed at his lace-up ankle boots, straightened his cloak, and didn't move from certain sculptural postures.

"Go on, continue," he said to me, when I stopped giving him the news.

But I couldn't go on anymore. Having entered the realm of the inextricable, the marvelous, I believed everything was possible. I thought that there was no reason why, seeing as he had come to visit me in the temporal world, I shouldn't be taken with him to the eternal one. I was absorbed with this idea. For a man who had just digested his dinner and is waiting for the club to open, death is the ultimate irony.

If only I could escape . . . I jumped up: I told him that I was going to a ball.

"A ball? What type of thing is a ball?"

I explained it to him.

"Ah! To see them dance the pyrrhic!"

"No," I corrected him, "the pyrrhic is a thing of the past. Each century, my dear Alcibiades, changes dances just as it changes ideas. We no longer dance the same dances as the last century; the twentieth century will probably not dance the same ones as this century. The pyrrhic is gone, just like the men of Plutarch's *Lives* and the deities of Hesiod."

"Even the deities?"

I repeated that yes, paganism had ended, that the academies of the past century had taken them in, but without conviction, without soul, and that even the Arcadian drunkenness—"Evoë, father Bacchus! Evoë! etc."—the honest pastime of a few peaceful high court judges, even this was cured, radically cured. From time to time, I added, one poet or another or one prose writer or another alludes to the remains of the pagan theology, but only does so for pomp or decoration; even science has reduced all of Olympus to symbolism. Dead, everything was dead.

"Zeus, dead?"

"Dead."

"Dionysius, Aphrodite?"

"All dead."

Plutarch's man stood up and paced about, containing his indignation, as if he were speaking to himself and imitating his interlocutor:

"Ah! Well, as long as I'm there along with my fellow Athenians!"

"Zeus, Dionysius, Aphrodite . . ." he murmured every so often.

I then remembered that he was once accused of profanation of the gods, and I asked myself where all of this posthumous and, naturally, artificial indignation came from. I had forgotten—me, a devoted student of Greek!—forgotten that he was also a refined hypocrite, an illustrious dissembler. And I almost didn't have time to make this observation, because Alcibiades, unexpectedly checking his speech, declared that he would go to the ball with me.

"To the ball?" I repeated, stupefied.

"To the ball. We shall go to the ball."

I became terrified, and told him no, that it wasn't possible, that they wouldn't admit him in those clothes. He would look crazy—unless, of course, he wanted to go there to present some comedy of Aristophanes, I added laughingly, in order to mask my fear. What I wanted to do was leave him at the house, and once

I was out in the street I wouldn't go to the club at all, but to see Your Excellency. But that devil of a man would not budge: he kept on listening to me with his eyes on the ground, pensive and deliberate. I shut up and began to think that this nightmare was about to end, that this figure was going to disappear, and I would be left there with my pants, my shoes, and my century.

"I want to go to the ball," he repeated. "Seeing as I'm already here I will not go back without first comparing the dances."

"My dear Alcibiades, I don't think that such a desire is very prudent. Certainly, I would take the greatest honor, the greatest pride in introducing at the club the most noble, the most charming of all Athenians. But the other men nowadays, the young lads, the young women, the elderly . . . it's impossible."

"Why?"

"Like I've said already, they will think you are a madman or a comedian, because this outfit is . . ."

"What's the matter with it? I can change clothes. I will dress after the manner of this century. Don't you have some clothes you can lend me?"

I was going to tell him no, but it soon occurred to me that it was most urgent that we leave the house, for once in the street there would be plenty of opportunities for me to escape him, so I told him yes.

"Well then," he replied as he got up, "I shall dress after the manner of this century. I only ask that you dress yourself first, so that I can learn how and imitate you afterwards."

I rose as well and asked him to accompany me. But he didn't move immediately: he was astonished.

I perceived that only now had he taken notice of my white trousers; he looked at them with mouth and eyes wide open. At last he asked me the reason why I wore those two cloth tubes. I responded that it was for comfort and added that our century, more modest and practical than artistic, had determined to dress

in a manner that was compatible with its decorum and solemnity.
Furthermore, not everyone is an Alcibiades. I believe that I
flattered him with this; he smiled and shrugged his shoulders.

"Well, then!"

We continued to my dressing room and I began to change
clothes, hurriedly. Alcibiades seated himself lazily on the divan,
but not without praising it, and not without praising the mirror,
the straw chair bottoms, the paintings . . . I dressed myself, as I
said, hurriedly, anxious to get out into the street, to hop into the
first coach that passed by . . .

"Black tubes!" he exclaimed.

I had just put on my black trousers. He cried out and let out a
laugh that mixed surprise with scorn, which greatly offended my
modern sensitivities. Because you will note, Your Excellency, that
even though our age appears to be worthy of criticism, and even
of execration, we do not like it when an ancient comes and makes
fun of it to our faces. I didn't respond to the Athenian; I scowled
and continued to button my suspenders. He then asked me why
I used such an ugly color . . .

"Ugly, but serious," I told him. "Look, however, at the beauty
of the cut, look how it falls over the shoe, which, even though it
is black, is polished, and wrought to perfection."

And seeing that he shook his head, I said to him:

"My dear, you can certainly insist that your Olympic Jupiter
is the eternal emblem of majesty: he is the height of ideal,
disinterested art, superior to the ages that pass by and the men
that accompany them. But the art of dress is another thing.
What appears to be absurd or inelegant is perfectly rational and
beautiful—beautiful in our manner, for we do not walk through
the streets to hear the rhapsodists reciting their verses, nor the
orators their speeches, nor the philosophers their philosophies.
Even you, if you become accustomed to seeing us, will end up
liking us, because . . ."

"You scoundrel!" he cried, throwing himself at me.

Before I understood the reason for the scream and the gesture, I was scared stiff. But this was merely a misunderstanding. I had pulled the necktie around my neck and was beginning to tie it, and Alcibiades supposed that I was going to strangle myself with it, as he explained to me later. And to tell the truth, he was pallid, tremulous, and breaking out in a cold sweat. Now it was my turn to laugh. I laughed and explained to him the use of the necktie, and even noted that it was white, not black, even though we also use black ties. Only after everything was sufficiently explained did he consent to return the necktie to me. At last I tied it, then put on my vest.

"In the name of Aphrodite!" he exclaimed. "This is the most remarkable thing that I have ever seen, alive or dead. You are dressed entirely in the color of night—a night with only three stars," he continued, pointing to the buttons on my chest. "The world must be going about in immense melancholy if it chooses to use a color so dead and so sad. We were more cheerful, we *lived* . . ."

He couldn't finish his sentence. I had just put on my dress coat and the consternation of the Athenian was indescribable. His shoulders fell, he had trouble breathing and couldn't articulate anything, and his eyes, large and open wide, were fixed on me. To be sure, Your Excellency, I was afraid, and I rushed even more to get out of the house.

"Are you finished?" he asked me.

"No, there's still the hat."

"Oh! There's still something that can make up for all the rest!" replied Alcibiades, with a supplicating voice. "Come on, come on. So, all of the elegance we bequeathed to you is reduced to a pair of closed tubes and another pair of open tubes (this he said holding up my coattails), and all in this tiresome and negative color? No, no I cannot believe it! Here comes something that will make up for it. What is left to put on, did you say?"

"The hat."

"Put on what is left, my dear man, put on what is left."

I obeyed. I went from there to the hangar, took down the hat, and put it on my head. Alcibiades looked at me, staggered, and fell. I ran to the illustrious Athenian to help him up, but (it pains me to say it) it was too late: he was dead, dead for the second time. I implore Your Excellency to be so kind as to expedite your orders for the corpse to be transported to the morgue and to proceed with the *corpus delecti*. I also hereby make it known that it is only because of the profound shock that I have just experienced that I do not proceed to your house in person this very minute (ten o'clock at night), which at any rate I shall do tomorrow morning, before eight.

On the Ark: Three (Undiscovered) Chapters from Genesis

Chapter A

1. And Noah spoke unto his sons Japeth, Shem, and Ham: "We shall take leave of the ark, according to the will of the Lord; we, and our women, and all of the animals. The ark shall come to rest on the summit of a mountain; we shall descend to it.

2. "Because the Lord has fulfilled his promise, when he said: I have resolved to bring an end to all flesh; evil dominates the earth, I will cause all men to perish. Make thou an ark of wood; enter into it: thou, thy wife, and thy sons.

3. "And the wives of thy sons, and two of every animal.

4. "Now, thus was fulfilled the promise of the Lord, and all men have perished, and the floodgates of heaven have been shut; we shall go and descend onto the land, and live in the bosom of peace and harmony."

5. Thus spoke Noah, and the sons of Noah were overjoyed to hear the words of their father; and Noah left them to themselves, retiring to one of the cabins of the ark.

6. Then Japeth raised his voice and said: "What a pleasurable life we shall have. The fig tree shall give forth fruit; the lamb, wool; the cow, milk; the sun, clarity; and at night we shall have shelter.

7. "For we shall be alone on the earth, and all the land shall be ours, and no one will disturb the peace of a family that was saved from the castigation that fell upon all men.

8. "Forever and ever." And Shem, upon hearing his brother

speak, said: "I have an idea." To which Japeth and Ham responded: "Let us hear your idea, Shem."

9. And Shem spoke that which was in his heart, saying: "My father has his family; each of us has his own family; the land is abundant; we can live in separate tents. Each of us shall do what he deems best, and shall plant, hunt, cut timber, or weave wool."

10. And Japeth responded: "I find Shem's idea to be well thought; we can live in separate tents. The ark shall descend at the side of a river; my father and Ham shall descend to the side from whence the river flows; Shem and I to the side toward which it flows. Shem shall occupy two hundred acres of land, and I another two hundred."

11. But Shem said: "I find two hundred acres to be very little." Japeth rebutted: "Then let it be five hundred to each. Between my land and thine shall be a river that divides them in the middle, and thus the property shall not be confused. I shall remain on the left bank and you on the right.

12. "And my land will be called the land of Japeth, and yours, the land of Shem; and we shall visit one another's tents, and we shall share the bread of joy and harmony."

13. And Shem, having approved the division, asked of Japeth: "And the river? To whom shall belong the waters of the river and the current?

14. "Because we possess the banks, and have not established anything with regard to the river." And Japeth responded that they could fish from one side as well as the other; but his brother disagreed, and proposed to divide the river into two parts, by embedding a rod in the middle. Japeth, however, said that the current would sweep away the rod.

15. And, as Japeth had responded in this manner, his brother retorted: "Thus, if the rod does not serve you well, I shall possess the river, and the two banks; and so that there is no conflict, thou canst raise a wall ten or twelve cubits away from the bank on the side that was thine.

16. "And if in this thou losest anything the difference is not too great, and neither shall it mean that this matter is not settled, so that the peace between us is never disturbed, according to the will of the Lord."

17. Japeth, however, replied: "Go fool someone else! What right dost thou have to take away the bank, which is mine, and rob me of a piece of land? Art thou better than I,

18. "Or fairer, or more beloved of my father? What right hast thou to scandalously violate the property of another in this manner?

19. "Thus, I now say unto thee that the river shall remain on my side, with both of the banks, and that if you dare to enter into my land, I shall slay thee as Cain slew his brother."

20. Hearing this, Ham was much frightened, and began to calm his two brethren,

21. Who had eyes the size of figs and the color of flaming coals, and stared at one another full of rage and disdain.

22. The ark, however, continued to float upon the waters of the abyss.

Chapter B

1. Now Japeth, having contained his rage, began to foam at the mouth, and Ham spoke kind words unto him,

2. Saying: "Let us find a way to reconcile everything; I shall call for your wife and the wife of Shem."

3. Both one and the other, however, refused, saying that the case was a matter of rights, not a matter of persuasion.

4. And Shem proposed to Japeth that he would compensate for the ten cubits lost, measuring out others from the far end of his lands. But Japeth responded:

5. "Why not just as soon send me to the ends of the earth? Thou art not content with five hundred acres; thou wantest five hundred and ten, and that I should have four hundred and ninety.

6. "Dost thou lack all moral feeling? Dost thou not know what justice is? Dost thou not see that thou plunderest me impudently? Dost thou not perceive that I shall know to defend what is mine, even unto risking my life?

7. "And that if it becomes necessary for blood to be spilt, then surely blood will be spilt,

8. "To chastise your haughtiness, and cleanse your iniquity?"

9. Then Shem advanced toward Japeth; but Ham put himself between them, placing a hand on the chest of each one;

10. Meanwhile the wolf and the lamb, which during the days of the flood had lived in the sweetest serenity, heard the clamor of the voices and caught sight of the fight of the two brothers, and began to keep guard against one another.

11. And Ham said: "Now behold, I have a wonderful idea, one that will accommodate all;

12. "An idea inspired in me by love, which I have for all my brethren. I will sacrifice, therefore, the land appropriated to me by the side of my father, and I will remain with the river and the two banks, each of you giving me twenty acres."

13. And Shem and Japeth laughed with scorn and sarcasm, saying: "Go plant dates! Save your idea for the days of

your old age." And they pulled at the ears and nose of Ham; and Japeth, putting two fingers in his own mouth, imitated the hiss of the serpent, with an air of mockery.

14. Now Ham, ashamed and irritated, wrung his hands saying: "Let it be!" And he went from there to meet with his father and the wives of his two brethren.

15. Japeth, however, said to Shem: "Now we are alone, let us decide this grave case, be it by tongue or by fist. Either you cede to me the two banks, or I break one of your ribs."

16. Upon saying this, Japeth threatened Shem with closed fists, while Shem, bracing himself, said with an angry voice: "I cede nothing unto thee, thief!"

17. To which Japeth, irate, responded: "Thou art the thief!"

18. This said, they advanced one toward the other and grappled with each other. Japeth had a firm and skillful arm; Shem was strong in his resistance. Then Japeth, grabbing Shem around the waist, squeezed him mightily, shouting: "Whose river is it?"

19. And Shem responded: "It's mine!" Japeth made a move in order to fell him; but Shem, who was strong, shook his body and threw his brother far. Japeth, however, foaming with anger, turned to grab his brother, and the two fought hand to hand,

20. Sweating and puffing like bulls.

21. In the course of the fight they fell and rolled, punching each other; blood flowed from noses, lips, and cheeks. Now Japeth was winning.

22. Now Shem was winning; because their anger enraged them equally, and they fought with hands, feet, teeth, and fingernails; and the ark trembled as if the floodgates of heaven had been opened once again.

23. Then the voices and shouts reached the ears of Noah, at the same moment that his son Ham appeared to him,

clamoring: "My father, my father, if for Cain vengeance will be taken seven times, and for Lamech seventy times seven, what will it be for Japeth and Shem?"

24. When Noah asked what this meant, Ham spoke of the strife of the two brethren, and the anger that excited them, and said: "Let us run to calm them." Noah said: "Let us go."

25. The ark, however, continued to float upon the waters of the abyss.

Chapter C

1. Behold, Noah arrived at the spot whereupon fought his two sons,

2. And found them still clasped to one another, and Shem below the knee of Japeth who, with a closed fist, was hitting him in the face, which was purple and bloody.

3. However, Shem, lifting his hands, was able to grab the neck of his brother, who began to scream: "Let go of me! Let go of me!"

4. Hearing the screams, the wives of Japeth and Shem came to the scene of the fight and, seeing them in such a state, began to sob and say: "What will become of us? A curse has fallen upon us and our husbands."

5. Noah, however, said unto them: "Quiet yourselves, wives of my sons, I shall see what this concerns, and shall ordain that which is just." And, going toward the two combatants,

6. He shouted: "Stop the fight. I, Noah, your father, order and command it." Upon hearing their father, the two brethren suddenly gained control of themselves, and remained a long time frozen and mute, neither one of them standing.

7. Noah continued: "Rise up, o men unworthy of salvation, deservers of the castigation that fell upon all other men."

8. Japeth and Shem stood up. Both had cuts on their faces, necks, and hands, and clothes sprinkled with blood, for they had fought with fingernails and teeth, enraged by mortal hatred.

9. The ground was soaked with blood as well, as were the sandals of both, and the hair of both,

10. As if sin wished to mark them with the seal of iniquity.

11. The two wives, however, came to them, crying and caressing them, and one could see that their hearts were wounded. Shem and Japeth answered nothing, and were standing with their eyes lowered to the ground, afraid to face their father,

12. Who said: "Behold, I wish to know the cause of this fight."

13. This word ignited the hatred in the hearts of both. Japeth, however, was the first to speak and said:

14. "Shem invaded my land, the land upon which I had chosen to raise my tent, once the waters have disappeared and the ark has descended, according to the will of the Lord;

15. "And I, who do not tolerate plundering, said to my brother: 'Thou art not content with five hundred acres, and thou wantest ten more?' and he responded to me 'I want ten more and the two banks of the river that shall divide my land from your land.'"

16. Noah, upon hearing his son, had his eyes on Shem; and when Japeth finished, he asked the brother: "How do you respond?"

17. And Shem said: "Japeth lies, because I only took from him the ten acres of land after he refused to divide the river into two parts; upon proposing to him that I should

be left with the two banks, I even consented that he should measure off another ten acres at the far end of his lands,

18. "To compensate for what he had lost; but the iniquity of Cain was awoken in him, and he wounded my head, face, and hands."

19. And Japeth interrupted him, saying: "By chance didst thou not wound me as well? Am I not bloody, as thou art? Look at my face and neck, look at my cheeks, which thou hast ripped with thy tiger claws."

20. Noah, starting as if to speak, noticed that his two sons again appeared to challenge each other with their eyes. So he said: "Hear me!" But the two brothers, blind with rage, again commenced to argue, yelling: "Whose river is it?"—"The river is mine."

21. And only after much struggle could Noah, Ham, and the wives of Shem and Japeth contain the two combatants, whose blood began to gush in great abundance.

22. Noah, however, raising his voice, yelled: "Cursed be him who doth not obey me. He shall be cursed not seven times, not seventy times, but seven hundred times seventy.

23. "Behold, thus I say unto you, that before the ark descends, I do not want any discussion with regard to the place upon which you will pitch your tents."

24. After this he became pensive.

25. And raising his eyes to the heavens, for the small door of the ceiling was raised, he shouted with sadness:

26. "They do not yet possess the land and already they are fighting over the borders. What will happen when Turkey and Russia come into being?"

27. And none of the sons of Noah could understand these words of their father.

28. The ark, however, continued to float upon the waters of the abyss.

APPENDIX A

Note on Contemporary Brazilian Literature: Instinct of Nationality

He who examines contemporary Brazilian literature soon recognizes in it, as a fundamental trait, a certain instinct of nationality. Poetry, novel, all forms of literary thought seek to clothe themselves in the colors of the country, and it cannot be denied that such a preoccupation is a symptom of vitality and a promise for the future. The traditions of Gonçalves Dias, Porto Alegre, and Magalhães are thus continued by the present generation and the coming generation, just as they continued the traditions of José Basílio da Gama and Santa Rita Durão. The advantage of this universal agreement goes without saying. Interrogating Brazilian life and American nature, prose writers and poets will find a plentiful spring of inspiration and will go forth giving a unique expression to national thought. This other independence does not have a September 7th, nor an Ipiranga field; it will not be achieved in one day, but slowly, so as to be more lasting; it will not be the work of just one generation or two; many will work for it until it is totally perfected.

This instinct can be felt even in the manifestations of critical opinion, although still poorly formed, restricted in the extreme, hardly helpful, and even less impassioned in these matters of poetry and literature. In this opinion there is an instinct that principally tends to applaud the works that have national touches. Above all the literary youth takes pride in this point. Not all of them will have meditated on the poems of *Uruguai* and *Caramuru* with the attention that such works deserve, but the names Basílio da Gama and Durão are cited and loved as the precursors of Brazilian poetry. The reason for this is that they looked around themselves in search of a new poetry, and gave forth the first traits of our literary physiognomy, while others, Gonzaga for example, who, breathing nonetheless the air of the *patria*, never find out how to break free from the hold of Arcadia nor from the precepts of the era. One admires their talent but cannot forgive them their banners and their shepherdess; in this there is more error than achievement.

Even if the limits of this essay permitted me to do so, I would not take it upon myself to defend the bad taste of the Arcadian poets nor the fatal damage that this school produced in Brazilian and Portuguese literature. However, the criticism of our colonial poets, who were lured into that evil, does not seem just; nor equally just the criticism that they didn't strive for literary independence, when political independence still lay in the womb of the future and, more than anything, when, from the metropolis to the colony, the homogeneity of traditions, customs, and education was created. Even the works of Basílio da Gama and Durão sought to display a certain local color rather than strive to make Brazilian literature independent, which it has yet to achieve, and which it can only now begin to bring forth.

Upon recognizing the instinct of nationality that is manifested in the works of these recent times, it would be prudent to examine whether or not we possess all the historical conditions and motives of a literary nationality; this investigation (a point of divergence among the lettered), aside from being beyond my power, would result in something beyond the limits of this essay. My principal object is to attest to the current facts. This fact is the instinct of which I have spoken: the general desire to create a more independent literature.

The apparition of Gonçalves Dias called the attention of the Brazilian muses to Indian history and customs. *Os Timbiras*,

I-Juca-Pirama, Tabira, and the other poems of the distinguished poet excited imaginations; the life of the tribes, long since overpowered by civilization, was studied in the memoirs that the chroniclers left us, which were, in turn, examined by the poets, who each took something from them, an idyll from this one, an epic canto from that one.

Afterwards, there was a species of reaction. There began to prevail the opinion that the entirety of poetry was not to be found in the semi-barbarous customs that preceded our civilization—which was true—as well as the idea that poetry had nothing to do with the existence of that extinct race, so different from the triumphant one—which seems erroneous.

It is certain that Brazilian civilization is not linked to the Indian element, nor received from it any influx; and this is sufficient for us not to go searching among the defeated tribes for the titles of our literary personality. But if this is true, it is no less true that everything is subject matter for poetry, as long as it carries the conditions of the beautiful or the elements of which the beautiful is composed. Those who, like Mr. Varnhagem, deny everything from the first peoples of this country, can logically exclude them from contemporary poetry. It seems to me, however, that after the memoirs that Mr. Magalhães and Mr. Gonçalves Dias wrote on this subject, it would not be fair to exclude the Indian element from our intellectual efforts. It would be an error for it to constitute an exclusive patrimony of Brazilian literature, and its absolute exclusion would certainly be an equal error. The indigenous tribes—whose practices and customs João Francisco Lisboa compared with the book of Tacitus and found so similar to those of the ancient Germanics—have disappeared, to be sure, from the region that was theirs for so long; but the dominant race which had contact with them collected precious information and transmitted it to us as true poetic elements. Piety, putting aside other arguments of greater value, should at least incline the imagination of the poets toward those peoples who first drank in the air of these regions, including in literature those peoples who were excluded by the fatality of history.

This is the current reigning opinion. The literary imagination of our time has searched for scenes of singular effect in either unadulterated Indian customs, as we see in Gonçalves Dias's *Os Timbiras*, or the struggle between the barbarous element and the civilized, among which I will note, for example, *Iracema* by Mr. José de Alencar, one of the early works of this prolific and brilliant writer.

If we understand that the entire patrimony of Brazilian literature is not to be found in Indian life, but that this is only one legacy, as Brazilian as it is universal, our writers will not limit themselves to this one fountain of inspiration. The civilized customs, either from colonial times or today, equally provide fine and extensive material for study. No less than these, American nature, whose magnificence and splendor challenge poets and prose writers, invites study. The novel, above all, took advantage of all these elements of invention, to which we owe, among others, the books of Mr. Bernardo Guimarães—who brilliantly and ingeniously paints for us the customs of the region in which he was born—Mr. José de Alencar, Mr. Macedo, Mr. Sílvio Dinarte (Escragnolle Taunay), Mr. Franklin Távora, and a few others.

I should add that there is an opinion that is sometimes manifested on this point, which I hold to be erroneous: that which only recognizes national spirit in the works that deal with local subject matter; a doctrine that, to be exact, would extremely limit the resources of our literature. Gonçalves Dias, for example, would be admitted to the national pantheon with poems of his own. Yet, except for *Os Timbiras*, the other American poems, and a certain number of compositions, his verses belong, according to their subject matter, to all of humanity, of whose aspirations, enthusiasm, frankness, and pains he generally sings. Furthermore,

I exclude from this the beautiful *Sextilhas de Frei Antão*, for these belong exclusively to Portuguese literature, not only because of the subject matter that the poet extracted from the Lusitanian historians, but also because of the style, which he cleverly antiquated. The same goes for his dramas, none of which are set in Brazil. I could go on and on if I had to cite more domestic examples, and I would never finish if it were necessary to turn to foreign examples. But, since this will be published in America and England, I would simply ask if the author of *The Song of Hiawatha* is not the same author of *The Golden Legend*, which has nothing to do with the land which witnessed its birth, and whose admirable singer it is; and I would further ask if *Hamlet, Othello, Julius Caesar,* or *Romeo and Juliet* have anything to do with English history or the British territories, and if Shakespeare is not, nonetheless, an essentially English poet.

There is no doubt that a literature, especially a nascent literature, should nurture itself principally with the subject matter that its region offers to it; but we must not establish doctrines so absolute that they impoverish it. What should be demanded from an author, before anything else, is a certain intimate feeling that transforms him into a man of his time and his country, even when dealing with subject matter remote in time and space. Some time ago a notable critic from France, astutely analyzing a Scottish author named Masson, said, along these same lines, that one could be a Breton without always speaking of the furze flower; similarly Masson was very Scottish without uttering a word about the thistle. He went on to explain what he meant by this, adding that there was a certain interior Scottishism in him, different and better than if it were merely superficial.

It would be necessary for criticism to establish these and other points, if we had a criticism that was didactic, ample, and elevated, correspondent to what it is in other countries. We do not have it. There are and have been writings which deserve such a name, but they are rare, and only appear every once in a while, without the profound everyday influence that they should exercise. The lack of such criticism is one of the greatest evils from which our literature suffers; analysis must correct or enliven invention, the points of doctrine or history must be investigated, the beautiful must be studied, flaws must be pointed out, and taste must be perfected and educated, so it develops and strides toward the great destinies that await it.

APPENDIX B

Bibliography

"The Psychiatrist" ("O Alienista") was first published serially in the journal *A Estação: Jornal ilustrada para a família* (Rio de Janeiro), beginning with 15 October 1881 issue and ending with 15 March 1882 issue. It was also included in a volume of short fiction entitled *Papéis Avulsos*, published in Rio de Janeiro in November 1882.

"The Immortal" ("O Imortal") was first published serially in the journal *A Estação: Jornal ilustrada para a família* (Rio de Janeiro), beginning with 15 July 1882 issue and ending with 15 September 1882 issue. It was not published in a volume of short fiction in Machado's lifetime, but was eventually included in a two-volume collection of previously uncollected writings entitled *Relíquias de Casa Velha*, published in 1937 in Rio de Janeiro. It is interesting to note that an early, shorter version of this story was published a decade before, under the title "Rui de Leão," the name of one of the main characters in both stories. "Rui de Leão" was published serially in the journal *Jornal das Famílias* (Rio de Janeiro), beginning with the January 1872 issue and ending with the March 1872 issue, under the pseudonym "Max."

"The Dictionary" ("O Dicionário") was first published in the journal *Gazeta de Notícias* (Rio de Janeiro) in the March 1885 issue, under the title "Os Dicionários" ("The Dictionaries"). It was also included, under the title given here, in a volume of short fiction entitled *Páginas Recolhidas*, published in Rio de Janeiro in 1899.

"The Academies of Siam" ("Las Academias de Siam") was first published in the journal *Gazeta de Notícias* (Rio de Janeiro) in June, 1884. It was also included in a volume of short fiction entitled *Histórias Sem Data*, published in Rio de Janeiro in 1884.

"The Priest, or The Metaphysics of Style" ("O Cônego ou Metafísico do Estilo") was first published in the journal *Gazeta de Notícias* (Rio de Janeiro) in November, 1885. It was also included in a volume of short fiction entitled *Várias Histórias*, published in Rio de Janeiro in 1896.

"To Live!" ("Viver!") was first published in the third literary supplement of the *Gazeta de Notícias* (Rio de Janeiro) in February, 1886. It was also included in a volume of short fiction entitled *Várias Histórias*, published in Rio de Janeiro in 1886.

"Ex Cathedra " ("Ex Cathedra") was first published in the journal *Gazeta de Notícias* (Rio de Janeiro) in April, 1884. It was also included in a volume of short fiction entitled *Histórias Sem Data*, published in Rio de Janeiro in 1884.

"Voyage around Myself " ("Viagem a Roda de Mim Mesmo") was first published in the journal *Gazeta de Notícias* (Rio de Janeiro) on 4 October 1885. It was not published in a volume of short fiction in Machado's lifetime, but was included in a volume entitled *Outras Relíquias*, published in Rio de Janeiro in 1910.

"A Lady" ("Uma Senhora") was first published in the journal *Gazeta de Notícias* (Rio de Janeiro) on 27 November 1883. It was also included in a volume of short fiction entitled *Histórias Sem Data*, published in Rio de Janeiro in 1884.

"Trio in A Minor" ("Trio em Lá Menor") was first published in the second literary supplement of the journal *Gazeta de Notícias* (Rio de Janeiro) on 20 January 1886. It was also included in a volume of short fiction entitled *Várias Históras*, published in Rio de Janeiro in 1896.

"Wedding Song" ("Cantiga de Esponsais") was first published in the journal *A Estação: Jornal ilustrada para a família* (Rio de Janeiro) on 15 May 1883. It was also included in a volume of short fiction entitled *Histórias Sem Data*, published in Rio de Janeiro in 1884.

"A Visit from Alcibiades" ("Uma Visita de Alcibiades") was first published in the journal *Jornal das Famílias* (Rio de Janeiro) in October, 1876, under the pseudonym "Victor de Paula." An expanded, drastically modified version was included in a volume of short fiction entitled *Papéis Avulsos*, published in Rio de Janeiro in November, 1882. The latter version is understood to be the final, definitive version of the story, and was thus the source text for the translation included here.

"On the Ark: Three (Undiscovered) Chapters from the Book of Genesis" ("Na Arca—Três Capítulos (Inéditos) do Gênesis") was first published in the journal *O Cruzeiro* (Rio de Janeiro) on 14 May 1878, under the pseudonym "Eleazar." It was also included in a volume of short fiction entitled *Papéis Avulsos*, published in Rio de Janeiro in November, 1882.

"Note on Contemporary Brazilian Literature: Instinct of Nationality" ("Notícia da Atual Literatura Brasileira") was first published in volume 30 of the journal *O Novo Mundo* (New York) on 24 March 1873.

MACHADO DE ASSIS was born in Rio de Janeiro in 1839 and is widely considered Brazil's greatest writer. The only surviving child of working-class parents, Machado was descended from freed mulatto slaves, and became an autodidact in early youth in order to augment his meager education. At the age of fifteen he began publishing sonnets, and over the course of his illustrious career he produced poetry, drama, criticism, short fiction, and novels. A shrewd, versatile writer who numbers among the nineteenth century's most accomplished psychological realists, Machado's work is also ironic and conceptual, probing the depths of human ambiguity. Dubbed "Machado de la Mancha" by Carlos Fuentes, who considered him the only true follower of Cervantes in Latin America before Borges, Machado de Assis is an underappreciated master whose work prefigures some of the most audacious formal experimentation of literary modernity. He died in 1908.

RHETT MCNEIL is a scholar, critic, and literary translator from Texas, where he graduated Phi Beta Kappa from UT-Austin with degrees in English, Portuguese, and Art History. He completed an MA in Comparative Literature at Penn State University and is currently finishing a PhD in the same department. His translations from the Spanish and Portuguese include novels and short stories from some of the most innovative authors on the world literary scene, including Antônio Lobo Antunes, Enrique Vila-Matas, Gonçalo M. Tavares, João Almino, and A.G. Porta. Rhett has also translated short fiction by the Brazilian master Machado de Assis, who, along with Jorge Luis Borges, is the subject of his dissertation.

SELECTED DALKEY ARCHIVE TITLES

MICHAL AJVAZ, *The Golden Age.*
The Other City.
PIERRE ALBERT-BIROT, *Grabinoulor.*
YUZ ALESHKOVSKY, *Kangaroo.*
FELIPE ALFAU, *Chromos.*
Locos.
IVAN ÂNGELO, *The Celebration.*
The Tower of Glass.
ANTÓNIO LOBO ANTUNES, *Knowledge of Hell.*
The Splendor of Portugal.
ALAIN ARIAS-MISSON, *Theatre of Incest.*
JOHN ASHBERY AND JAMES SCHUYLER, *A Nest of Ninnies.*
ROBERT ASHLEY, *Perfect Lives.*
GABRIELA AVIGUR-ROTEM, *Heatwave and Crazy Birds.*
DJUNA BARNES, *Ladies Almanack.*
Ryder.
JOHN BARTH, *LETTERS.*
Sabbatical.
DONALD BARTHELME, *The King.*
Paradise.
SVETISLAV BASARA, *Chinese Letter.*
MIQUEL BAUÇÀ, *The Siege in the Room.*
RENÉ BELLETTO, *Dying.*
MAREK BIEŃCZYK, *Transparency.*
ANDREI BITOV, *Pushkin House.*
ANDREJ BLATNIK, *You Do Understand.*
LOUIS PAUL BOON, *Chapel Road.*
My Little War.
Summer in Termuren.
ROGER BOYLAN, *Killoyle.*
IGNÁCIO DE LOYOLA BRANDÃO, *Anonymous Celebrity.*
Zero.
BONNIE BREMSER, *Troia: Mexican Memoirs.*
CHRISTINE BROOKE-ROSE, *Amalgamemnon.*
BRIGID BROPHY, *In Transit.*
GERALD L. BRUNS, *Modern Poetry and the Idea of Language.*
GABRIELLE BURTON, *Heartbreak Hotel.*
MICHEL BUTOR, *Degrees.*
Mobile.
G. CABRERA INFANTE, *Infante's Inferno.*
Three Trapped Tigers.
JULIETA CAMPOS, *The Fear of Losing Eurydice.*
ANNE CARSON, *Eros the Bittersweet.*
ORLY CASTEL-BLOOM, *Dolly City.*
LOUIS-FERDINAND CÉLINE, *Castle to Castle.*
Conversations with Professor Y.
London Bridge.
Normance.
North.
Rigadoon.
MARIE CHAIX, *The Laurels of Lake Constance.*
HUGO CHARTERIS, *The Tide Is Right.*
ERIC CHEVILLARD, *Demolishing Nisard.*

MARC CHOLODENKO, *Mordechai Schamz.*
JOSHUA COHEN, *Witz.*
EMILY HOLMES COLEMAN, *The Shutter of Snow.*
ROBERT COOVER, *A Night at the Movies.*
STANLEY CRAWFORD, *Log of the S.S. The Mrs Unguentine.*
Some Instructions to My Wife.
RENÉ CREVEL, *Putting My Foot in It.*
RALPH CUSACK, *Cadenza.*
NICHOLAS DELBANCO, *The Count of Concord.*
Sherbrookes.
NIGEL DENNIS, *Cards of Identity.*
PETER DIMOCK, *A Short Rhetoric for Leaving the Family.*
ARIEL DORFMAN, *Konfidenz.*
COLEMAN DOWELL,
Island People.
Too Much Flesh and Jabez.
ARKADII DRAGOMOSHCHENKO, *Dust.*
RIKKI DUCORNET, *The Complete Butcher's Tales.*
The Fountains of Neptune.
The Jade Cabinet.
Phosphor in Dreamland.
WILLIAM EASTLAKE, *The Bamboo Bed.*
Castle Keep.
Lyric of the Circle Heart.
JEAN ECHENOZ, *Chopin's Move.*
STANLEY ELKIN, *A Bad Man.*
Criers and Kibitzers, Kibitzers and Criers.
The Dick Gibson Show.
The Franchiser.
The Living End.
Mrs. Ted Bliss.
FRANÇOIS EMMANUEL, *Invitation to a Voyage.*
SALVADOR ESPRIU, *Ariadne in the Grotesque Labyrinth.*
LESLIE A. FIEDLER, *Love and Death in the American Novel.*
JUAN FILLOY, *Op Oloop.*
ANDY FITCH, *Pop Poetics.*
GUSTAVE FLAUBERT, *Bouvard and Pécuchet.*
KASS FLEISHER, *Talking out of School.*
FORD MADOX FORD,
The March of Literature.
JON FOSSE, *Aliss at the Fire.*
Melancholy.
MAX FRISCH, *I'm Not Stiller.*
Man in the Holocene.
CARLOS FUENTES, *Christopher Unborn.*
Distant Relations.
Terra Nostra.
Where the Air Is Clear.
TAKEHIKO FUKUNAGA, *Flowers of Grass.*
WILLIAM GADDIS, *J R.*
The Recognitions.

JANICE GALLOWAY, *Foreign Parts.*
  The Trick Is to Keep Breathing.
WILLIAM H. GASS, *Cartesian Sonata*
    and Other Novellas.
  Finding a Form.
  A Temple of Texts.
  The Tunnel.
  Willie Masters' Lonesome Wife.
GÉRARD GAVARRY, *Hoppla! 1 2 3.*
ETIENNE GILSON,
  The Arts of the Beautiful.
  Forms and Substances in the Arts.
C. S. GISCOMBE, *Giscome Road.*
  Here.
DOUGLAS GLOVER, *Bad News of the Heart.*
WITOLD GOMBROWICZ,
  A Kind of Testament.
PAULO EMÍLIO SALES GOMES, *P's Three*
    Women.
GEORGI GOSPODINOV, *Natural Novel.*
JUAN GOYTISOLO, *Count Julian.*
  Juan the Landless.
  Makbara.
  Marks of Identity.
HENRY GREEN, *Back.*
  Blindness.
  Concluding.
  Doting.
  Nothing.
JACK GREEN, *Fire the Bastards!*
JIŘÍ GRUŠA, *The Questionnaire.*
MELA HARTWIG, *Am I a Redundant*
    Human Being?
JOHN HAWKES, *The Passion Artist.*
  Whistlejacket.
ELIZABETH HEIGHWAY, ED., *Contemporary*
    Georgian Fiction.
ALEKSANDAR HEMON, ED.,
  Best European Fiction.
AIDAN HIGGINS, *Balcony of Europe.*
  Blind Man's Bluff
  Bornholm Night-Ferry.
  Flotsam and Jetsam.
  Langrishe, Go Down.
  Scenes from a Receding Past.
KEIZO HINO, *Isle of Dreams.*
KAZUSHI HOSAKA, *Plainsong.*
ALDOUS HUXLEY, *Antic Hay.*
  Crome Yellow.
  Point Counter Point.
  Those Barren Leaves.
  Time Must Have a Stop.
NAOYUKI II, *The Shadow of a Blue Cat.*
GERT JONKE, *The Distant Sound.*
  Geometric Regional Novel.
  Homage to Czerny.
  The System of Vienna.
JACQUES JOUET, *Mountain R.*
  Savage.
  Upstaged.

MIEKO KANAI, *The Word Book.*
YORAM KANIUK, *Life on Sandpaper.*
HUGH KENNER, *Flaubert.*
  Joyce and Beckett: The Stoic Comedians.
  Joyce's Voices.
DANILO KIŠ, *The Attic.*
  Garden, Ashes.
  The Lute and the Scars
  Psalm 44.
  A Tomb for Boris Davidovich.
ANITA KONKKA, *A Fool's Paradise.*
GEORGE KONRÁD, *The City Builder.*
TADEUSZ KONWICKI, *A Minor Apocalypse.*
  The Polish Complex.
MENIS KOUMANDAREAS, *Koula.*
ELAINE KRAF, *The Princess of 72nd Street.*
JIM KRUSOE, *Iceland.*
AYŞE KULIN, *Farewell: A Mansion in*
    Occupied Istanbul.
EMILIO LASCANO TEGUI, *On Elegance*
    While Sleeping.
ERIC LAURRENT, *Do Not Touch.*
VIOLETTE LEDUC, *La Bâtarde.*
EDOUARD LEVÉ, *Autoportrait.*
  Suicide.
MARIO LEVI, *Istanbul Was a Fairy Tale.*
DEBORAH LEVY, *Billy and Girl.*
JOSÉ LEZAMA LIMA, *Paradiso.*
ROSA LIKSOM, *Dark Paradise.*
OSMAN LINS, *Avalovara.*
  The Queen of the Prisons of Greece.
ALF MAC LOCHLAINN,
  The Corpus in the Library.
  Out of Focus.
RON LOEWINSOHN, *Magnetic Field(s).*
MINA LOY, *Stories and Essays of Mina Loy.*
D. KEITH MANO, *Take Five.*
MICHELINE AHARONIAN MARCOM,
  The Mirror in the Well.
BEN MARCUS,
  The Age of Wire and String.
WALLACE MARKFIELD,
  Teitlebaum's Window.
  To an Early Grave.
DAVID MARKSON, *Reader's Block.*
  Wittgenstein's Mistress.
CAROLE MASO, *AVA.*
LADISLAV MATEJKA AND KRYSTYNA
    POMORSKA, EDS.,
  Readings in Russian Poetics:
    Formalist and Structuralist Views.
HARRY MATHEWS, *Cigarettes.*
  The Conversions.
  The Human Country: New and
    Collected Stories.
  The Journalist.
  My Life in CIA.
  Singular Pleasures.
  The Sinking of the Odradek
    Stadium.
  Tlooth.

FOR A FULL LIST OF PUBLICATIONS, VISIT:
www.dalkeyarchive.com

JOSEPH MCELROY,
  Night Soul and Other Stories.
ABDELWAHAB MEDDEB, *Talismano.*
GERHARD MEIER, *Isle of the Dead.*
HERMAN MELVILLE, *The Confidence-Man.*
AMANDA MICHALOPOULOU, *I'd Like.*
STEVEN MILLHAUSER, *The Barnum Museum.*
  In the Penny Arcade.
RALPH J. MILLS, JR., *Essays on Poetry.*
MOMUS, *The Book of Jokes.*
CHRISTINE MONTALBETTI, *The Origin of Man.*
  Western.
OLIVE MOORE, *Spleen.*
NICHOLAS MOSLEY, *Accident.*
  Assassins.
  Catastrophe Practice.
  Experience and Religion.
  A Garden of Trees.
  Hopeful Monsters.
  Imago Bird.
  Impossible Object.
  Inventing God.
  Judith.
  Look at the Dark.
  Natalie Natalia.
  Serpent.
  Time at War.
WARREN MOTTE,
  *Fables of the Novel: French Fiction
    since 1990.*
  *Fiction Now: The French Novel in
    the 21st Century.*
  *Oulipo: A Primer of Potential
    Literature.*
GERALD MURNANE, *Barley Patch.*
  Inland.
YVES NAVARRE, *Our Share of Time.*
  Sweet Tooth.
DOROTHY NELSON, *In Night's City.*
  Tar and Feathers.
ESHKOL NEVO, *Homesick.*
WILFRIDO D. NOLLEDO, *But for the Lovers.*
FLANN O'BRIEN, *At Swim-Two-Birds.*
  The Best of Myles.
  The Dalkey Archive.
  The Hard Life.
  The Poor Mouth.
  The Third Policeman.
CLAUDE OLLIER, *The Mise-en-Scène.*
  Wert and the Life Without End.
GIOVANNI ORELLI, *Walaschek's Dream.*
PATRIK OUŘEDNÍK, *Europeana.*
  The Opportune Moment, 1855.
BORIS PAHOR, *Necropolis.*
FERNANDO DEL PASO, *News from the
  Empire.*
  Palinuro of Mexico.
ROBERT PINGET, *The Inquisitory.*
  Mahu or The Material.
  Trio.
MANUEL PUIG, *Betrayed by Rita Hayworth.*

  The Buenos Aires Affair.
  Heartbreak Tango.
RAYMOND QUENEAU, *The Last Days.*
  Odile.
  Pierrot Mon Ami.
  Saint Glinglin.
ANN QUIN, *Berg.*
  Passages.
  Three.
  Tripticks.
ISHMAEL REED, *The Free-Lance Pallbearers.*
  The Last Days of Louisiana Red.
  Ishmael Reed: The Plays.
  Juice!
  Reckless Eyeballing.
  The Terrible Threes.
  The Terrible Twos.
  Yellow Back Radio Broke-Down.
JASIA REICHARDT, *15 Journeys Warsaw
  to London.*
NOËLLE REVAZ, *With the Animals.*
JOÃO UBALDO RIBEIRO, *House of the
  Fortunate Buddhas.*
JEAN RICARDOU, *Place Names.*
RAINER MARIA RILKE, *The Notebooks of
  Malte Laurids Brigge.*
JULIÁN RÍOS, *The House of Ulysses.*
  Larva: A Midsummer Night's Babel.
  Poundemonium.
  Procession of Shadows.
AUGUSTO ROA BASTOS, *I the Supreme.*
DANIËL ROBBERECHTS, *Arriving in Avignon.*
JEAN ROLIN, *The Explosion of the
  Radiator Hose.*
OLIVIER ROLIN, *Hotel Crystal.*
ALIX CLEO ROUBAUD, *Alix's Journal.*
JACQUES ROUBAUD, *The Form of a
  City Changes Faster, Alas, Than
  the Human Heart.*
  The Great Fire of London.
  Hortense in Exile.
  Hortense Is Abducted.
  The Loop.
  Mathematics:
  The Plurality of Worlds of Lewis.
  The Princess Hoppy.
  Some Thing Black.
RAYMOND ROUSSEL, *Impressions of Africa.*
VEDRANA RUDAN, *Night.*
STIG SÆTERBAKKEN, *Siamese.*
  Self Control.
LYDIE SALVAYRE, *The Company of Ghosts.*
  The Lecture.
  The Power of Flies.
LUIS RAFAEL SÁNCHEZ,
  Macho Camacho's Beat.
SEVERO SARDUY, *Cobra & Maitreya.*
NATHALIE SARRAUTE,
  Do You Hear Them?
  Martereau.
  The Planetarium.

ARNO SCHMIDT, *Collected Novellas.*
Collected Stories.
Nobodaddy's Children.
Two Novels.
ASAF SCHURR, *Motti.*
GAIL SCOTT, *My Paris.*
DAMION SEARLS, *What We Were Doing*
and Where We Were Going.
JUNE AKERS SEESE,
Is This What Other Women Feel Too?
What Waiting Really Means.
BERNARD SHARE, *Inish.*
Transit.
VIKTOR SHKLOVSKY, *Bowstring.*
Knight's Move.
A Sentimental Journey:
Memoirs 1917–1922.
Energy of Delusion: A Book on Plot.
Literature and Cinematography.
Theory of Prose.
Third Factory.
Zoo, or Letters Not about Love.
PIERRE SINIAC, *The Collaborators.*
KJERSTI A. SKOMSVOLD, *The Faster I Walk,*
the Smaller I Am.
JOSEF ŠKVORECKÝ, *The Engineer of*
Human Souls.
GILBERT SORRENTINO,
Aberration of Starlight.
Blue Pastoral.
Crystal Vision.
Imaginative Qualities of Actual
Things.
Mulligan Stew.
Pack of Lies.
Red the Fiend.
The Sky Changes.
Something Said.
Splendide-Hôtel.
Steelwork.
Under the Shadow.
W. M. SPACKMAN, *The Complete Fiction.*
ANDRZEJ STASIUK, *Dukla.*
Fado.
GERTRUDE STEIN, *The Making of Americans.*
A Novel of Thank You.
LARS SVENDSEN, *A Philosophy of Evil.*
PIOTR SZEWC, *Annihilation.*
GONÇALO M. TAVARES, *Jerusalem.*
Joseph Walser's Machine.
Learning to Pray in the Age of
Technique.
LUCIAN DAN TEODOROVICI,
Our Circus Presents . . .
NIKANOR TERATOLOGEN, *Assisted Living.*
STEFAN THEMERSON, *Hobson's Island.*
The Mystery of the Sardine.
Tom Harris.
TAEKO TOMIOKA, *Building Waves.*

JOHN TOOMEY, *Sleepwalker.*
JEAN-PHILIPPE TOUSSAINT, *The Bathroom.*
Camera.
Monsieur.
Reticence.
Running Away.
Self-Portrait Abroad.
Television.
The Truth about Marie.
DUMITRU TSEPENEAG, *Hotel Europa.*
The Necessary Marriage.
Pigeon Post.
Vain Art of the Fugue.
ESTHER TUSQUETS, *Stranded.*
DUBRAVKA UGRESIC, *Lend Me Your*
Character.
Thank You for Not Reading.
TOR ULVEN, *Replacement.*
MATI UNT, *Brecht at Night.*
Diary of a Blood Donor.
Things in the Night.
ÁLVARO URIBE AND OLIVIA SEARS, EDS.,
Best of Contemporary Mexican Fiction.
ELOY URROZ, *Friction.*
The Obstacles.
LUISA VALENZUELA, *Dark Desires and*
the Others.
He Who Searches.
PAUL VERHAEGHEN, *Omega Minor.*
AGLAJA VETERANYI, *Why the Child Is*
Cooking in the Polenta.
BORIS VIAN, *Heartsnatcher.*
LLORENÇ VILLALONGA, *The Dolls' Room.*
TOOMAS VINT, *An Unending Landscape.*
ORNELA VORPSI, *The Country Where No*
One Ever Dies.
AUSTRYN WAINHOUSE, *Hedyphagetica.*
CURTIS WHITE, *America's Magic Mountain.*
The Idea of Home.
Memories of My Father Watching TV.
Requiem.
DIANE WILLIAMS, *Excitability:*
Selected Stories.
Romancer Erector.
DOUGLAS WOOLF, *Wall to Wall.*
Ya! & John-Juan.
JAY WRIGHT, *Polynomials and Pollen.*
The Presentable Art of Reading
Absence.
PHILIP WYLIE, *Generation of Vipers.*
MARGUERITE YOUNG, *Angel in the Forest.*
Miss MacIntosh, My Darling.
REYOUNG, *Unbabbling.*
VLADO ŽABOT, *The Succubus.*
ZORAN ŽIVKOVIĆ, *Hidden Camera.*
LOUIS ZUKOFSKY, *Collected Fiction.*
VITOMIL ZUPAN, *Minuet for Guitar.*
SCOTT ZWIREN, *God Head.*